fallen angel

Also by Eden Bradley

The Lovers

fallen angel

Eden Bradley

HQN™

Recycling programs
for this product may
not exist in your area.

ISBN-13: 978-0-373-77717-4

FALLEN ANGEL

www.Harlequin.com

Printed in U.S.A.

To Sam, thank you for putting up with my creative meltdowns and writing burnout, for talking this book through with me over and over, and for understanding that sometimes the best thing to do is to slide a plate of food in front of me and tiptoe away. Without your patience and support this book would never have been written.

ACKNOWLEDGMENTS

Thanks to my agent, Roberta Brown,
who was just as excited about this rather strange idea
as I was. And also to my editor, Susan Swinwood,
for allowing me to stretch my writing wings.

I must thank, in no particular order, my writing friends
R. G. Alexander, K. B. Alan, Crystal Jordan, Lilli Feisty,
Jax Cassidy and Gemma Halliday for reading my proposal
and chapters and giving me the encouragement I needed
to write this book, and for their cheerleading
when I was afraid I'd gone too far off track.

Thanks to James Buchanan for guidance early on about
writing in the horror/suspense genres, and encouraging me
to include some of those elements in my work.

A huge thank-you to fellow author
and L.A. city police officer Kathy Bennett
for sharing her knowledge of police procedure.

Many thanks to Sam and my girls, R. G. Alexander,
K. B. Alan, Rachel Jameson, Vivienne Westlake
and Sabrina Darby for support, karaoke, lunch, knowing
the value of retail therapy and always, for the cabana boy.

CHAPTER ONE

MIST SWIRLED AROUND HIS FEET, obscuring the hard-packed sand as Declan Byrne took his morning walk down the rugged beach. The sun was just beginning to rise, a faint amber glow casting the first golden rays of the day, barely touching the cresting waves of the Pacific Ocean. He loved it here, loved to come when it was still nearly dark, picking his way over the craggy rocks, the piles of driftwood and seaweed, the empty sound of the thundering ocean soothing him.

Liam, his enormous black mastiff, trotted beside him, his only company. Declan preferred it that way. He reveled in the loneliness, the isolation of this place. It was a big part of why he'd come back here six years earlier. He'd needed the quiet. He'd needed to heal. Maybe he still did.

Abby...

No, don't think about her now.

Don't think about her, period.

He turned instead to the sea, watched as Liam chased the edge of the incoming waves, sniffing, backing away as the water surged onto the sand. This was their daily ritual. How Declan got his head on straight before beginning work, before he had to interact with other people, something he'd been lousy at the past few years. He much preferred his dog, the ocean, the rough and lonely Mendocino coastline, to people.

His work as a forest ranger didn't require much human contact. This particular job included making sure trails were cleared, keeping order in the campgrounds, the occasional lost hiker, and sometimes training new rangers. But most of the time it was just him and the forest, the lone stretches of beach and rugged cliffs that made up the national park's coastline. Probably the biggest reason why he'd taken the job. That, and something about his father having worked in this area as a ranger most of his life, up until he'd retired a couple of years ago.

Following in the old man's footsteps, no matter how he felt about him. But this place was home to him. His gruff father was home to him, even though they'd barely spoken since his mother died.

Don't think about that, either.

The sun was coming up fast, warming the damp air as he and Liam climbed over the rocks to the next crescent of sand. Declan stopped and looked out to sea, tracking the rising sun, the surge of the gray-and-green water, and felt that brief moment of peace he sought each day. He breathed in the sharp salt air, filling his lungs. Watched as a lone gull flew in low over the water on silent wings, skimming the surface beyond the waves. Peace here, yes. He didn't want to stop to consider why he needed it so desperately.

A hard thump sounded behind him; shocking, how loud it was, how it made the ground shake. Declan spun around, his heart hammering while Liam went off, barking like crazy.

A woman lying on the sand before him. He nearly tripped over her in the half light, had to dig his heels into the rocky beach to steady himself. The crashing of the cold surf faded into the background as he tried to grasp what he was seeing. Liam had stopped barking and was sniffing her limp body, his huge black head dwarfing her.

He grabbed for the mastiff's collar. "Liam, off!" *What the hell?*

She was naked, bleeding, one leg caught on the rocks, twisted at an impossible angle. His brain shifted into high gear as he bent over her, adrenaline swamping his veins in a hot, speedy current.

Where the hell had she come from? He looked up, peering through the pale light, his gaze wandering up the ragged cliff side, but he saw nothing, no one.

"Jesus," he muttered as he pulled out his cell phone and dialed 9-1-1.

As the phone rang his gaze roamed her body, trying to assess the damage in the diffused light of the rising sun. Pale, wavy blond hair down to her knees. There were strange symbols painted all over her: her stomach, her thighs, across her bare breasts. They were lush and round, he couldn't help but notice, then cursed himself. The woman was half-dead, for God's sake. He leaned in closer, trying to hear her breathing. He didn't want to touch her. No, he *wanted* to touch her. He didn't dare.

What the fuck is wrong with you?

There. A small, gasping breath rattling in her chest.

Thank God.

An operator finally answered the phone, and he quickly told the man who he was, gave him details, his location.

He hung up to wait for the rescue team, finally dared to reach out and lay his fingertips on her wrist to check her pulse. Bones like a bird, isn't that what the saying was? She was so delicate…

She was alive, her breath shallow, but she was taking one after another. There was blood everywhere; he could smell it even over the tangy ocean scent in the air, but beneath the mess he could see a lovely, angelic face. Hard to tell how old she was. Early twenties? Closer inspection showed him bits of twigs—herbs, maybe?—and small bones woven into her hair. On her upturned palms were penta-grams painted in red.

Who the fuck would have done something like this?

Liam was standing next to him, over the girl, peering into her face as though he were trying to figure it out, too.

Declan had never seen anything like it. He never wanted to again.

He fought back the sense of horror that made bile rise, made his throat want to close up.

So much blood...

He pulled off his jacket and covered her, glad it was spring and, although the beach was damp, it wasn't too cold. He had no idea what else he could do for her. He waited, his pulse racing, his jaw grinding hard. And no matter how he fought against it, his mind began to fill with memories, flashing images he couldn't seem to forget.

The heat of Bahrain, the dry, acrid desert scent he'd never smelled anywhere else in the world. He hated that scent. Hated the Middle East. But it was his job to be there.

It was your job to protect them.

Yeah, great job he'd done. The girl was dead and he was mind-fucked for the rest of his life.

His jaw clenched so hard it hurt.

And now this girl.

He reached out and touched his fingertips to

her cool cheek, then pulled back, feeling like some kind of asshole for touching her. Some kind of pervert. But he hadn't been able to help himself. She hadn't stirred. He knew enough to realize she would probably die. Who could survive a fall like that? Those cliffs had to be a good fifty, sixty feet high. Her lungs must be compressed, other internal injuries, he was certain. Sadness tied his gut into a knot.

And anger.

Who was she? What had happened to her? Someone had pushed her off that cliff. Had done some pretty weird shit to her before that, by the look of it. No one could have done this to themselves. Could they?

Where the fuck was the damn rescue team?

He breathed deeply trying to calm himself.

Liam whined and Declan focused once more on the girl's still figure, her solemn face. He knelt beside her, the damp sand soaking through the knees of his jeans. She was so broken.

He rubbed a hand over his jaw, his fingers automatically finding the ridge of the old scar there. He didn't need this. This…trauma. This horrible sight.

He watched as she drew a rattling sigh into her damaged lungs.

She didn't need it, either.

Liam hadn't taken his eyes off her. Well, neither could he, for more than a few moments. Unbelievably flawless face. If it weren't for the blood matting her hair, the cuts all over her skin, she would almost look as if she were asleep. He reached out and touched her cheek once more. Like cool satin under his fingers.

What was he thinking?

Christ.

He forced his brain to shut down, to let the thunder of the ocean drown out all thought, and waited.

PAIN AND PAIN AND PAIN. Breathless. Why couldn't she breathe? She was falling through the dark. Alone. The wind whistled by her, whipping her hair against her cheeks, stinging her skin. *Falling,* not flying. She had some idea of what that meant. But alone? She couldn't bear that. Where was he?

"Asmodeus!"

Silence, but for the sound of the wind and her own heart beating faintly. Tears stung her eyes.

Had she failed again? The Grandmother would be so disappointed. She had lived for this moment. They both had. And this was the fourth attempt. Her last chance.

Her heart was a hammer in her chest, a wild thunder carrying pure, stark panic. She couldn't stand this sense of being utterly alone, even though she'd spent most of her life by herself, other than The Grandmother. And *him.*

She tried once more. "Asmodeus!"

She felt him before she saw him. He was with her, the heat of him radiating like a shield. He was glorious, as always, gleaming in the dark as though he were made of light. His hair so pale it shimmered like transparent strands of the finest silk around his shoulders. His skin was golden and shining, a hard shell around his massive body. Exoskeletal. Beautiful. Perfect. And his eyes, black as midnight, black as coal, and hotter than any fire could possibly burn. Just black, no pupils, so that she never knew what he might be thinking. She could feel the heat on her naked flesh.

Asmodeus.

Her teacher. Her lover. Her enemy.

He shimmered before her, his lush mouth curving into a welcoming smile. Or perhaps it was a mocking smile. It was impossible to tell with him. Her body surged with yearning, the same yearning she had felt in his presence since she'd first seen him. How long ago had that been? She'd just reached puberty when The Grandmother had shown Asmodeus to her. And she had loved and feared him, craved his touch, the timbre of his deep voice, ever since.

Light shone through the darkness behind her eyelids, and he faded away, the flame that was his presence, his essence, dimming. Her eyes burned as she tried to pry them open.

Sunlight. Pale, gray, but cutting through the dark. A shadow moved over her.

Focus.

His head was enormous, his black fur shining. His eyes were two dark orbs, glittering with a knowing intelligence. Not as dark as Asmodeus's eyes. Not as bottomless. But the pupils were large. His gaze seemed almost soft to her, not what she'd expected. She wanted to reach out, to ask for entrance, but her arm wouldn't obey her brain.

I am failing.

That dark head moved in closer, until she could feel the heat of his breath. And in the distance was a dull roar that she understood was the sea, waves hammering on a shore. Was that salt she smelled? Water on her skin? She was so cold…

She let her eyes close, dared to hope…and fell, once more, into the darkness.

"Asmodeus!"

The darkness was illuminated by his golden body. He was naked, as she was, his body flawless in only the way that of a fallen god could be. They were always naked together. Desire pulsed in her system, even through the haze of pain.

"My beauty." His voice was deep, as deep as the darkest caves beneath the ocean floor. She had read about such things.

He reached for her, but didn't touch her. He never did.

Instead, he ran his long fingers up the length of his always erect cock, his fingertips feathering against the solid shaft. He sighed, his expression never changing as his tongue darted out to lick his beautiful lips. Her breasts ached, needing to be touched. But she held her arms where they were, wrapped around her body. Even her need couldn't overcome her fear, her sense of desolate desperation.

"I thought I'd made it," she told him, her voice shaking. She was so tired. "I saw Cerberus at the Gates. I swear I did."

"No." His face was somber.

Her heart seized in her chest. Pain again.

"I tried."

"Did you?"

"I did, I swear it!"

He shook his head.

She knew he was right.

"What happens now?" she asked. "This was my last turn. If I've been rejected again, what happens now?"

"That does not concern me. I have served my purpose. It was up to you to serve yours."

"Will I be here forever, then? With you?" She wiped at a strand of her hair, caught against her mouth by the wind. The idea was frightening. But at least he was familiar to her, her demon lover. And she wanted him, as always.

"I would keep you with me for eternity. But it is up to you. Choose. Choose to stay and fall with me. Or choose to go."

"Go? But I wouldn't see you again! Is that true? You're…all I have left. I love you."

"I love you, in my way. Do you understand?"

"I understand that you are greater than I can ever be. That your love is precious."

"Yes. But you were not created for me. Nor were you trained for me. I have been nothing more than a catalyst."

"You have been the most important thing in my life. You and The Grandmother. And I won't return to her now, will I?"

She remembered the pungent fragrance of herbs drying in The Grandmother's kitchen, the sweet air of the high, walled garden that was her one haven. She remembered The Grandmother's silent, stony presence in the evenings as they sat by the fire, reading or sewing. Her lined face, ancient and weary, the beady gray eyes, as sharp as a steel blade and twice as cruel, yet familiar. As familiar and cruel as her hands could be, her hard, ancient voice. Cruel and cold, yet her heart twisted. Ached. She knew what the answer would be.

"No. She is done with you."

"Does that mean you are, as well? How do I choose if I don't know what I'm choosing?"

"Every choice is a risk."

"Please, Asmodeus… Tell me what you mean. Tell me what to do."

He remained silent for several moments. Then, "Choose."

His face grew cold, hard. Her pulse throbbed with fear. With desire. With life. She chose.

DECLAN DIDN'T KNOW HOW LONG he sat and stared at her before Liam went off again, and he saw the rescue team making its way down the treacherous path that led to the far end of the beach. Endless moments as he waited for them to run down the narrow strip of sand, while he felt some odd twisting in his gut about handing the girl over to them.

He dialed his cell phone while they put a cervical collar on her, slid a backboard under her and started strapping her to it, placed an oxygen mask over her face. His father answered after one ring.

"Oran Byrne." Sharp as a military commander, even at barely 6:00 a.m.

"Dad. I need you to do me a favor."

"Okay."

He was grateful his father wasn't going to mention that it had been years since he'd asked him for anything.

"I need you to come and pick up Liam."

"Is he hurt? Where are you?"

"I'm at the beach, below Gualala Point. Something really bizarre just happened. There's this woman…" How to explain it? "I…found her on the beach. I need to go to the hospital. Can you meet me there and take Liam?"

"Yeah, sure."

"Thanks."

"You going to tell me what happened when I get there? Or do I have to get the story from the sheriff's office?"

Grumpy bastard. Declan had to admit he and his father didn't exactly communicate well, and it wasn't all the old man's fault. But this wasn't the time to think about all that.

"I'll tell you everything. Just meet me at the hospital."

He snapped his phone shut and followed the EMTs back up the beach, along the steep path that wound up the cliffs.

"She needs the helicopter," he muttered to himself, knowing there was no way a helicopter could have landed on the tiny strip of sand down there. Probably wouldn't make a difference, anyway. The girl would likely die before they reached the hospital.

Pain cut into him like a knife. Why did it matter, anyway? He didn't know this girl. But he couldn't get her face out of his mind. Beautiful. Angelic…

He kept one eye on the girl as she was loaded into the ambulance, the other on the sheriff pulling up and jumping out of his car.

Tim Bullock's brown hair stuck up in clumps, as though he'd been pulled out of bed. He probably had. "Declan, you the one who found her?"

Declan nodded. "But I didn't exactly find her. More like she found me."

"You can tell me more down on the beach. Backup should be here soon."

"Tim, I'm going to the hospital."

"We have an investigation to deal with. You're our only witness."

Declan set his jaw. "I can tell you I was walking on the beach and she landed on the sand, like a goddamn catapult had launched her off the cliffs. I didn't see anyone. I didn't hear anything. You're welcome to ask me more questions after we get her to the hospital, but I'm going."

"They'll take care of her, Declan. What the hell is wrong with you?"

What the hell *was* wrong with him?

"I'll see you at the hospital, Tim."

He yanked open the door of his truck and whistled to Liam. The dog jumped in, and he swung his long legs in after him.

The sheriff rubbed his eyes with one hand. "Shit. Okay. Only because it's you, Dec."

Declan hit the gas and took off after the ambulance as it pulled out onto the coast highway, cursing all the way to the hospital.

And somewhere behind the curses was a small prayer that she'd make it.

The scenery went by in a blur of grays and greens and the beginnings of a blue sky. The radio was tuned to the local country station, and an old Patsy Cline song came on. He flipped the sound off roughly.

"Don't need to hear that on a day like today," he grumbled to Liam.

The day was bad enough, and would probably get worse. He didn't need a song to remind him of his mother on top of everything else.

Don't think. Just drive. Just get there.

He pulled into the emergency parking lot at the hospital as they were unloading the stretcher into the E.R. bay. Rolling the windows down for Liam, Declan jumped out and followed the stretcher and the team of EMTs in, but once inside the E.R. doctor, Stephen Kane, a man he'd known since high school, stopped him.

"We need some room to work, Declan."

"I found her, Stephen. I want to make sure she's okay."

"I'll let you know." He pushed Declan back with a gentle hand on his shoulder.

Declan glared at him. Stephen pushed harder. He let his muscles relax, knowing he wasn't going to be of any help in there. "Okay. Okay. Take good care of her."

He watched as the doctors and nurses worked on the girl in a frenzy. Everything was moving so fast, he couldn't tell what was happening. Orders were shouted, equipment hooked up. He was acutely aware of the smell of disinfectant, the metallic scent of blood he hadn't been able to get out of his nostrils since she'd fallen at his feet on the beach. His ears still echoed with that hard thump as her body had hit the damp sand. So damn hard her blood had splashed the legs of his jeans, which he hadn't noticed until now. He dropped his head, rubbing the back of his neck.

Jesus.

His head buzzed, went a little empty. He dug his fingers into his hair.

A hand on his arm steadied him, and he was surprised to see it was his father.

"Dad."

Oran Byrne was shorter than his son, but still a commanding figure. His features were rugged, a little worn with age. His hair was all gray now, but still thick. He wore it a little too long. His mother would have hated that.

Small pang at the thought of his mother, dead now from cancer for more than ten years. Too many reminders of her today.

"What's going on, Dec?"

"I was walking, like I do every morning. Someone threw this girl off the cliffs."

"Threw her off? Jesus. And she's alive?"

"Barely. Something weird going on, though—"

"Throwing someone off a cliff isn't exactly typical, Dec."

"Yeah. But look at her."

He gestured with his chin. Even from where they stood, with the medical team buzzing around her, they could clearly see the strange marks all over her body.

"What the hell is all that?" his father mumbled.

Christ, there was blood everywhere. Even worse than it'd been on the beach, the red so stark against the white linoleum, the doctors' scrubs, their latex gloves. He didn't know how much longer he could stand the damn scent of it.

Blood everywhere, like a crimson flood flowing out of her neck. That bastard grinning at him victoriously before the band of them took off with Abby's purse. The feel of her body heavy in his arms. The warmth of her blood beneath his hand as he pressed over the wound. Fucking impossible to stop it, her neck sliced all the way across. Her brown eyes staring at him helplessly. She was still in there, damn it!

Don't go...

Too damn late. Too late before it even happened.

"Dec? You okay?"

His father's voice cut through the images playing in his mind like a movie he couldn't shut off. He was sweating. Shaking. Fucking awful that his old man had seen him like this.

He shrugged his father's hand from his arm. "Yeah, what? I'm fine. Fine."

He took a few steps away from his dad, whose hands were raised, palms up, as if warding off his son's anger. He didn't blame him. But he had to fucking distance himself. Catch his breath.

He looked back at the young woman on the table. Her long, blond hair hung over the edge, nearly touching the floor. He wished she wasn't going to die. Wished he could know her, that he could have saved her. Moving to the window, he touched the glass. He knew from experience that wishing wasn't enough. But he was doing it anyway.

Who was this girl? He would probably never know.

Another flurry of activity as her heart monitor flatlined. His own heart hammered in his chest, slamming into his lungs. He could barely breathe. He couldn't look away, even though he knew he was watching her die.

Too damn late. Too late before it even happened. Again.

DECLAN RUBBED AT HIS grainy eyes. He couldn't believe she'd survived the night, but somehow, she had. A glance at his watch told him it was 7:00 a.m. The hospital ward was just beginning to stir, a metal cart with breakfast trays rolling down the halls, leaving a trail of starchy scent in its wake.

They'd taken her from the E.R. and admitted her late last night. Not even into ICU. How could she have lived through a fall like that?

He was stiff from having spent the night in the hard, blue plastic chair in the sterile hallway. But he was not going to leave her. His father had tried to talk him into going home and getting some rest, and they'd had some words. No surprise there.

The local cops had shown up, as promised, some baby-faced kid and his even younger side-kick, neither of them guys he knew. He'd gone over what had happened a dozen times before they realized he really didn't have any more to tell aside from the sparse details they'd already written down in their notebooks. They'd finally left with a promise to come back when the woman woke up.

If.

Declan ran a hand over his stubbled jaw. He needed a shave. A shower to wash the stink of hospital from his skin. Desperately needed a cup of coffee. But he wasn't going anywhere until he talked to someone about her.

It was another hour before the doctor showed up. He was glad to see it was someone he knew.

Declan stood, took a moment to clench his jaw against a wave of exhaustion-induced dizziness. "Stephen. How is she?"

"She's doing well, considering."

"Considering what, exactly? I want to know everything. No one would tell me yesterday. And the people on the night shift were even more close-mouthed."

"We were too busy working on her yesterday. And last night there still wasn't much to tell."

"I know." He shrugged impatiently. "So, tell me now."

"Her right leg was broken pretty badly, but I think you knew that. Surgery is scheduled for later today. Her right shoulder was dislocated, but that was easy to fix. The wrist is sprained. Plenty of cuts and bruises. Several small facial wounds and a severe concussion, which is what I'm most concerned about. But the strangest injuries are these two cuts along her shoulder blades, about six inches long. And they were put there on purpose, cut clean, right along the edge of the scapula."

"That's where all the blood was coming from?" Declan asked.

Stephen nodded. "Most of it. Some from the head wound. But those weird incisions… Any deeper and the tendons would have been cut through."

"Jesus. What else?"

"Tox screen shows a significant amount of drugs in her system. Hallucinogens. Peyote, belladonna, something else we haven't identified yet. And plenty of tranquilizers, too. She should be dead just from that, frankly."

Declan ran a hand through his hair. Amazing that the girl had lived. "What kind of damage do you expect when she wakes up?"

"*If* she wakes up. It's still too early to say. We'll run some scans today before the leg surgery. There's definitely brain activity, but will she come out of this whole, with her mind intact? We just don't know. I'd sure like to know what the hell happened to her, though." The doctor paused, massaged the back of his neck for a moment. "I know we're a small town, but this is the strangest damn case I've ever seen. Oh, and by the way, those pentagrams on her hands? When we washed her off, we found that beneath the paint they've been tattooed there in red ink. And from what I can see, the tattoos have been there for years."

Declan's mind was working at a hundred miles an hour suddenly. "Do you think there's any chance she did this to herself?"

"I don't know what to think. Maybe she's one of those people who are into weird stuff. Witchcraft. But she couldn't possibly have put those cuts on her own back. We may never know if she doesn't wake up."

Declan nodded, but his mind was already else-where. He had to get ahold of the sheriff, find out if he'd discovered anything new looking around the beach and the cliffs. Find out if there'd been any kidnappings in the area lately. See if there were any APBs out that matched the girl's description. He'd talked to Tim last night before those children in state police uniforms had shown up, told him everything he'd seen, brainstormed with him, but they'd come up with nothing. He knew Tim would be doing everything he could, but Declan wanted to look into this himself. Do it right. This case would be too much for a small-town sheriff's of-fice to handle. They didn't have the staff, the fund-ing, to investigate this kind of case. And as much as he hated to admit it, he knew his father could help. Oran had connections he didn't.

"I have to go order some pre-op tests, Dec," Stephen said, giving him a pat on the shoulder. Declan flinched. He didn't like people touching him. Couldn't stand it.

"Yeah, sure. Thanks for the information." He drifted back across the hall to watch her through the open door to her room. He couldn't bring him-self to go inside.

Too close.

No, better to watch from a distance. Better not to allow himself to get too near her, where his body could respond to her again. She really had the most beautiful face he'd ever seen. And he couldn't get the image of her bare breasts, ripe and pale in the morning light, out of his mind.

Sick bastard.

Yes. But any man would have to be crazy not to respond to a woman who looked like she did. Innocent and so damn lovely it almost hurt to look at her. When had he ever used the word *lovely?* But it fit. She really was some ethereal creature, like a fallen angel tumbled from the sky.

Her monitors gave a beep and he saw that her pulse and respiration had sped up. He stepped into the room, found himself at her bedside before he had a chance to think about it. He knew the nurses would come if she were in any danger. Maybe the change in her heart rate meant she'd wake up soon?

She was even prettier up close. Skin like pale satin. Flawless. He wanted to touch her. Wanted to reach out and stroke her cheek with his fingertips again. He remembered exactly what it felt like, but he forced his hands to stay still at his sides.

Don't do it.

His gaze fell to her hand, turned palm-up on the blue hospital blanket, and he saw the red pentagram tattoo. It almost hurt to look at it. To see the tattoo. The bandaged wrist. The cuts and bruises. To imagine the things that must have been done to her. How she'd been hurt in the fall.

Christ, this girl was really getting to him.

Finally, it was too much. He lifted his hand, touched the tip of one finger to her face. Warmth washed over him, his groin tightened.

God, like some kind of pervert!

One of her monitors beeped and he yanked his hand back. He looked into her face, watched as her eyes fluttered, then opened. Unbelievable. Eyes that were all cloudless blue summer skies. That innocent. That clear and sweet. She was looking right at him. His heart lurched.

She moved her lips, but for a long moment nothing came out. Lips lush and cherry-pink, despite her condition. Finally she whispered, "Save me."

His heart hammered. Broke wide-open. He leaned in, looking into her eyes, willing her to see him, hear him. "Anything. Anything for you."

He meant it. And that scared the hell out of him. This girl scared the hell out of him. Because she was the first person in six years he'd felt anything for.

"Who are you?" he asked her, his voice low, almost as though he were asking himself. But her eyes had closed again. He wasn't even certain she'd really spoken to him, or if he'd imagined it, a combination of exhaustion and shock. He was surprised he was even still capable of being shocked. He sure as hell wasn't capable of feeling much else anymore, other than resentment, anger.

But looking down at the pale figure with the

beautiful face, he knew that was a lie. It was more than anger surging through his veins. Beneath the anger, the shock, was a deep need to protect this girl, this stranger. To avenge her.

He would find out who had done this to her. No matter what it took.

CHAPTER TWO

SHE COULD SEE CERBERUS'S HEAD, enormous and black as midnight. He was just out of reach, over the next dune of windswept sand. She followed him, running as fast as she could, so fast grains of sand kicked up onto the small of her back, the back of her thighs, stinging her bare skin. But he was faster.

Was he leading her to the Gates? Did this mean she wasn't rejected, after all?

She'd been to the Gates before, or nearly there. She had seen them from a distance, anyway, black and shining against the smoky red sky that never seemed to end. But they were always just out of reach, just like their guardian.

He was running, faster and faster, and she was breathless, trying to keep up as he led her into a dark cove, the rocky peaks towering above her on either side. The sand narrowed to a small pathway, twisting and turning so that she couldn't see what was ahead or behind her, other than the flash of black fur she followed after.

Her heart was burning, her legs pumping, her lungs on fire as she ran. And suddenly she knew she was lost, that he was gone. That she'd failed again.

Her chest ached with sorrow. With a purely physical pain she didn't understand. She stopped, turning around and around, but everywhere was rocks and sand and emptiness. Panic shook her, making her dizzy.

The sky was fading from red to gray, the rocks disappearing in the mist. Light shone through. She peered into the shadows. Someone was there.

Not Asmodeus. Not Cerberus.

He had a hard, kind face. Beautiful in its own way. Not the sharp perfection that was her demon lover. More…real. And she found her racing pulse calming.

There was something about his eyes…they were a pure, dazzling blue. And fierce with…what? She sensed no anger from him there, not toward her, at least. But he burned, this man.

Her mind was blurring, and she forced herself to stay with him, to focus. He reached out, and her pulse raced as he touched her face. The gentlest of touches, making her body warm all over.

She had never before been touched by a man. Had never seen one other than Asmodeus, and he wasn't really a man at all.

Her body ached. It was the pure and lovely ache

of desire beneath the wrenching pain that was building, until she could barely breathe through it.

He was fading again. She wanted to hang on to him. *Needed* to. This was what she'd chosen. But she felt too weak, too tired, to hold on. She couldn't do it. Not alone.

She tried to tell him, but the words wouldn't come out.

Save me.

She tried again, but her lips refused to move. She was going numb all over: her body, her mind. She felt an odd sinking sensation, as though she was being pulled into the very center of the earth.

She didn't want to do it, but she called on the only one who was familiar to her.

"Asmodeus!"

"I am here."

Relief flooded through her at the sound of his voice. Then his heat enveloped her and she saw the golden glow that often preceded him. Just a clear, gleaming light that seemed to come from his hair and his body, cut through only by the burning, bottomless black of his eyes. More beautiful and deadly than a snake.

"Asmodeus, where am I?"

"You are here, with me." His voice was a deep, soothing echo, one she could never quite catch. But it wrapped around her like a full-body caress.

"But...I remember choosing."

"Yes. You chose."

"Yet here you are anyway. With me again."

"My loyalty is astounding."

She hung her head, her hair falling around her face, covering her naked breasts. "More so than my own. There are reasons why I've been rejected by the Dark God."

She looked up, and the demon nodded, his black gaze on hers.

"Is this to be my punishment?"

"Being with me is a punishment? I have guided you, taught you. Loved you."

"No, I…I meant to be in this nowhere place. To feel such pain."

"I am with you. As always."

"Asmodeus…"

She was full of sadness. Full of fear.

"I would comfort you, little one. I would put my arms around you. But you are untouchable."

"Even now? Now that my body is no longer sacred?"

"I did not say your body was not still sacred, still consecrated."

"Yet you cannot touch me."

His voice was low, seductive. "I would touch you in the way I always have."

"Yes, Asmodeus."

She took a step toward him, absorbing the fiery

heat of his body, the hard shell gleaming with desire, his dark golden cock rising.

"Tell me what you desire, my beauty."

"To be touched," she answered, as she so often had.

"I will tell you how I would touch you, how you would touch me."

"Yes…"

Already her sex was plumping, filling, her breasts aching.

The demon's hand began a slow stroking motion, up his rigid shaft, down again. He was pure beauty, her demon lover. His skin was like polished gold, impossibly smooth. And his hair was pale, pale silk, the long strands floating weightlessly about his broad shoulders, his perfect face. But at this moment, nothing was more beautiful to her than his hand on his cock, the flawless instrument of pleasure that was ever denied her. His long fingers brushed at the swollen head, and her mouth watered.

"I would put my lips there, Asmodeus, and taste you," she told him while the heat built in her system, scorching her with need.

"Yes. And I would wrap my hands in your long hair, wrap it around and around my fist, holding you tight, pushing my flesh down your lovely throat."

"And you would be sweet on my tongue…"

"Show me how I would touch you while you sucked me, beauty."

"Oh…"

Her hands went to her breasts, teasing the nipples. They went hard as two stones immediately. But she needed more. With one hand she parted the lips of her sex, looked up at Asmodeus as pleasure seeped into her system, warming her all over.

"The perfect pearl," the demon told her. "I would taste you, as well." His tongue darted out, the luscious pink tip running over his full lips. "I would drink from you, my tongue pushing into you, suckling you. You would grow hard in my mouth."

"Yes…"

She used her other hand to tease at her entrance, to tug on her clitoris. She watched as he stroked his thick member, the head growing darker, like burnished copper. With his other hand he smoothed his fingertips over one of his dark, bronze nipples.

"You would put your lovely mouth on me here," he continued. "And here." He arched his hips into his fisted hand.

"I want you, Asmodeus."

"As always, my beauty." He pumped into his fist, faster and faster. His eyes burned like the darkest coal, brighter with his pleasure. "Spread your pretty thighs for me, little one. Press onto that needy nub of flesh, rub at the entrance to your tight, virgin center with your fingers. Yes. Beautiful."

She did as he told her, her fingers teasing, pushing in the slightest bit, then slipping out again. With her other hand she circled her clitoris, hard and aching and needing release.

Their hips arched together, into the cool air that separated them, and always would. And as the demon's gaze burned red, then blue with fire, his roar reverberated in her body as he came. The roaring made her tremble inside, with need, with fear. Like some deep, unearthly vibration, bringing her closer to the edge.

Asmodeus was still roaring, his voice hurting her ears, her head. The ache grew, fanned out, enveloping her. But this was no sharp stab of desire, no exquisite release. It was pain and pain and pain. Drowning her.

She gasped, her hands going to her head, trying to hold it still in the screaming light blinding her eyes, numbing her mind. She couldn't see, didn't know where she was.

Was Asmodeus still with her? She didn't know.

The light pierced, and behind it was a veil of shadows. She blinked, and saw *his* face once more.

Her stranger who was not a stranger. He blinked at her, his blue eyes fringed in dark lashes. She felt the strength in his face. The concern.

She tried to focus on him, but the pain was too

much. She couldn't bear it. She closed her eyes, called out for Asmodeus in the dark.

The pain faded, and Asmodeus was with her once more. His skin shone golden in the enveloping blackness, like some sort of guiding light.

"Asmodeus. I saw someone. A man."

The demon's dark brows drew together, his mouth going tight. "Would you choose him over me?"

"Who is he?"

His voice burned with a simmering fury. "I am the one who comes when you call, am I not?"

"Yes. Of course. But he was here…or somewhere. And I think he is…my protector, somehow."

"Ha!"

"Please, Asmodeus. Won't you give me some answer?"

"Do you not love the Dark One?"

"Of course!" she said, fiercely, but knew in her heart some of the fierceness was to cover the lie.

"We must all suffer for love," the demon said. "You chose to suffer."

"I did not know that was what I was choosing."

"You chose to turn your back on the Dark One. You chose to turn your back on me."

She couldn't answer him. His fiery gaze burned into her.

"Is it too late to change my mind? To choose differently?"

He shook his head, and faded away, leaving her alone among the rocky cliffs once more, the light fading with him, until all was dark as night once more. Pain gripped her, terrible pain. Cool steel touched her skin, cut into it. She bled. She wanted to call out for him, Asmodeus, but her mouth wouldn't work. Her *head* wouldn't work. She was blind, unable to move, unable to scream.

Was this what she had condemned herself to? This empty place, with nothing but her own failure, her guilt, the endless and abiding love she had been raised for unanswered? That was the worst part of all. Her mind worried over that, until the physical pain surged, her lungs pressing down on her, filling, taking her under like a heavy tide she couldn't resist.

FOUR DAYS. AND FOUR LONG nights, listening to the quiet beeping of her monitors. Waiting for her to wake up. And the whole time Declan had been certain she was in there, that she would wake up and be whole.

Or, as whole as someone who'd been through the weird shit she had could be.

Stephen had warned him she might never wake up. Or that she could wake up with nerve damage, brain damage. Still, Declan couldn't argue away the impossible hope he'd been hanging on to after that first night with her here, in the stifling, sterile white and linoleum and illness of the hospital. As silent and still as she'd been, he felt some strange connection to her.

You've been living alone too long. Starting to lose it....

Maybe. Or maybe there was something special about this girl. This young woman.

He hadn't for a moment been unaware that she was a woman. Even now, with her life hanging by a thread, he was aware of the curve of her lush breasts beneath the white sheet. The beauty of her face under the tubes and bandages. From his seat in the big, beige, vinyl chair the nurses had brought in for him the second night, he watched the gentle rise and fall of her breathing, moving with the rhythm of the machines that were keeping her alive.

She's in there somewhere, my fallen angel. If only I can find her.

Find her? He didn't even know what he meant by that. Giving himself too much credit. As if there was anything he could do to pull her out of wherever her mind was. So why was he so convinced he could? That staying with her every moment was so damn crucial?

God, he was tired. Tired and apparently delusional.

He rubbed at the stubble he'd allowed to grow on his chin, his cheeks. He hadn't been willing to take enough time away from her bedside to do more than grab a quick shower, check on Liam, who was safe and cared for at his father's place.

His father.

They'd hardly spoken since his mother died. He'd avoided the house, had only seen Oran when they'd inevitably run into each other in their small town. His father called every now and then, but it had been less the past year or two. The old man had finally had to give up, he guessed, in light of his son's constant rebuffs. Or maybe part of it was that he knew damn well Declan wouldn't like that Oran had a new girlfriend. Well, not so new anymore. But a hell of a lot newer than the woman he'd been married to for almost twenty-five years.

It had been harder and harder not to think of his mom. Not to remember her in a room in this same hospital, pale and suffering, swollen from the chemo and the aftereffects of her surgeries, her dark hair gone. She'd been sick for over a year, but round after round of chemo hadn't allowed it to ever grow back. It had bothered her. She hadn't complained, but he'd caught her once, standing in front of the vanity mirror in her bedroom at home, smoothing her hand over her bald head, tears in her eyes. He hadn't said anything. He'd wanted to allow her the dignity of privacy with her grief.

That was right after they'd learned that more chemo wasn't going to help. Right before she'd signed the DNR order.

"Damn it," he muttered, rising from the chair to look out the window, trying to ignore the way his gut still twisted up whenever he remembered what she'd gone through. His own helplessness to do anything about it. To help her.

Calm down.

The morning was heavy with fog, as it was year-round on this part of the Northern California coast. Beyond the rows of cars in the parking lot he could see the trees, dense and dark green against the gray-and-blue skyline.

His mother had loved the fog, which was one reason he'd had to escape after she was gone. There was a span of years when he couldn't stand to see it: the fog, the ancient redwoods, the wet and the green of the Mendocino coastline. All the things she'd loved so much. He'd joined the military to get as far away as possible. And he had. He'd gone to the other end of the goddamn earth.

Not that that had been any better. In the Middle East he'd merely traded one grief for another.

He turned back to the woman in the bed, barely alive, kept that way by the breathing tube and Lord knew what other machines they had her hooked up to. He had to wonder if his optimism meant she'd really make it, or if he was screwed up enough that he had to make something up. Something to believe in rather than watching another woman die before her time.

"Hey, Dec."

He turned at his father's voice, annoyed that he'd been caught in this condition: brooding, worried. Weak.

"Dad." His father's gray eyes were watchful, taking everything in at once, making Declan even more self-conscious. He gestured to the chair. "Do you want to sit down?"

"You look like you need to sit more than I do. You been here all night again?"

"Damn right." Why did he feel the need to lash out? Defensive?

Oran let out a small sigh. "Well, that's nice of you, son. Nice of you to sit with the girl. Any news about who she is yet?"

"I figured you'd know more than I would, being part of the old-boy loop."

"I haven't heard a thing yet."

"Neither have I." Declan's hands fisted at his sides. He pulled in a breath, reminding himself that everything didn't have to be a confrontation with his father. He rubbed the back of his neck. "I'll come and get Liam soon."

"No need. He's fine at my place. I like having him around. He's good company. And Ruth likes dogs."

He tried to ignore Ruth's name being brought up. It wasn't that Declan disliked her. He didn't even know her. But he resented his father trying to replace his mother. He knew it was ridiculous. It had been ten years, and that was a long time to be alone. But even if his father was ready to move on, Declan wasn't. But the man didn't have to care for his dog, so he'd keep his mouth shut about his girlfriend and be grateful. "Yeah, well…thanks for looking after him."

"Sure. Like I said, it's no problem." His father moved closer to the bed. "How is she?"

"No change. They've set her broken bones, repaired the internal injuries. They don't know at this point if she won't wake up because of the injuries or the drugs in her system. Both, maybe."

Oran shook his head. "She's a beautiful girl. Hard to think of anyone wanting to do this to someone. It's crazy. I've never seen anything like it. I heard state police took over the investigation."

"Yeah. State park jurisdiction."

"And you don't like that."

"I don't want to be left out of the loop, and right now Tim won't talk."

"Tim's local sheriff—he's probably being kept in the dark for now, as much as anyone else."

"Yeah, I guess so."

"You should go home, get some sleep. You can't have slept much in this chair."

"I keep telling you, I'm fine. I'll head home to shower in a while."

His father jammed both hands in his pockets, his lips setting in a hard line for a moment before he blew out a long breath. "Okay, Dec. Call me if she wakes up, will you? Call if you need anything."

"If you can just keep Liam a little longer…"

"I'll keep him as long as you need me to."

Declan could see the unasked questions in his father's eyes. They were always there. He wanted to know why his son had pushed him away, why he couldn't forgive him. Yeah, well, maybe his dad would have those answers when Declan did.

He looked back at the woman in the hospital bed. He was a real shit to be thinking about his own problems right now.

"I'll see you later, Dec. Try to get some rest."

"Okay. See you later."

He hated that he acted like some surly teenager around his father. He didn't hate the man. But he couldn't let the old blame go. Or maybe he'd never really tried very hard. But it was too hard to think about all that now. He was damn tired. His mind reeling with a thousand thoughts about the girl. Who the hell had done this to her. If she would survive.

A machine beeped and he turned to the bed, but she slept on. Sleeping Beauty. Blonde and sweet, like someone out of a fairy tale, and this never should have happened to her, goddamn it.

The anger was rising again, sharp and burning in his chest, his throat. He swallowed it down. Anger wasn't going to do him any good. It never had.

"Good morning, Declan." A nurse came bustling in, a chart in her hands. "This might be a good time to head home for a bit while I change her dressings."

"Okay. Thanks, Liz. I think I will. You have my cell if anything changes?"

"Of course."

"All right..."

Liz stepped toward him, laid a hand on his arm. He had to steel himself not to jerk away from this nice woman. "You need sleep. Take a nap while you're there, too, will you? She's not going anywhere. We'll take good care of her. You're dead on your feet, and no good to her like this. Promise me you'll stay home and take care of yourself for a few hours?"

"Yeah, okay. Maybe you're right." He managed to slip out of her soft grasp. "I didn't sleep much last night."

"I am right, Declan. Shower. Rest. And do it now. Go on."

The nurse smiled and stayed put, her arms crossed, until he'd grabbed his keys and the worn copy of *Animal Farm* he'd brought with him and walked out the door and into the wide hallway. He moved down the corridor, through a set of automatic doors and down another long hallway without thinking about it. He knew the route by heart.

Outside, the sun was just coming through the cloud cover, casting soft golden light on the road, tipping the tall, dusky pines lining the highway. He swung up into his truck and started the engine, let it rev for a moment before he pulled onto Highway One and headed south.

It would be an hour's drive or more to get home, but he didn't mind. He switched on the iPod he had plugged into the truck's stereo and flipped through his collection of rock and country until he found a playlist of classical music. He needed something soothing. Soft. Life had been too intense lately. He didn't need intense music.

The road was a blur of charcoal-gray against the backdrop of trees. He rubbed his eyes, gripped the steering wheel.

Liz was right. He needed rest. He was exhausted. He didn't really sleep in the chair beside her bed. He stayed up most of the night, watching her face, listening to her breathe, dozing off for maybe twenty minutes at a time. Praying she would open her eyes. That she would be okay.

He didn't even know this woman. Didn't know her name, where she'd come from. It didn't matter, hadn't mattered since the moment he'd laid eyes on her. There was something about her…he felt connected to her.

He knew the psychology involved. Hero saves damsel in distress. Yeah, he'd fucked that up the last time, hadn't he? Were his feelings about this girl nothing more than the need to redeem himself? And if so, what was the insane physical attraction about? Because not one moment had gone by that he hadn't wanted to touch her, *really* touch her. Lay his palms over her breasts. Kiss her mouth.

Get a grip.

Or maybe get some sleep. Shower. Pull himself together. Then go back to the hospital. He couldn't stay away for long.

By the time he reached the long gravel driveway to his house his eyes were heavy, and he was glad to be done with the drive. He pulled up in front of the rambling wood-sided cabin with its red door and green painted shutters and got out. Strange, to come home to such silence, without Liam there. He'd go to his father's place and see him tomorrow.

He let himself in, closing the door behind him with a heavy thud. The place felt empty, musty, as though the house itself could sense that it had been left mostly empty for several days. He'd always liked the quiet; he couldn't understand why it bothered him now.

You're just tired.

He *was* tired. He couldn't remember ever being this wiped. The shower would have to wait.

He moved across the wood floors, his toe catching on the edge of the throw rug. He grumbled, kept moving down the short hallway, tearing his dark blue thermal shirt over his head as he went. Reaching the bed, he sat down to pull his boots off, stood again to remove his jeans. Then he yanked the covers back and just stared at the white sheets for a moment before lying down and throwing the dark brown quilt over his body. He felt himself sink into the down ticking, pure luxury to his stiff and aching muscles.

"Ah…"

His eyes burned, so he closed them, sighing once more. He felt himself drifting, tried to fight it simply because he'd gone so long without sleep that staying awake felt like the right thing to do. But in moments he was giving over to the urge to sleep. To dream. He let his body sink into the bed. It felt so damned good. The sheets soft against his skin.

Skin…

Her skin was like pale satin, like fresh butter beneath his hand. He knew already the curve of her cheek. Wanted to know the curve of her breasts that he'd seen outlined beneath the hospital sheets.

That he'd seen on the beach in the chiaroscuro light of dawn.

He knew he shouldn't be thinking of her this way. But he couldn't help himself. She was too damn beautiful and he was too exhausted to fight it. So exhausted he couldn't fight the images of her in his head. Or was she right in front of him?

Her face shimmered before him, then her body, as if she were under water. There, yet insubstantial. She reached out for him, touched him. Just her fingertips grazing his arm, but his body was on fire instantly.

He knew he couldn't touch her. But she was smiling at him, her hands sliding over her sides, cupping her naked breasts, inviting him.

Can't touch her.

"Touch," she whispered, her voice as soft and quiet as a feather on the air.

Her own hands went between her thighs, and her long lashes lowered to her cheeks, her mouth making a small O of pleasure as she sighed.

He followed her lead, letting his hand slide down over his stomach, the muscles tight with desire already. Then lower, to his stiffening cock. He was hard as steel, just watching her, hearing her voice. He wanted to touch her so badly he could hardly stand it. He wanted to bring her pleasure. To make her cry out in ecstasy.

Her nipples would come up hard beneath his

fingertips, growing darker and darker pink as he caressed them. They'd be firm and sweet in his mouth as he sucked.

She looked at him with her sky-blue gaze, her hands coming up to smooth over her full breasts, her fingertips teasing the hardening nipples.

Need poured into his system like the ocean, a powerful, roaring white noise in his head.

Her mouth was pink, so, so pretty, and he knew how soft her lips would be around his cock…

"Ah…"

Sucking, sucking, while his fingers found the sweet cleft between her thighs, delved between the silken folds. She would be wet, his fingers sliding. And then inside her…oh, yes…pushing into her tight, sweet body.

He stroked himself, his fisted hand moving up and down, his hips beginning to thrust. Pleasure knifed through him, hot and sharp. He could almost smell her desire. Could smell his own. He was going to come soon.

"Ah, God…"

If only he could touch her. He would spread her pretty thighs, move down between them, his tongue pushing into her. He could almost hear her moans, feel her muscles tightening as desire rose, her hard nub of flesh in his mouth, her sweetness on his tongue.

"Yes…" She smiled at him, all lovely, sweet innocence, along with an almost unbearable sensuality. Too damn beautiful, this girl.

His hips arched, his hand gripping his cock until it nearly hurt. But it felt too damn good.

He would make her come, with his hands, with his mouth, her head thrashing. And then he would fuck her. Just slip between her thighs, spread those full, pink pussy lips and slide inside.

"Ah, God…"

Was that him crying out? Was it her?

Pleasure stabbing into him as he drove into her, drove into his palm. Heat and need arrowing deep into his belly. And it was her face, twisted in exquisite agony, her lovely body he was fucking, fucking…

"Angel!"

He came, his body clenching, bucking. He shivered, pleasure a pure, driving force, taking him over, blinding him to everything but her face.

Angel.

His angel.

He woke, sat straight up. His hand, his stomach, were sticky with his seed.

"Fuck."

Breathless still, he rolled onto his side and pulled some Kleenex from the box there, wiped himself off impatiently.

This was wrong. *Wrong.*

But she was so beautiful. His heart was already

beating in anticipation of seeing her again. Even if all he could ever have of her was in his dreams.

Must be losing my goddamn mind.

Maybe he was. But he wasn't going to stay away from her. Not a chance.

WHERE HAD HE GONE? SHE still couldn't open her eyes, but she knew he wasn't there. She sensed it. And Asmodeus had abandoned her, too. She was alone, in some strange place. Not the falling darkness where she met with her demon lover. Not back at the compound, in her bed in The Grandmother's house, with its familiar, earthy scents. Here everything smelled…white.

The pain was tolerable. If only she could move, see where she was, then maybe she would know what was going to happen to her. She had no idea if she would exist in the shadow places with Asmodeus, or in some new place, on some new plane. Perhaps in that place of piercing light? But that was where *he* was, her stranger.

If only he would come back to her, the man whose face she'd seen. He would care for her. He *did* care for her. She'd seen it in his clear blue eyes, even in that one brief glimpse.

She heard the muffled sound of footsteps, but it wasn't him. His were sharper. She felt hands on her, gentle female hands, doing…something. It hurt, but she knew it wasn't made to hurt on purpose. She wanted to force her eyes to open. She wanted to ask questions. But her body wouldn't cooperate with her brain. The feet shuffled away, leaving her in silence once more.

Please come to me...

She wanted to cry, but she couldn't do that, either. Not that she ever cried anymore. She'd stopped crying years ago. What had been the point?

She didn't feel sorry for herself, either, no matter how difficult her tasks. The Grandmother had taught her that self-pity was worthless. That everyone had to accept their lot in life, to do their duty. That it was hard for everyone. That those who were among the chosen had the hardest lives of all, but the greatest rewards, if they succeeded on their paths.

She had not succeeded.

A sharp surge of pain in her chest at the thought. "No!"

"Hey...you're awake. Are you trying to talk?"

His voice was deep and smooth. Rich. Like honey and gravel. Was it him?

She struggled to open her eyes once more, and it was as though every muscle in her body worked to make it happen, every ounce of her strength.

"Angel?"

His hand on her face, warm and lending her courage. She took a breath, tried again. And felt the whispering flutter of her lashes against her cheeks for a moment before she was able to raise them.

His eyes were that startling blue, bluer than the sky. They were the deep, nearly purple-blue of the iris that grew in The Grandmother's garden.

She smiled. "It's you," she managed to whisper. Her throat burned as though she'd swallowed fire.

"Jesus Christ. You *are* awake."

"Awake? Is that where I am?"

"I can't believe it."

He was gone in an instant, and there was too much noise as someone else appeared over her: a woman's face. Then she was gone and a moment later there were more people. Pain again as they touched her, moved things around. It reminded her of the ceremonies, the sacred nights of prayer and sacrifice. Only she'd been tied down then, the earth cool and solid beneath her naked back...

Chanting loud in her ears and the salt being scattered like chunks of pure quartz crystal. She couldn't see their faces; they were all robed and hooded, standing in a circle around her.

The Grandmother bent, her ancient back curving as she reached the ground to paint the sacred symbols there, within the edge of the circle of salt. Then to paint them on her body. The brush was made of twigs; it scratched into her skin, hurting her. She pulled against the ropes, but they were too firmly tied to the stakes to allow her to move. She had nowhere to go, anyway. All that happened to her was inevitable.

Then The Grandmother's face over her, her wrinkles like the deep valleys of shadow between the hills where they lived as she spoke the prayers. The Grandmother leaned in closer, and she could smell the sharp tang of herbs on her breath. Then the bitter liquid being poured down her throat. She knew better than to fight it, as she had when she was little, when she had first come to this place.

Had she not always been in this place?

The time before was a blank, emptiness. *Now* was an unanswered question, as hands moved over her flesh. As pain washed over her in waves.

Be with me…come back.

"I'm here."

Not Asmodeus, though those were the words he often said to her. No, it was *him*. The man with the blue eyes. He was holding her hand.

She wept then. She didn't know why. But the tears poured out, hot on her cheeks, sliding down over her jaw, onto her neck.

"Ah, don't cry. Don't be afraid. I'm here. I won't leave you. I won't. I promise."

She heard the sincerity in his voice. Felt his fierce protection. Knew he was the one who had saved her. Gratitude suffused her. For what he had done. For what he would be to her. For what he was already.

She blinked the tears from her eyes, and truly saw him for the first time.

He had a beautiful face. Not the kind of perfection that was her demon lover, but more beautiful, perhaps, because of the humanity he wore. His cheekbones were high, his chin square. His mouth was all firm lines, but there was a softness there. Along his jaw there was a scar, old and pale. She knew the beauty of it, from her own scars. Knew they always meant something, were another layer of who a person was. That they were earned through strife, and therefore valuable.

Her hands felt as though they weighed a thousand pounds, but she managed to lift one, to reach up and touch that scar.

His lips parted, but he didn't say anything as she explored it with her fingertips, her body lighting up with need. Yes, he was pure beauty, this man.

This *man*.

The first man she had ever touched.

Her heart raced. Her sex thrummed with wanting, even through the confusion, the pain.

She knew then that she must give herself to him. That *this* was what she had to live for. She could still make a gift of her innocence, herself. She was not without purpose. Life was not without the beauty she was raised to believe in.

"Are you in pain?" he asked, his dark brows drawn.

"A little. It hurts to talk."

He smiled at her, his face lighting a bit, but still heavy with shadows. He was sad, this man.

"That's because you had a breathing tube down your throat for a few days."

She didn't understand what he was saying, only that he was trying to reassure her. She smiled to show her appreciation.

"Ah…Jesus, I don't know how you can smile," he murmured, "after everything you've been through."

She wanted to tell him she was smiling because she was happy, but she was so sleepy. She had to close her eyes once more. Had to rest. To dream…

She was back with The Grandmother. They were in the garden. The sun was shining, warm on her face. She loved the garden. The place smelled of the rich earth newly overturned as she bent over a row with her trowel. The Grandmother had taught her to plant and care for the herbs and vegetables when she was so small it took both of her hands to hold the trowel, and she could barely manage the tall shovel. The earth was familiar to her, and the plants. She knew their cycles: when to plant, when to harvest, what each one was for. Basil and thyme to flavor food, black sage for backache, yarrow for toothache, wormwood and chamomile to calm. Datura and salvia and the mushrooms to dream.

Was she dreaming now? But everything was so familiar. She was safe within the walls of The Grandmother's garden. This was where she belonged.

Not anymore.

Shadows loomed in the garden as the sky went dark. And then there was nothing but the dark. She was falling, falling...

"Asmodeus!"

But the empty air whistled past her ears, tangling her hair, and she remained alone.

CHAPTER THREE

"WHAT'S HAPPENING TO HER?"

A nurse gently but firmly moved Declan aside. The monitors were beeping, the noise jangling his nerves. She was too damn pale, her breath coming out in short gasps. He'd tried to wake her again, but when she wouldn't open her eyes he'd called for the nurse. It was as though she was lost somewhere in there.

The tears rolling down her cheeks were killing him.

"Can't you do something?"

"She's just a little agitated," the nurse answered. "Probably dreaming."

The nurse reset the monitors, straightened the pillows. And his angel calmed, her breath a steady whisper now.

"She's okay?"

"She'll be fine. Her body's just working off the heavy sedation from her surgeries."

The nurse shuffled out, her soft-soled shoes whispering across the linoleum floor. He went back to his place at the side of her bed, standing over her. The damn tears were still slipping down her face, over the small cuts on her cheeks, the bruises on her jaw. He wiped them with his thumbs, his heart beating like thunder in his chest.

What was it about this girl? They'd barely exchanged a dozen words, and most of them didn't make sense. But she'd gotten under his skin. He shouldn't care so much. But he did.

She moaned and he held her cheek. "Wake up. Come on, Angel. You're dreaming. You just need to come out of it."

Anxiety was like a piercing heat in his veins. Desire just as strong, but he ignored it.

Her eyes opened, that summer-sky-blue.

"Hey. You're back."

"Yes."

He held perfectly still as she stared up at him. Her lashes were long and dense, a dark golden-brown. Like doll eyes. Except they were filled with light and warmth as she searched his face.

"You're real, then," she said softly.

"What? Of course I'm real."

"It's difficult to tell sometimes, what's real and what's not. I was just in the garden…and then it went away. I wanted to call for you, but I don't know your name."

She had the strangest way of talking.

"It's Declan. Declan Byrne."

"Declan Byrne," she repeated.

She blinked up at him. Then she lifted her hand and covered his. And it was only then he realized he still held her face in his hand. Her palm was warm, her fingers brushing over his, making him heat all over. He pulled his hands back, stuck them in the pocket of his jeans.

"Can you tell me your name?" he asked her.

"I have no name." Her gaze drifted out the window as thunder rumbled outside. The sky was an ashen gray.

Her injuries must have really rattled her. Stephen had warned him she might not be all there when she woke up. *If* she woke up. But here she was, awake and at least partially alert. "That's okay. You'll remember after you've had a chance to recover."

"I remember. I remember that I have no name."

"I...don't understand."

She was still looking out the window, watching as the rain started to come down, tiny droplets spattering the glass. "I am The Gift. The Consecrated. Those are my only names, but they are not mine. There is nothing which belongs to me."

He straightened up. She seemed sane enough. Or, he wanted to believe she was. But this was some weird shit. He ran a hand through his hair. "You're telling me you don't have a name, just... titles?"

She turned her head to look at him again. She seemed perfectly calm. Too calm, maybe. "If that is how you wish to think of it."

"No one has ever called you something else?"

"Only you. You call me an angel."

He was surprised to feel himself blushing. "You heard that?"

"Yes."

"What else… Never mind. I'm just glad you're awake."

"So am I. What is this place? Is this your place?"

"What? No. It's the hospital."

"Hospital…" She seemed to be testing the word on her tongue. "You do not live here?"

"Only lately."

Her brows drew together in confusion.

"Sorry. I was making a joke."

"I don't understand."

"Yeah, neither do I. Look, something has happened to you. You've been hurt pretty badly. But you're going to be okay."

"What I am going to be remains to be seen. I've not been told yet."

"For now you'll stay here, in the hospital, until you're well. You'll be taken care of. I'll make sure you're taken care of."

Where had that come from? But it felt ridiculously important to him, to protect this girl. From what, he wasn't sure, exactly. But he needed to find out.

"Do you remember who did this to you?"

She turned her face away from him once more, pressing her cheek into the pillow, her jaw clenching, her eyes squeezing shut. Another tear slid down her cheek.

Shit.

He leaned in closer, said quietly, "You don't have to tell me right now. Okay? That can wait. Just rest. Get better."

"It hurts," she said quietly.

"Are you in pain? I'll get the nurse, have her give you something for it."

"It hurts to know I've failed. That I did this to myself."

"Angel, it's not possible for you to have done these things to yourself."

She shook her head. "It is my own fault, my own failings. If I'd been good enough…"

He was angry now, at whoever had put these ideas into her head. "No one deserves what happened to you," he said fiercely. "No one."

She turned to look at him, her eyes glossy with tears. "You don't know that."

"I do." He stared down at her, willing her to believe him. "I don't know very much about you, but I know that."

She was silent for several moments, then her

face lit in a slow smile that dazzled him. She nodded her head. "Thank you."

He was speechless, overcome by her beauty, by the innocence of her face. By the depth of her blue eyes, as though even in that sweet face, she was a thousand years old, somehow. And beneath that sweetness was a sensual earthiness he couldn't explain. But his body knew. His body knew the flawless heat of the skin on her cheek, her hand. He was going hard, even as he berated himself for it.

"The doctor is coming in to see her," the nurse said, bustling into the room. "We're going to be taking her out to run some tests. Maybe you want to go get some food, Declan? Come back later?"

"Yes, sure." He turned back to the young woman in the bed. "I'll be back in a little while."

She reached for him, and he took her hand in his. She was still smiling at him. He had to force himself to give up her hand, to step out of the room.

Ridiculous.

This obsession with her was crazy. But he'd never met anyone like her. Hell, he didn't know the girl, didn't even know what he meant by that, exactly. She was like some unearthly creature. Truly like an angel come to earth.

It had to be some sort of weird amnesia—the way she talked, that she thought she had no name. He'd talk to Stephen about it after he'd had a chance to examine her, run the tests, whatever they planned to do now that she was awake. Meanwhile, he'd see what anyone had found out about who had done this to her, who she was. He'd focus on getting information. And he'd damn well get his body under control.

He went down the hall and outside, the fresh air cool on his face as he made his way to his truck, pulling out his cell phone as soon as he sat down.

"Hello?"

"Dad."

"Hi, Declan. What's up?"

"I need your help." There was a long silence on the other end of the line. "Look, I know I've been a total shit and I don't deserve anything from you—"

"Cut the crap, Dec. Tell me what you need."

"Just like that?"

"I'm not the one who's been angry."

His father's voice was gravelly, low. It always had been, but it had become even rougher as he'd grown older. Declan didn't like to think about him aging. Growing weak. It made him feel as if he was running out of time.

He ran a hand through his hair. "Yeah. Yeah, you're right."

"We don't have to talk about it now. You called for a reason."

"It's the girl…she woke up. And she has no idea who she is. She says she doesn't have a name. She wasn't making a whole lot of sense, but I got the feeling she was alert. Hard to say with her injuries, I guess. But nothing is adding up. And the sheriff's office still isn't telling me anything. I want to know, Dad. I want to know who I can talk to. I need to know where she came from, who did this to her."

"I thought you might. I've been doing a little digging through some old connections."

"And?"

"Nothing so far. She sort of came out of nowhere. No missing-persons reports fitting her description. And no leads as to who did this. A boyfriend, maybe?"

"I don't think so. There's more to it than that. Unless her boyfriend is some total psycho."

"That's possible, isn't it?"

"Maybe."

"Can you talk to her again?"

"Yes. But I don't want to push her too hard yet. I don't want to upset her. And enough time has passed that whoever did this has probably left the area already."

"Dec, it's likely we'll never find them," Oran said quietly.

"I know that. Do you really think I don't know that, Dad? But I have to try."

"Jesus, Dec. Why do we have to do this now? You need my help and I'm willing to give it. For the girl. Hell, for *you,* whether or not you want to believe it."

"Fuck." He ran a hand over his hair, dug his fingers into his scalp, squeezed his eyes shut. "Okay. Okay. I'll put a lid on it. I appreciate your help."

He heard his father huff out a breath. "It's no problem. I'll help with this however I can."

"Thanks. I'll be by to pick up Liam tonight. How's he doing?"

"Fine. He hangs out on the porch all day, eats like a horse. He's good company."

"Good. Good. Okay, I'll see you later, then."

"I can bring him by your place. You've got plenty going on."

"You don't have to do that, Dad."

"I know."

He heard the stubborn tone in his father's voice. Knew there was no point in arguing. Knew Oran understood perfectly well that he had his reasons for avoiding the house all these years.

Declan flipped his phone shut, stared at it for a few moments. He damn well hated to ask his father for anything. But this wasn't for himself. It was for *her.* He'd do anything he had to for her.

There it was again, that crazy idea. But he couldn't shake it. He wasn't sure he wanted to.

Shades of the way he'd felt about Abby. But this was different. He was different.

Yeah, a hell of a lot more bitter.

It was true. But he'd lived with that bitterness long enough that he was used to it.

God, he was thinking in circles. He must still be tired. But he had things to do. Like go harass Tim Bullock for information again.

He stuck the key in the ignition and the big truck roared to life. He pulled onto the road, rolling the windows down, letting the scents of sea and cypress roll in.

A mile down the highway he caught himself humming. That was new. What the hell was wrong with him? Or maybe something was right for once, which would sure as hell be hard to recognize.

She made him feel good, the beautiful girl in the hospital bed. Good about himself. Just good, in general.

Must be some sort of savior complex. But there would be plenty of time to psychoanalyze himself later. He was on a mission. He could help this girl. His angel. Be of some fucking use to someone again.

Was that what he really wanted? To be of use to someone? Or was it something more?

He refused to think of Angel as a substitute for Abby. And even if that had been partly true in the beginning, things had changed. Even just watching her sleep, waiting for her to wake up, praying she would come out of this whole. It made him feel a deeper connection to her than should be there, maybe. But the moment she'd opened her eyes and talked to him, it all felt all right. And for the first time in a long time he didn't want to question anything. He could allow himself to feel good.

It had been years. Too long, probably, and he had plenty of regrets. His relationship with his dad, although he wasn't ready to resolve that yet. He wasn't ready to let go of resentments held too long. He regretted relationships with women he'd passed up because he just couldn't handle it. So, why now? Why her? Why was it so damn important to him that whatever happened with her, there would be no regrets?

She was a mystery to him. Yet he felt like he *knew* her in some strange way. He couldn't explain it.

He didn't like anything he couldn't explain. He was too goal-oriented to leave anything hanging in the air unanswered. But he almost didn't mind when it came to Angel. He wanted to find out who had hurt her. But the rest—the strangeness about her, his response to her—didn't bother him as much as it should.

A shadow flickered over the truck and he looked up in time to see a hawk gliding across the road, wings spread, soaring. He didn't know why it made him think of Angel. She was very much a part of the earth, but it was as if she wasn't quite tethered to it.

Jesus, he was getting philosophical now.

He wanted to see her again, talk to her. He could hardly wait.

Ridiculous.

But she'd gotten beneath his skin, deep down, and he couldn't shake her. He didn't even want to. He didn't know what he'd do when it was time for her to leave the hospital.

And where would she go?

Don't even consider it.

But she had nowhere to go, no family that anyone knew of, no way to take care of herself.

He couldn't stand the idea of her alone in the world. He could give her money to get an apartment, maybe. And hire someone to help care for her. She'd need that. And he could still see her…

He stepped on the gas, hard, and the truck lurched forward.

He'd go back to the hospital after he'd talked to Bullock, tell her that he'd help her.

If only he knew who was going to help him get over this girl. This woman. His angel fallen from the sky.

SHE DIDN'T LIKE IT WHEN Declan was gone. The others—the nurses—were nice to her. But she only felt safe and happy when he was with her.

The men had come to talk to her. Police, they'd told her they were called. She didn't like the questions they asked her. She'd turned away from them, closed her eyes, pretending to sleep until they went away. She'd heard them tell the nurse they'd be back another time. She hoped Declan would be there. She didn't want to face those men without him. They'd tried to be kind, but their faces were too hard, too eager. She didn't like it. And she didn't want to answer their questions. She wasn't going to talk to the men about The Grandmother. Asmodeus. She would tell Declan, maybe, once she was feeling stronger.

He said he'd come back. She hoped it would be soon. She was awake now, and unsure what to do with her time.

She'd spent a few hours simply taking in everything around her. It was a barren place, this hospital. The walls were white, with just one small picture of flowers in a watering can. It only made her miss her garden more. She hoped someone would care for her plants, her herbs and flowers. She hoped someone would care for The Grandmother. She was getting old, and her body hurt. Who would mix her tinctures? Cook for her? Help her from her chair in the evenings?

Maybe there would be another girl, a new Gift. She'd known there were other girls in the compound, even though she wasn't allowed to see or talk with them. She could hear their young voices over the garden wall sometimes. Had heard The

Grandmother make some muttering reference to
them when she was not quite asleep or in pain. It
made her feel better, knowing The Grandmother
wouldn't always be alone.

She knew what alone was. If it hadn't been for
The Grandmother and Asmodeus she would have
always been alone. As she was now. And she was
too awake to call for Asmodeus; he only came to
her when she was dreaming.

She missed him. Her body craved his voice,
his instruction, even in pain as she was. But her
body had a new yearning. For Declan. Her body
and her heart.

She understood he had saved her. She would always be grateful to him. And he was beautiful to
her, maybe more so because of her gratitude. His
touch set her on fire, even his fingertips on her
cheek, and she knew she would have responded to
him this same way no matter the circumstances.

But she would have to wait until her body had
healed to show him how she felt. If he would give
her the chance. She hoped he would not reject
her, too. But she would try and try, as she'd been
taught, until she was certain of her failure.

She turned to the window to watch the twilit
sky. The rain had stopped, leaving the fog behind.
It rolled along the branches of the trees, soft in its
shadow colors, shades of gray and white. It made
her think of the stories she'd read, about the spir-

its of the trees who lived in the forest, hiding in the mist. It made her think of the sparrows who lived in the trees in The Grandmother's garden, the hummingbirds who drank from the flowers, the call of the ravens, who were black as night.

She was growing bored with her own thoughts when Declan returned.

"Hey. You're awake."

"Yes."

His smile was warm, his lips lush, his teeth strong and white. She saw the scar on his jaw again, felt a small twinge for whatever he had suffered. But it was hard to feel bad with him smiling at her.

"How are you feeling? Is the pain under control?"

"For the most part. My shoulder blades hurt where they were cut, but I can bear it. My leg is not bothering me. The medicine they give me helps."

"That's good. What have you been doing, Angel?" he asked, stepping closer.

"Telling myself stories."

"Stories? What kind of stories?"

"Pretty tales of birds and rabbits. You know."

"I'm not sure I do."

"I remember stories I've read, and then I take parts of them and put them back together again. In my head. It passes the time."

He seemed puzzled. "Ah. Why don't you just turn on the TV?"

"TV?"

"The television."

She shook her head, confused.

"You…don't know television?" he asked, gesturing to a box with a dark window in it, mounted somehow close to the ceiling.

"I don't know this thing."

"Jesus."

Declan ran a hand through his dark hair, sat in the chair beside her bed. She wanted to touch his shining hair, to see what it felt like beneath her fingers. But she thought it better to wait until he no longer seemed so concerned.

"Angel, you have no idea what a television is," he said, his tone low, his brows drawn together.

She wasn't sure why this was so important. She shook her head again.

"You really are an innocent, aren't you?"

"Yes. I am innocent, untouched." She felt excitement that he would broach this subject with her. Her body surged with wanting.

"What?"

"I am untouched by man, as I should be."

He flinched. Why did he seem so surprised? She didn't understand.

"Declan, should I not have said this to you?"

"No, it's fine. Fine."

But he was running his hand through his hair again, which she recognized already as a sign of agitation.

"Angel. Have you thought about what you'll do when you get out of here?"

"Leave the hospital?"

"Yes."

"This is not to be my place, then?"

"No, of course not."

"Oh."

She let her gaze wander to the window, where she could see the cool green treetops. She knew she should be paying closer attention, but this was all so confusing.

"Angel?"

She turned back to Declan. "Yes?"

He sighed. "You'll have to live somewhere after they let you go. I want to help you."

"I am to live with you, then? In your place?"

"What? No. I meant I'd get you set up in an apartment, or a small house somewhere."

"Without you?"

"I… Yes."

Her heart was hammering in her chest, like the short, sharp clattering of the baby sparrows that had hatched in the garden one year.

"Please do not ask me to go without you, Declan."

"Angel…look, I live alone in a house pretty

much in the middle of the forest. It's just me and my dog. It wouldn't be appropriate."

"Why would it not be appropriate?"

"Because you've just come through a trauma. You need to be taken care of."

"Will you not take care of me, Declan?"

His hand went into his hair again. "I don't… You need a nurse or something. And I have to work most days."

"Oh. I don't want to be a burden to you. You have work to do, of course. I understand."

Disappointment beat a sad, steady cadence in her chest, but she would not tell him.

"Angel, you really will need a nurse for a while."

"I can nurse myself. I always have. I cared for The Grandmother when she was ill."

"Is that who you lived with? Your grand-mother?"

"Not *my* grandmother. She is The Grandmother. The leader. She is my guardian. She was…"

He pulled one of the small, hard chairs to her bedside and sat down, resting his palms on his knees. He wore blue jeans. The Grandmother had sometimes worn blue jeans. She had given her a pair of her own once, but she'd found them too re-strictive. She much preferred dresses.

Declan touched her arm briefly, making her focus on him once more. "Angel? Do you know how long you were with her?"

"As far back as I remember. Almost."

"Almost?"

She didn't like to think of the time before. It was a blur, dreamlike. A happiness just out of reach. Too insubstantial to hold on to.

Declan's gaze was bright, intense, his brows drawn together.

"Are these things important, Declan?"

"Yes. I think they might be. Can you tell me about her? The Grandmother?"

She sighed, running the fingertips of her unhurt hand over the edge of the white sheet. "She is very old. So old her skin is like the bark of the oak tree. Her eyes are dark and shining. She knows all there is to know. She taught me the ways of growing things, the herbs to heal and hurt. She taught me to cook, so that I can nurture the human body. She gave me books to study, and then she would ask me questions to be certain I learned as I should. All things. Of the earth and the sky. How to do things. What things are made of. She gave me books to read of strange people and places. Stories, so that I came to know *people.* Humans. She wanted me to know our faults. Our beauty. She guided me in all things."

She thought briefly, longingly, of Asmodeus, of his sensual instruction, his teachings about her body. How to please the body of a man. She thought of his low voice, the way it seemed to caress her skin, even though he never touched her. Looking at Declan, she let her gaze wander to his mouth, then his hands. She wanted to touch his mouth, to press her lips to his. To feel his hands on her. Not only her cheek, her arm, but all over her body. Her breasts, between her thighs… "She taught me nearly all things…"

She wanted Declan so badly she ached with it. But he seemed interested only in talking with her now. Perhaps when she had healed he would want her. When she was strong enough to take a man into her body, as she had waited her entire life to do. She squeezed her thighs together to ease the ache there.

"I'm sorry, Declan. What did you ask?"

"I asked if you're feeling up to talking about this. The Grandmother. Your life with her."

"It hurts to think of her. That I will not see her again." She paused, her fingers twisting in the sheet. "That I have been cast out."

"That's what happened to you? You were cast out?"

She shrugged. "Yes. I will never go back there, to the compound. To The Grandmother. Even if I knew my way back. I don't know what I will do now, what my life will be."

"I'll help you figure that out. We just need to find a place for you when you're released in a few days. I'll talk to your doctor, figure things out from there. Okay?"

"Yes. Thank you, Declan."

She reached for him, took his hand. Surprise rippled across his face, then his fingers closed around hers, his skin warm and dry. And an arc of desire flickered over her skin. She could see in his face he felt it, too. He tried to draw his hand back, but she held on as tightly as she could.

"Angel..."

"Don't let go, Declan. Don't let me go."

He stared at her, his lips parted. She wanted more than ever to feel his kiss on her lips, her flesh.

He cleared his throat. "I have to go. I have to talk to the doctor now."

She sighed. "But you'll be back?"

"Yes. I promise."

She released his hand, but her body was still filled with wanting. And she was so tired. She was always tired now, it seemed.

"I think I will sleep while you're away."

"I'll shut off the light on my way out."

He smiled, stood and left the room. Left her system humming with need.

She lay in the dark, wishing sleep would come so she could call to Asmodeus to satisfy her needs. But sleep eluded her.

Instead, she let her left hand, the one undamaged, wander beneath the cool white sheet, over her body. She touched her breasts, her fingertips feathering over the hardening nipples, imagining Declan's touch. Her breasts grew full, warm, her nipples like two stones, the flesh rising to meet her fingers. She pulled on them lightly, then harder, as Asmodeus had often instructed her, bringing them to two fine points.

She spread her thighs and dipped her hand between them, desire swarming her as her fingers slipped in the wetness there. She rubbed the lips of her sex, felt them swell beneath her touch.

What would Declan's hands feel like between her thighs? His mouth?

"Ah…"

Pleasure stabbed deep, simply thinking about his head between her thighs, his tongue hot and wet. Asmodeus had often told her how this could be done. Her hips arched and she slid one fingertip inside her sex, careful not to probe too deeply, not to breach her maidenhead. But how she wanted that sensation of being filled. By Declan.

She pictured his face once more, looking at her body. Would he keep his gaze on hers as he entered her? Or would his eyes clench shut in ecstasy?

She shivered, need shimmering through her in small waves that grew moment by moment. She pressed the heel of her hand against her mound, hard over her tight clitoris.

Declan…

Would he kiss her as he drove into her body? Would he put his hot mouth on her neck? Take her nipples into his mouth?

"Ah…"

Her hips were pumping up to meet her hand, her sex growing wetter and wetter. And in her mind it was Declan's hands on her, his mouth, drawing her nipples in, his tongue swirling over the tips while he pressed deep into her flesh.

Her climax shimmered like a mirage in the distance, then roared through her, taking her by surprise. Hard and fast, the spasms of pleasure taking her over, blinding her.

Declan…

Asmodeus's voice resonated in her head.

Come, girl. Come for me.

"No, not for you. For him," she whispered.

Declan.

Only for him.

She thought she heard Asmodeus's roar, but her climax was like thunder in her ears, dazzling her, deafening her.

It left her trembling, only that first keen edge satisfied. She wanted him still. She was meant for him, she was certain of it.

Comforted, her body relaxed, and finally she slept.

CHAPTER FOUR

DECLAN PULLED UP IN FRONT of the hospital and stepped out of his truck. It was a classic Mendocino spring day, the air damp and still heavy with fog, even though it was nearly noon. He patted Liam, who was standing in the truck bed, his stumpy tail wagging, his big tongue lolling.

"Hope you aren't opposed to change, boy," he told the dog, knowing full well he was the one who was anxious about it.

He was taking Angel home today. To *his* home. He still couldn't quite believe it. Still wasn't certain it was the right thing to do. But what other options were there?

He'd talked to Stephen, to the nurses. She'd need some care for a while, and he could take some time off work, hire a nurse to come in to check on her between doctors' appointments. That wasn't a problem. But to have her in his house, where her sweet, earthy body tempted him beyond anything he'd experienced before…

He could handle it. *Would* handle it. She really had no place else to go.

There was no one else to take responsibility for her. The county didn't want to deal with her, do anything for her. And both Stephen and his dad seemed to think this was the best option for her.

He made his way down a long hallway to the elevator, pressed the button.

The local psychotherapist they'd assigned her to was Ruth Hehewuti, who had evaluated her and had agreed Angel should go to Declan's house until she was able to care for herself. Ruth was also his father's girlfriend, which he didn't like much.

Still, Ruth was one of a handful of qualified therapists in the small coastal town, and Stephen had highly recommended her, so that was something. He'd met her a few times when he'd run into Oran and Ruth at one of the local diners, the grocery store, the farmers' market. He'd never done more than offer a gruff greeting to the woman. He'd certainly never made an effort to get to know her. He knew he was being a jerk about it. The way he felt about his dad and his dad's relationship with her wasn't Ruth's fault. But he hadn't been able to help it. Seeing them together always made his blood boil.

He'd had one meeting with her the other day to discuss Angel's case, and he'd had to put his issues aside for Angel's sake. She seemed like a nice enough woman, he had to admit grudgingly. She was a lot nicer to him than he probably deserved. A Hopi healer and shaman, Stephen had told him, in addition to being a practicing therapist. He wasn't sure how he felt about all that spiritual stuff, but Angel was going to need some help adjusting to a world that was strange and new to her. Some help dealing with the trauma of her past, although she didn't seem to be particularly traumatized by it. She accepted it all pretty calmly, other than being sad about leaving behind that crazy old woman— the woman who had held her captive for what the police and her doctors figured was a good sixteen years, since she was around five years old.

The elevator doors opened and he stepped inside, pressed the button for the fourth floor.

He'd been able to piece together some bits of information during some of her more coherent moments. The picture painted from the things she said, the injuries, the marks on her body, was pretty damn ugly. Unbelievable, still, no matter how many times he went over it in his head.

The nursing staff was really coddling her. Not that he didn't think she deserved to be coddled, but nurses were usually made of stern stuff, and they all clucked over her like a bunch of mother hens. Anyone in the hospital who knew anything of Angel's story was horrified. Even the police he'd spoken with seemed shocked. Hell, so was he.

Shocked by what she'd been through. By what that grandmother woman had done to her, for years. But Angel was attached to her.

Stockholm Syndrome, Ruth had told him it was called, the weird, psychological phenomenon where victims came to love their kidnappers. He found it hard to relate to, but he'd done some reading and had at least a basic understanding of it. He was trying, anyway, for Angel's sake. She would definitely need some help with that. It seemed like some pretty twisted shit to him.

The doors opened and he moved down the hall, grateful it was the last time he'd have to see this place for a while. Too many memories here of his mother's last days. Too many memories of Abby's body in the hospital morgue in Bahrain. He fucking hated hospitals.

The nurses nodded to him as he passed their station. He'd been coming here for two weeks, and knew most of them by name.

He paused at the door to her room, took a deep breath. His life was about to change. He hadn't wanted this kind of responsibility for another human being. It scared the shit out of him frankly. But he wouldn't turn his back on her.

The fact was, he *couldn't.*

When he stepped into the room she was there, sitting on the edge of the bed, her casted leg resting on a chair that was pulled close. The pale sunlight came through the open blinds, gilding her long hair so that it looked more silver than gold. She was dressed in a long-sleeved dress that was the same summer-blue as her eyes. He'd never seen her in real clothing before. She looked different to him. More real. But her smile was the same as ever: brilliant, trusting, innocent and sensual all at the same time.

Lust kicked him hard in the gut. He had to suck in a breath, command himself to calm down.

"Declan! I go home with you today."

"Yes."

"I am so happy."

"Me, too."

He smiled back at her. He couldn't help it. She was so beautiful, this girl. So vulnerable. He would do anything for her. He stepped closer.

It wasn't the first time that thought had passed through his mind. Better not to think about it now, to analyze it. Just get her to the house, get her settled in. He could think about all that other shit when he was alone later in his room. In his bed…

Don't even go there.

"How are you doing today? Feel okay?"

"I'm just excited." She paused, her smile fading. "Sheriff Bullock came again today with that policeman."

She never said the investigating officer's name—she didn't like him.

His stomach tightened. He didn't like to hear when the guy was questioning her without him being there. But at least Tim had been. "Want to tell me about it?"

She glanced away, her fingers smoothing the edge of the sheet on the bed. "He always asks the same questions. He doesn't like that I only have the same answers."

"No, I guess he doesn't. Don't worry about him right now, okay?"

She sighed. "Okay."

"Are you all ready, Angel? Do you have your stuff together?"

She'd accepted the name. So had her nursing staff, the doctors. The courts, when one of the social workers sent by the hospital had helped to file the paperwork last week that would give her an identity. It fit her.

"Yes. Liz gave me dresses and sweaters and shoes. Some of the other nurses gave me nightdresses and a brush for my hair and lotion for my skin. It smells so pretty, like my old garden. Here, smell."

She held her hand to his face and he inhaled automatically.

God, it was *her* beneath the faint scent of lavender and lemons. He couldn't imagine her smelling like anything else.

Except the raw scent of desire…

Stop it.

An orderly came in with a wheelchair, and the nurses all said their goodbyes, many of them hugging Angel. Then they were riding the elevator down, his arms piled with plastic bags holding her scant belongings. He couldn't imagine what that was like, to go into life with nothing. Nothing to hold on to, no certainty.

Except for him.

If he thought about it too long the sense of responsibility was overwhelming. He'd chosen not to think about it much.

They reached the ground floor and the orderly wheeled Angel out to his truck. Liam was there, tail-stub wagging like crazy, but he knew not to try and jump out.

"Oh!"

"Angel, are you afraid of dogs? I didn't think to ask. Shit. I'm sorry."

"Oh, no. The Grandmother has dogs. I liked them. It's just that…I *know* him. I saw him. I thought he was Cerberus. I thought…but he's not. He's yours."

Cerberus? The three-headed dog who guarded the gates of hell? She was confused, that was for sure. But he guessed that was normal. Ruth and Stephen had both told him that having to leave the hospital today was going to be another shock for her.

"Liam can ride in the back of the truck. I'll make sure he doesn't bother you."

"Can he sit with me? Is there room?"

"You want him to sit with you? He slobbers like crazy."

"Yes. Please, Declan. He is my protector, just as you are."

She was smiling, holding her hand out, trying to reach for Liam as the orderly helped her to stand up. The dog came to the edge of the truck bed, laid his face in her palm, nuzzling her, his brown gaze on her, adoring.

What the hell had gotten into the dog? He was always friendly, but this... He'd never seen him act this way with anyone.

"If you're sure." She sent him a dazzling smile. He really could not refuse her anything. "Okay, let's get you into the truck, then we'll get Liam."

He helped her into the cab, laying her crutches in the truck bed, then whistled to Liam. The dog jumped in, settled himself politely next to Angel, his big muzzle resting against her cheek. She was murmuring to the big animal, smiling. Declan shook his head as he went around and got into the driver's seat.

He thanked the orderly, started the truck and pulled onto the Shoreline Highway.

Some of the fog had cleared; trees and ocean whizzed past on either side as they headed south.

He pointed out landmarks to Angel: a local inn, the junior college, but she wasn't really paying attention.

"This has to be pretty overwhelming for you," he told her after a while.

"I almost remember riding in a car. I know I have…"

"I keep forgetting how limited your life has been. And I'm sure I don't know the half of it. Ruth told me everything would be new to you, but it's hard to comprehend until I see it happening."

"Yes, for me, too. She told me to trust you. That you would guide me. Liam will guide me, too."

She rubbed her hand over the dog's massive, black head.

"Looks like you two are going to be friends."

"Yes." She smiled again, and he had to force himself to watch the road rather than her.

Her face was healing, the cuts and bruises mostly faded, leaving her pure beauty shining through. Her hair was pulled back in some sort of clip, away from her face, revealing her high, rounded cheekbones, her fine jawline. Her mouth was even more lush, more pink, now that her health was returning. But it was her eyes that always got him: big and blue, so pure and innocent, but with a thousand lifetimes in there in some weird way.

Concentrate on the road, buddy.

"Angel, do you want me to put on some music?"

He knew the nurses had played music for her during her weeks in the hospital. Liz had brought in her own iPod and speaker dock for Angel to use.

"I love music."

"What do you like? Anything other than Liz's country music?"

"Everything."

Everything. It was all so simple with her. He pushed in the CD he'd been listening to on the way to the hospital, an old Kenny Loggins album. He glanced at Angel, found a small smile on her lips as she smoothed her hand over Liam's neck rhythmically.

"This is happy music. I like it," she said.

"I'm glad. What else do you like? Besides music, I mean. I guess I've never asked."

She shrugged. "I love the garden, growing things. I love the scent of the earth. I like to work it, to feel it in my hands, to encourage things to grow."

"I can make a place for you to garden at the house, once your leg is better, if you want."

"I would like that very much."

"What else? What kind of things are you interested in?"

"I love the birds. And we sometimes had rabbits in the garden, although The Grandmother would often catch them to eat for supper. I didn't like that, but I understand the circle of life. We must find sustenance where we can."

He wanted to ask more about the old woman, but figured it was Ruth's job now. And thinking about the crazy old bitch who had kept Angel prisoner sickened him.

"Anything else? What did you do at night?"

"I cooked meals, cleaned The Grandmother's house. I knitted blankets and socks. I liked to draw, when I could. I love to read books. I wasn't given many, never enough. Do you have books, Declan? And may I look at them?"

"I have tons of books. And of course you can read them. Read whatever you want. If there's something you want to read and I don't have it, I can get it for you."

"How will I know what you don't have until I see it?"

She wasn't being facetious, he understood that. But he didn't have an answer for her. He figured searching the internet would be a completely alien idea to her.

"We'll figure that out as we go, I guess."

"Thank you, Declan, for the offer of your books. For sharing your home with me."

"You're welcome."

He didn't know how to handle all this gratitude. He was doing this because he felt compelled to.

Not forced. But he couldn't imagine *not* taking care of her.

"We have at least another half hour before we get to my house. Are you comfortable enough? Is your leg okay?"

"Yes. Thank you, Declan."

Angel settled back into the seat, Liam warm and solid beside her. She felt the most absolute sense of safety she'd ever felt in her life, with Declan on one side of her and Liam on the other. Her protectors. Both strong and beautiful, in their own way.

She was excited to see where she would live. But this car journey was exciting, too. Everything moved so quickly; she barely had time to focus on a house or a tree before it was gone. She experimented with squinting her eyes, letting everything outside the window blur into a smear of green. It was a strange sensation, not unlike falling with Asmodeus, but brighter, with more color. And full of hope.

He hadn't visited her in a number of days, and she hadn't called him. She was half-afraid to at this point. She knew he would be angry with her. There was so much she wanted to ask him, but she didn't dare. And she felt a strange sense of freedom without him, as much as she did the fear. Uncertainty. She didn't know how to go about learning about her new life, taking in all the strange and wonderful things: television, the way her bed moved up and down simply by pressing a button. More important things like talking with Ruth, with Liz and the other nurses. Getting to know people, truly, for the first time, in some real way, rather than by reading books about them. And most of all, knowing Declan, which was wonderful and a little frightening at the same time. But of course, she could never ask Asmodeus about him. He would be too angry. Too…jealous of Declan. Strange to think of the nearly omnipotent demon as envious of anything, but she knew it to be true.

Declan had replaced Asmodeus in her fantasies. Her body craved him now, instead of her demon lover. Most of the time. And even when she yearned for Asmodeus's hard and burning touch, her mind immediately turned to Declan.

She turned her head to watch his profile as he drove. He was so masculine. She knew already every angle and plane of his face. Every expression. And every line, every look, was beautiful to her.

He felt *right*. Asmodeus never had. Of course, she'd always known he was temporary, that his job was to prepare her. She just hadn't known what it was he would prepare her for. She understood and accepted now that it was not to be the Dark One. But she no longer felt sad. Because now she had Declan. He was her destiny, she was certain of it.

All her training, her dedication and effort, were to prepare her for *him*.

He appeared not to know it, and she understood he would be resistant. But that seemed to be an organic part of this dynamic. She knew it would be a process. She was prepared to wait.

The truck rolled down the highway, and despite her fascination with all she saw, her eyelids soon grew heavy. She slept.

Asmodeus came to her almost as soon as her mind was enveloped by the darkness.

"I heard you call to me, girl."

She was naked, as always, the wind sweeping over her bare skin, twisting her hair into long, floating coils. They were nowhere, in the falling, weightless dark, as they most often were. It used to feel like a cocoon to her, womblike. Now it simply felt empty. Even Asmodeus could no longer fill up that empty space.

"I did not call you, Asmodeus."

"You said my name. That is enough."

"Only in my head."

"Do you think I am not there, little one? I am in your every thought. I always have been."

"Is that true?"

"Think on it."

"I…I don't know."

"You begin to question me. I do not care for it."

His eyes blazed, a pair of black-and-red coals in his flawless face.

"I'm sorry," she told him, remorseful. Afraid.

"Do you not still love me?"

"Of course. Once loved, always loved. You yourself taught me that. I believe it to be so."

"Do you still desire me?"

His skin glowed, that lovely, burnished gold, his erect cock standing tall and strong. Her body surged with need, as it always had.

"Yes," she whispered.

He moved closer, stroking his shaft with long, slow sweeps of his hand. The head swelled, glistened at the tip.

"Tell me you want me, my beauty."

Her nipples were stiffening, her sex filling with desire.

"I want you," she said quietly. "As always, Asmodeus."

He fisted his long-fingered hand and pumped into it. Desire pooled deep in her belly, even as her mind shied away, trying to reject the sensation. Still, she was unable to deny it was there.

"Tell me again."

"I want you."

"Show me how you want me. Show me how you would have me touch you."

She started to raise her hands to her breasts, but they stilled, as if of their own accord.

"Show me how you would have me suckle your breasts. Spread your thighs for me and show me the honey of your wet desire."

She could not move. Despite the hunger gnawing at her belly, her breasts, her sex. She was swollen with it, yet immobilized. She could not do as he asked.

She could not do it.

"Asmodeus, I—"

"You deny me?" he roared, his hand giving his hard flesh another savage yank. "You reject me, girl?"

"No."

"Your body will not obey me. I can smell your desire, yet you are still as a statue."

"I'm sorry."

She was shivering now. With unmet need, with fear. Goose bumps lined her skin.

"Go to your human male, then." Asmodeus spit the words out.

"I… How do you know about him?"

"I see it all, little one. You cannot hide. I see your need for him. Your desire to please. Your attentions are diverted from me, and you do not fight it."

"Asmodeus, it feels right. He feels right."

"You are mistaken."

She raised her chin, looked into the scorching black depths of his eyes. "I am not."

"Foolish girl."

He began to stroke himself again, growing thicker, longer. His nipples swelled into two dark, luscious pads of flesh as he fingered them with his other hand. Her body responded, her sex growing wet. But her heart was not with him any longer.

She shook her head. "No."

His brows drew together in his golden face. She felt his fury like heat on her naked skin, searing her. His lush mouth set into a grim line as he stroked himself faster and faster.

"You will want me."

Tears blurred her vision. "No, Asmodeus."

He stroked faster, his fist a savage, driving motion, the tip of his rigid flesh beginning to glow with brilliant blue light. His gaze was hard on hers, his flawless face intent. His mouth pulled into a grimace and she knew he was close to his peak. And for the first time she did not want it, did not want anything to do with it.

"I said no, Asmodeus. No!"

She came awake, Declan's hand on her shoulder. The truck was stopped and he was leaning over the seat toward her. On her other side, Liam's big face was close to hers; she could feel the warmth of his breath on her cheek. He whimpered, and she reached up to smooth her palm over his head.

"Angel, are you okay?"

"I… Yes. I'm well."

"You're sure?"

"Yes. Yes."

She drew in a breath, forced her racing pulse to calm. She was here with Declan now. Asmodeus could not reach her on this plane. She was safe.

She hadn't talked with Declan—or anyone—about Asmodeus. She wasn't ready to bring him into this new life. She didn't know how he would fit in this place, outside of her life with The Grandmother. She didn't know yet how *she* would fit. All she knew was that Declan would help her.

"We're here," Declan said. "At my house."

"Oh."

She turned to look out the window, shaking off the edges of the dream, getting her body, her mind, to settle.

Oh, it was lovely. The house looked like something out of a book she'd read when she was very young. It was all made of wood, with a stone chimney and a peaked roof. The green shutters made the windows look happy somehow, and the red door was a welcome in itself. Trees towered on either side, and as Declan opened her door, calling Liam out before helping her from the truck, she could hear the chirping murmur of birds, the soft sigh of wind in the boughs. The outdoor sounds she had missed so much during her time in the hospital.

"This is your place? This is to be my place? It's beautiful."

"Well, I don't know about beautiful, but it's comfortable and quiet."

"It *is* beautiful," she insisted.

Declan grabbed her crutches from the back of the truck and handed them to her. "They showed you how to use these?"

"I'm not very good at it yet."

"You won't be on them forever. I can help you get up the stairs."

She smiled her thanks and began the arduous task of making her way the few yards from the truck to the small flagstone path, Liam trailing along beside her. It was exhausting, with her heavy cast on her leg and her shoulders burning with the healing wounds there, but she was proud of herself when she made it to the foot of the steps. "I think I can go up the stairs myself."

"I don't know, Angel. I don't want you to get hurt."

"I can do it."

She placed her good foot on the bottom stair, shifted her weight on the crutches and brought them up, tried to swing her cast up, and tumbled backward, into Declan's arms. The crutches fell to the ground.

"I've got you."

He did. His arms were strong and solid around

her. Her body heated, going soft and warm all over: her legs, her belly, even her shoulders, her chest. Her heart thumped an unsteady beat as she looked up into his iris-blue eyes. He stared back silently, his lips parted.

She took in a breath. So did he. And she felt as though they breathed together for several moments. Then his features went dark. She felt him shutting down, pulling back, even though he still held her.

"I shouldn't have let you try the stairs," he said, his voice gruff.

"No, I was being stubborn."

He smiled then, a small tilting at the corners of his lush mouth. "Yes, you were."

"Will you help me, Declan?"

"Hold on," he said before lifting her in his arms and carrying her up the four stairs to the door.

It was as much physical contact as she'd ever had with a man, and it made her dizzy. With desire. With a breathless wanting that went beyond desire.

He sat her down on a wooden bench on the porch, went down to collect her crutches, brought them back to her and unlocked the door, held it for her while she hobbled in.

He made a gesture with one hand that she thought was a little self-conscious. "This is it."

She looked around at the house. Declan's house.

The floors were smooth wood, covered with a

few worn area rugs. There was a couch in a dark
green fabric, a big brown leather chair by the enormous stone fireplace. The mantel was a solid beam
of rough-hewn wood, flanked on either side by
shelves filled to overflowing with books, making
her smile in anticipation. And scattered among the
books was a collection of small, wooden figures,
animals and birds and trees, each one carved in
exquisite detail. Everything in the room was clean
and neat, the colors warm and earthy, the colors
of the outside: trees and earth, moss and ferns,
wood and sunlight. It was larger than The Grandmother's house, and didn't have the same clutter.
Yet somehow it was warmer.

"Are you tired, Angel? Do you want to go to
bed and rest? Or would you rather see the rest of
the house? There's not much to it."

"I'm not too tired. I would like to see your
house."

Declan nodded. "Through here is the kitchen.
You still okay on the crutches?"

"Yes, I can do it. It's easier inside."

He led the way through an open doorway to
the right. The kitchen was smaller than the one
she was used to, but had a large, old white stove
with a griddle in the middle, like the one she had
always cooked with. The cabinets were knotted
pine, and a pine table with two chairs sat beneath
a window. Again, it was simple but felt like home.

Maybe because this was Declan's home. Because she knew it would be hers.

"It's not much," Declan repeated, "but I can cook a few things in here. I make a good spaghetti sauce."

"I don't know spaghetti sauce," she said, carefully pronouncing the unfamiliar word, "but I look forward to trying it. But, Declan, I can cook myself. The Grandmother found my cooking to be pleasing."

"You let that leg heal first. All you have to do right now is lie around here and get better. I'll take care of the rest."

"I have rested quite a lot already, in the hospital."

"And you're not done just because they let you go home."

There was a scolding tone in his voice, but she knew it was nothing serious. And he had called this place "home," which made her happy.

"I will rest, then."

"Let me show you your room. It's just down the hall."

She followed him back across the living room, watching the easy swing of his narrow hips, his broad shoulders. She'd had the opportunity to see a number of other men at the hospital—doctors, nurses, orderlies, visitors—and she still thought

Declan the most beautiful, the most finely built
of all.

There was a door on either side of the hallway.

"This one is my room," he said. "The bathroom
is at the end of the hall. The one on the left is
yours."

He held the door open and let her pass through.

The room had one low window hung with white
curtains, a big bed covered in a light blue-and-
white quilt. On the night table was a lamp, a tiny
deer carved from wood, made with the same great
care and attention to detail as the figures she'd
seen in the living room, and a small vase filled
with wildflowers in pink and purple and yellow.
She made her way to the table, picked up the vase
and brought the flowers to her nose, inhaled.

"Thank you, Declan, for the flowers."

He shrugged, shoved his hands into his pockets. "Sure. I just found them growing around the
place."

She smiled at him. "Because you knew I would
like them."

"Yeah." He shrugged again, looked away for
a moment, then back to her. It was strange to see
this apparent shift in his usual absolute confidence.
"Do you need anything? More pillows?"

"Everything I need is right here," she said.

It was true. He had given her a home. *His* home.
A safe place. And more, a place close to him. She

hoped to get closer, hoped he would allow her to do so. Wanted it perhaps more than she had wanted anything in her life.

She didn't understand what she was feeling exactly, other than this burning desire to be with him, to please him. She had never experienced such feelings before, nothing with such strength.

Dizzy suddenly, she sank onto the edge of the bed. He was at her side in an instant.

"Angel, are you all right?"

He took her chin in his hand, tilted her face up, and she felt her cheeks go warm.

"Yes. I think perhaps I am tired, after all."

"I thought you might be. This is a big day for you."

"Yes. Maybe I will rest for a while."

"Here, let me help."

He pulled back the bedcovers, propped up a pillow while she sat at the foot of the bed and kicked off her single shoe.

"Declan, I cannot reach the zipper."

"I… Okay, turn around. I'll get it."

She shifted on the bed, felt his hands behind her. Felt the air hit her bare skin as he slid the zipper down. His fingers brushed the skin at the small of her back, and need shimmered through her system. She closed her eyes, pulled in a breath, pulled in his scent along with the air. He smelled of the woods, all greens and browns and fresh air.

She held his scent in her lungs for a moment. He hadn't moved behind her, his hands still on the lowered zipper.

She wanted him to take her in his arms again. She wanted to be naked with him, to lie next to him, flesh to flesh. But this moment was too good: just his body close to hers, his fingertips grazing her skin, the scent of him surrounding her.

"Declan…"

He stood abruptly. "Get some rest. I'll come and check on you in a while, bring you lunch when you wake up. And I'll bring your things in from the truck."

She nodded, her body consumed with wanting, but just as much with fatigue. He was right, the day had tired her more than she'd expected.

"Thank you, Declan."

He left the room and she removed her dress, folded it and carefully laid it at the end of the bed before climbing under the quilt in her cotton slip. She propped her casted leg on a pillow, letting it stick out from beneath the covers, and lay back.

She was tired, sleep threatening to overtake her. But she wanted a few more moments to savor it all: being in Declan's house, in this lovely, soft bed that was her own. The comfort of knowing that Declan and Liam were nearby.

She stared out the window at the shaded view of trees and sky, trying to distract herself from the heat of her body, the aching fullness of her breasts Declan's touch had left.

She cupped her breasts, brushing her thumbs over the nipples, a surge of pleasure humming through her. But she was so tired.

She blinked hard, kept her eyes on the view outside, tried to focus.

She was afraid to sleep. Afraid to meet Asmodeus in the dream world. Afraid of his fury. Of his ability to seduce her.

He had once been the only desire she had known. The only male figure in her life, if one could even call him that. But it had all changed the moment she'd opened her eyes and seen Declan.

Her stomach knotted. The truth was, it had all changed the minute The Grandmother had chosen to be rid of her.

She had come to understand, in some indefinable way, that it had been The Grandmother's choice to dispose of her. It hurt, cutting deep into her heart. Every bit as deep as the cuts made on her shoulders, and done with as much purpose. Despite what she'd had to do in service to The Grandmother, in the name of the Dark One, she loved the old woman. She had been her only family, her only sense of connection aside from Asmodeus, who had no presence in the waking world. If not for Declan and Liam she would be entirely alone now.

Tears stung her eyes, but she blinked them back. She would not cry. She had no reason to. She was safe and cared for. Perhaps in a way she never had been before. She would be grateful, *was* grateful. She would count her blessings, as The Grandmother had taught her, as meager as they had been before she'd come here.

She lay in the soft bed, twisting the end of a lock of hair, twirling it around and around her fingers. Trying to list in her head all the wonderful new things in her life to be thankful for. But it was hard to get her mind to work as sleep threatened to overtake her.

She gave up the task, saving it for later, and turned her head to look at the flowers on the table. The flowers Declan had picked for her: the pink honeysuckle, the ceanothus, like small puffy blue clouds, the yellow buttercups, the tall spikes of purple lupine. She knew the names; The Grandmother had taught her the wildflowers, along with the trees and the herbs. The flowers to eat, like nasturtium and pansy. The ones for scent, like lavender and rose. The ones to heal, like blue tansy. The ones to poison, like the oleander one of the dogs had eaten, and died from.

No one had ever picked flowers for her before, although she'd always kept The Grandmother's house full of fresh flowers. She wasn't sure what it meant, but there was something special about it.

But she was too tired to figure it out. Too tired to take in all the happenings of the day, the complexity of the heat of Declan's touch and his apparent need to back away from her whenever he got too close. Too tired to do anything but close her eyes and sleep.

CHAPTER FIVE

DECLAN OPENED THE DOOR, careful to be quiet. She slept, her face and hair silhouetted in the dim light of the setting sun coming through the window. Her hair was like pale gold in the misty light, spread out over the pillows, the bed. He'd never seen such long hair on anyone before. There was something...pure about it. Sensual. He wanted to touch it. He always wanted to touch it. His groin was going tight, just looking at her hair, for God's sake. And he could see the rise and fall of her breasts as she inhaled, exhaled softly. He curled his hands into fists, clenching his fingers.

Stop it.

His gaze went back to her face, so peaceful in the half dark.

She'd been napping since they got home. He hadn't wanted to wake her, figuring her body needed the rest to heal. But it had been pure torture, knowing she was here, in his house, so close by. He wanted to wake her, to talk to her.

Ridiculous.

He shook his head, closed the door, then opened it a few inches in case she woke and called for him before going to sit at his big oak desk in the living room. He sank low in the chair, his back aching from too many hours in it already that day. Picking up a small wooden figure of an owl he'd made from a piece of manzanita, he rubbed his thumb over it, the ridges that made up the face, the feathers. Liam, who was lounging on the floor next to the desk, his big head resting on the rug, gazed up at him with a halfhearted thump of his stubby tail.

Declan leaned down to rub his nose. "Yeah, I know. What the hell am I going to do with myself? I'm a mess over this girl, aren't I?"

His cell phone rang, piercing the quiet of the evening, and he sat up, checked the caller ID before picking up.

"Hey, Dad."

"Dec, hi. I'm calling to see how Angel's doing."

"She's been sleeping all day."

"That's good, I guess. But it leaves you at loose ends. You must be getting antsy. What have you been up to to keep yourself entertained?"

How was it his father knew him so well, after all these years of Declan keeping his distance? It was irritating. He rubbed a hand over his jaw, the beard stubble rough on his fingers.

"It's hardly been entertaining, Dad."

"Come on, Dec. I'm trying to work with you here."

He blew out a breath. He had to calm down. As much as he hated it he needed Oran's help with this.

"Yeah. Sorry. Look, I've been online and on the phone for hours. I've called every law enforcement agency I can think of, researching the databases on the internet, trying to find someone who gives a damn about what happened to her. But the fact is, no one's really interested in pursuing the case. Or even in talking to me about it, other than Tim Bullock. But since the case was taken out of his hands by the state police, Tim doesn't know any more than I do."

"My friends in Sacramento made sure they ran fingerprints on her first thing," Oran said. "But there's nothing. Not that there would be unless she'd committed a crime. There was some speculation about that initially because of the drugs in her system. But there was no way she could have done all of this to herself."

"Yeah, those crazy cuts on her shoulder blades…"

"I know. A lot of cops work by the book. Treat each case as a protocol, instead of as individual cases. That's why I never became a cop. And I liked the forest and the beaches better than people."

"Me, too."

Christ, had he just admitted to his old man how alike they were? Out loud?

"Dec? You still there?"

"What? Yeah. Just thinking. Do you know anyone you could convince to run her information through the National Crime Information Center? See if something pops up?"

"Yes, pretty sure I do. Should have thought of it before. But if she was taken as a kid, that was what? Probably 1994? 1995? The systems weren't nearly as sophisticated. Even if there was a kid who disappeared then, especially if it was outside of California, it might not have been cross-referenced so that she'd show up in a search."

"Yeah, I know. Can you try anyway?"

"I'll get on it first thing tomorrow. But, Dec, don't hold out a lot of hope. You know how these cases can go. There were no witnesses to any actual crime, so the department—whatever department is working the case—prefers to pretend there *was* no crime."

"I was there."

"But you didn't see it happen. Didn't see anyone there but her."

"Yeah, Tim's already rammed that fact down my throat. I don't need you to do it again."

"Cut it out, will you, Declan? I'm not ramming anything. The fact is, you didn't see anything but her. There's not much the cops can do with no information to go on. Not unless she remembers something substantial. Maybe Ruth will help her with that."

"Maybe."

He really did not want to talk about Ruth Hehewuti right now. Didn't want to think about his father's relationship with her.

"I have to go, Dad. Call me tomorrow if you find out anything. If you find someone who will talk to me."

"Will do. And, Dec…"

"Yeah?"

"This is a good thing you're doing. Taking care of her." His father's voice was gruff. "I'm not going to give you a bunch of crap about why you're doing it. I know it comes from a good place."

Declan shifted in his chair, his hand going into his hair. Why was his father being so damn nice to him?

"Yeah, well, anyone would have done the same."

"No, I don't think so. Anyway, we'll talk tomorrow."

"Okay. Thanks."

They hung up, leaving him wondering why it galled him so much to thank his father. He had to get over this old resentment. But no matter how firmly he understood, on a logical level, that his anger with his father was worn out and ultimately a purely emotional reaction that made little sense, he couldn't seem to let it go.

He'd bet Ruth the psychologist would have a field day with the complexities of his relationship with his father. Hell, she'd probably already spent hours analyzing the situation. The idea pissed him off.

Liam whimpered, got up and nudged his hand.

"What is it, boy?"

The dog whined again, dancing a little, his heavy paws thumping on the hard floor.

"You need to go outside?"

He got up and headed toward the door, but Liam took off down the hallway. Declan followed him into Angel's room.

The bedside lamp was on, casting light and shadow across the bed. Angel was sitting upright, carefully moving her leg, supporting the weight of it with both hands.

"Here, let me help." He grabbed one of the bed pillows and used it to prop her foot higher. "Is that better?"

"Yes. Thank you, Declan." She settled back against the wood headboard and winced.

"Shit. I'm sorry. We should put a pillow behind you."

"It's not that bad anymore. I am used to it, I think. But a pillow would be nice."

He went to the closet and pulled an extra pillow from the shelf, placed it behind her back with great care.

"Better?"

"Yes, that's lovely." She smiled.

"So…you sleep okay?"

"I think I slept a long time. I did not sleep well. But I never sleep well."

Her strange honesty always took him by surprise. He supposed he'd get used to it. If she was here long enough. But where else was she going? He didn't even like to think of it, but someday she would need to be on her own.

"Do you need some pain medication?" he asked her. "They sent you home with some. I put it right here on the nightstand."

"No, I don't need it. And I don't want it. I don't like the way it makes me feel. It makes me dream."

"Is that why you can't sleep, Angel? Because you dream?"

She turned away, her gaze on the darkening window. She said so quietly he could barely hear her, "Yes."

He took a few steps into the room and sat on the edge of her bed. He could still smell the delicate scent of the lotion: lemon and lavender.

"Bad dreams?"

"Yes."

"I have bad dreams sometimes. A lot, actually." He paused, watching her face in profile. She blinked a few times, but didn't respond. "Do you want to tell me about it?"

"Maybe…"

"You don't have to."

"No, I want to. But I don't know how to make you understand."

"Try me."

She turned to look at him and he was struck, as he always was, by her sheer beauty: the blue of her eyes, the pink pout of her mouth. He kept his gaze away from the swell of her breasts in her white cotton slip.

"I dream of the one who taught me. He is in my dreams, nearly always. I used to welcome him. But now things have changed. I don't need him to teach me any longer. His job is done. My purpose with him is done. Now he makes me sad." She stopped, her fingertips grasping the edge of the sheet. She glanced down at her hands, then back up at him. "And he makes me afraid," she said more quietly.

"I don't understand. *Who* taught you? What did he teach you?"

"His name is Asmodeus. Do you know of him?"

"It sounds familiar. I don't know why."

"He is the demon of all things carnal. A prince of his kind, the demon of lust."

He could see that she was perfectly serious. He didn't know what the hell to make of it. Was she delusional? Was this an aftereffect of her head injury? It would be better, no doubt, to let her talk this out with her doctor, or with Ruth, but she seemed to want to talk to him. This demon stuff was pretty damn alarming. But as alarming as it was, he was curious, too, about what went on in her head. He knew already that her life had been strange in ways he never could have imagined. And it was getting weirder and weirder. But he thought he should know, whatever it was. He was trying to stay calm, not to overreact.

"You see him when you sleep?" he asked her.

"When I dream, whether in sleep or with the drugs. I have seen him since I was a child. I don't remember a time before him. He trained me in the ways of love."

"He 'trained' you?"

He wasn't sure what she was saying. He wasn't sure he wanted to know. What had she been through?

"I am The Gift. Or, I was…I was trained to perfection. That was the goal my entire life. That was my purpose. Who better to teach me than the prince of lust himself? It is an honor. But he is also the prince of rage. And not only did I fail in my task, but now…I no longer desire him as I once did. As he expects of me. And he is angry."

She was becoming more and more agitated as she spoke, color rising in her cheeks, her breath coming faster.

Declan took her hand, held it tight. "Angel, he's only a dream."

"Is he? I'm not certain what he is any longer."

"He doesn't exist outside of your dreams, does he?"

"He is not present in this realm. Does that mean he does not exist?"

She had a point. Maybe. If she did, it was in some skewed, purely philosophical way. But he couldn't say that to her. She was too distraught. And while he had to concede the theory, he didn't actually believe it.

Still, that whole thing about some demon training her in the ways of love—that might explain her earthiness, that sense of raw sensuality he felt from her. Even if this demon was a figment of her imagination, the drugs she'd been fed, *she* believed it. That much was obvious. And so the effect was still the same.

She had responded with desire earlier, when he'd unzipped her dress. No doubt about it. He'd tried to tell himself it was some twisted wishful thinking. But he'd felt the heat of her skin, heard the quickening of her breath.

"Declan, you're holding my hand so tightly."

"Ah, I'm sorry." He released her fingers, pulled his back.

"No, it's all right." She reached out, took his hand tentatively in hers. "I like it when you hold my hand. It makes me feel safe. Safe enough to tell you more."

"Sure. Anything you want."

Her fingers gripped his, the flesh of her palm soft and smooth. He tried not to focus on the sensation, just to listen.

"Asmodeus has never touched me. I am untouched by man. Until now. Untouched by any but The Grandmother. She and Asmodeus have been my only companions, other than the birds and rabbits in the garden, The Grandmother's dogs. And both of them, Asmodeus and The Grandmother, I have loved and hated. Adored and feared. Depended on. The Grandmother has rejected me. And I thought he had, but he behaves as if I have rejected *him*. Perhaps I have. It's all so confusing. Declan—" she held his hand tighter, an intensity in her blue eyes, her golden brows drawn low "—do you believe it's possible to both love and hate simultaneously? Or is that some fault within me?"

He thought for a moment of his father. And even before he said the words, he knew it didn't really apply. He was angry as hell, resentful. But he'd never actually hated his father, had he? But the theory still held true, in his mind. "I believe it's possible. I believe we humans are complicated creatures. That we love and hate all the time. I've never known anyone who actually loved unconditionally, except maybe Liam here." He nodded with his chin to the dog curled up on the floor.

"Dogs are simple," she said. "Perhaps that's why I like them. They demand nothing and love you, anyway."

He said quietly, "Angel, you've never had anyone in your life who didn't demand something from you. Have you?"

"I have had no one but The Grandmother."

"But you weren't always with her. Do you remember anything about your life before her?"

"No, nothing. Just that there was a time before."

"You're certain? You were fed a lot of drugs. Maybe you were with her from birth."

"You think my perceptions have been altered by the drugs? I've been given those drugs, made to dream, my entire life. But, Declan, because of that I have had to become very clear on the difference between altered reality and the truth."

He shook his head. How was she so self-aware? And the details of her life were getting weirder and weirder. "I don't understand. From what you've told me, it sounds like they wanted the two to blend together for you."

"Yes. But I have always fought it. I didn't realize until my time in the hospital that that's what I was doing. And ultimately, why I've been rejected. Why I was removed from the only life I have ever known. The familiarity of my home, my garden.

Why everything was taken away from me. I'm trying to remember that none of these things were ever truly mine to begin with. That it was all The Grandmother's. But I think it might be natural for me, for anyone, to have to find something to hold on to, make my own."

He shook his head. Talking with her was like a series of small shocks. Good and bad. The most simple and the most bizarre. "How do you know all this, Angel?"

She shrugged, and his gaze was drawn to the pale, curving rise of her breasts, covered too little by the white fabric. "Some things I simply know, as we all do."

He didn't know what to say to that. He was blown away by her. And when her grip on his hand softened and she turned it over, tracing her fingers over his palm, his body swarmed with need, making it impossible to think.

"Declan, I think you know some of these things, too. But you don't accept them. It makes you unhappy."

"Yes."

She asked softly, "What will make you happy, Declan?"

His gaze rose to meet hers, those sky-blue eyes. So damn pretty. Her eyes. Her face. Her cheeks were flushed, her pupils enormous. He should pull his hand away. But he couldn't do it.

Without meaning to, he answered, "You make me happy, Angel."

Had he really said that to her? But he realized then it was true. Was it some neurotic need to fix someone, leftover from what had happened with Abby? But he didn't like to think of it that way. He didn't like to think of Angel that way. He'd sensed the moment he'd seen her that there was something special about her, and the more he got to know her, even in these small bits, the more amazing a woman she was to him. Truly like some angel, a creature who existed on some other plane.

He couldn't even believe he was thinking of anyone in those terms. But he was.

Her gaze still on his, she lifted his hand and placed a soft kiss on his open palm.

The heat was like a rush of pure lust, kicking him in the gut, making him go hard all over. He still couldn't take his hand away.

"Angel—"

"I am happy with you, Declan. I want to be here, more than anywhere else on this earth. I'm grateful for all you've done for me. But it's not only gratitude. It's *you*."

His pulse was racing, his heart a hammer in his chest. What the hell was she saying? Why did he need to hear it from her so badly?

"Angel, you don't know me."

"But I do."

He shook his head, but she'd pulled his hand to her mouth once more, those plush, pink lips, and was kissing his fingertips. When had anything like this, such a small gesture, turned him on so much he could hardly fucking see straight? All the blood had rushed from his head to his groin. If she didn't stop he was going to climb on top of her, press her down into the mattress, strip off that innocent white slip and crush her full breasts beneath him...

He groaned, pulled his hand back, finally.

"This isn't right."

"Why is it not right?" Her gaze was fevered, her breath coming in small, ragged pants.

"Because I'm trying to *help* you, damn it."

"Be with me, Declan. That will help me."

He stood, willing his body to calm down. "I can't."

He turned and strode from the room, into his, shutting the door behind him.

Goddamn it. Damn *him*.

He shouldn't have let her touch him that way. He shouldn't be responding to her the way he did. She was an innocent girl, for Christ's sake. A virgin, if what she'd told him was true. And she had to be, what, twenty-one years old? Which made him, at thirty, some old pervert.

He was still hard as stone. He pressed his hand over his erection, but that only made it worse.

He should have stepped back sooner, looked

away. But he could smell her excitement, coming off her like waves of heat. And when she'd laid her lips on his palm…

He moaned, moved farther into the room, stripping his T-shirt off as he went, unzipping his jeans. He caught his reflection in the wood-framed mirror over the low dresser, pulled his cock free. It stood firm between his thighs, the head swollen. And the more he tried to force his mind away from images of Angel, the harder he became.

"Fuck it."

He let his fingers graze the swollen tip and jerked back at his own touch. It was too much. He was too hard. He had to take a breath in before wrapping his hand around the rigid shaft.

God, her face. That sweet face, so fresh and still so purely sex to him. Sometimes he wanted to kiss her. Just *kiss* her. But that idea only led to others.

He watched his reflection in the mirror, at his hand fisted around his cock as he stroked. And he pictured her there, her golden head coming down, her sweet mouth taking him in, sucking.

He stroked faster, harder.

What would it be like to sink between those thighs, to be the first one inside her? She would be so damn tight.

He was panting, trying not to groan aloud. But he was going to come any moment.

Angel…

His body went rigid as pleasure took over, sharp, stabbing jolts, deep into his belly. He came, his climax like some sort of shock to his system. He had to bite his lip to keep from crying out. The one word echoing in his head.

Angel.

When it was over he fell back onto the bed, used his discarded shirt to wipe himself off as he tried to catch his breath.

He needed to get himself under control. And he needed to set some boundaries with her.

After he apologized to her for running out of the room like some scared kid.

Ridiculous.

He sighed. How many times had he said that to himself since he'd met her?

He was going to have to accept this insane attraction to her, as well as the need to protect her that was so fierce it made him crazy. He'd have to accept it so he could deal with it. Get it under control.

He'd spent most of his adult life with every aspect under control. Work. Family. Certainly his personal life—what there had been of it. He could handle this, too.

That's what he kept telling himself, anyway.

SHE COULDN'T FIGURE OUT what she'd done to chase him away. Didn't a man want a woman to want him? Wasn't that what she'd been taught? By the demon of lust himself. Surely he would know.

She *knew* he desired her; she'd felt it from him. There was no denying it, no wondering if she'd made that up. He wanted her. And yet, he'd rejected her. She was confused. Hurt.

And in need.

Her body burned for him.

She spread her thighs, shoved her hand in between, rubbing at her tight clitoris urgently. She needed to come, and quickly.

Pleasure washed over her, sharp and clean, clearing her mind of everything but him.

Declan...

She remembered the feel of his hand on hers. His forest scent. The heat of him. She wanted him more than ever.

She rubbed harder, circling that hard, needy nub with the heel of her hand. Desire rose, the lips of her sex filling, her clitoris pulsing. Her hips arched hard as her climax rolled through her. Wave after wave, pleasure sweet and sharp in her body.

It passed quickly. She felt limp, exhausted. Still needing him.

And she felt sad. She didn't want to—didn't want to taint her feelings for him with anything negative. She tried to distract herself with light touches on her breasts. Her nipples hardened, but it wasn't enough.

She wanted to know why he'd left the room the way he had. Wanted to know if she'd done something wrong.

She sighed, dropped her hands.

He would come back eventually; she knew that. Until then, she must still herself and wait.

She forced her mind to calm, as well as her body, wishing she had taken one of the books from the shelves in the living room to distract her. Maybe she should get up and go find a book. Declan had said she could read anything she wanted.

She sat up, her body still languid, buzzing, a little weak. But she found her crutches leaning against the side of the bed and heaved herself to her feet. The wood floor was cool and smooth beneath her. She tucked her hair behind her ear and made her way to the door. Declan's was closed. But there was a light on in the living room and she followed it.

Liam was lying next to a large wood desk at the far end of the room. He wagged his short tail when he saw her, and got up and followed her to the bookshelf, where she leaned against the back of the leather chair to steady herself while she looked, stroking the dog's head.

So many books! The shelves were filled with more books than she had ever seen in one place. The Grandmother had never brought more than a handful at a time. She had never imagined there was such overwhelming choice in things to read about.

She recognized books on wildlife, geology, building things. She was pleased to find several books she had read: *Moby-Dick,* the stories of Charles Dickens. Much of the rest she did not recognize. Not knowing where to begin, she pulled out a book about growing roses and began to page through it.

"Angel?"

She turned and saw Declan standing in the hallway. He was wearing a pair of plaid flannel pajama bottoms and a white T-shirt, his skin a beautiful golden-brown against the stark white. She smiled tentatively.

He moved closer. "Look, I'm sorry about earlier. I just don't think it's right that I… You're under my care. I'm responsible for you. I can't take advantage of you."

She closed the book, held it against her stomach. "How can you take advantage if it's what I want?"

He shook his head. His dark hair was a little mussed. She liked it that way. Liked the dark stubble lining his jaw.

"Angel, I think we have to set some ground rules here."

"All right." She was used to rules.

"I need to keep some appropriate distance. That's the only way this will work."

"If that's what you want, Declan." She was trying not to let her heart sink. She knew he wanted her. Perhaps he simply needed some time. Or some encouragement. She'd give him the time first. "I will respect your wishes."

"Angel, you're a beautiful girl. A beautiful woman. It's not that."

"I know."

She'd always been told she was beautiful. By The Grandmother, who rarely gave any other sort of compliment, and even then it was most often muttered under her breath as she prepared her for a ritual. And by Asmodeus, who, in his unearthly perfection, had no reason to tell her so if it wasn't true. It hadn't occurred to her that Declan might not find her so.

He nodded. She could see he still wasn't satisfied with the arrangement. But then, neither was she. But she could be patient.

"You found something to read?" he asked her, his hand going through his dark hair, then into the pocket of his pants.

He was fidgeting, something she'd often done to annoy The Grandmother. Not that it annoyed her when he did it. But she wished he was more comfortable with her.

"Yes. Gardening. I wasn't sure where else to start. You have so many."

Declan came to stand by her, looking at the

bookshelf. His broad shoulders still held some tension. "What do you like to read?"

"I don't know. Everything, I think. There's so much to learn about the world, especially now that I am to be a part of it. I want to know…everything. Places and people and animals. I want to know what people do in their everyday lives. I heard fragments of conversations in the hospital. The nurses and visitors talking about their families and so many things I didn't understand." She shook her head, trying to figure out how to explain to him how strange she found the world. "I have no context for most of it. It was confusing. Tempting. I want to know more. For instance, can you explain to me about television? I tried to watch in the hospital, but it was too overwhelming."

"You're not missing much."

"No? But it seems it's something everyone does. Or at least, that everyone knows."

"I'm not sure how to explain it in a way that would make sense to you. You just need to do it. After you get settled we can turn on the TV and I'll sit with you and try to explain. But frankly, I'm not sure I get it myself."

"You like books better." That made her smile, for some reason.

"Yeah. I guess I do."

"What books do you like, Declan?"

"Everything." He laughed, and she realized

it was the first time she'd heard his laughter. It
sounded a little rough, as though he wasn't used
to it. "I like to read classic literature." He pulled
the volume of Dickens she'd been looking at earlier from the shelf, held it in his hand. His thumb
caressed the worn spine. "And I like to read about
the earth and how it was made. What it's been
through, you know? What people were like a thousand years ago. Humans at their most basic. When
I was a kid I wanted to be an archeologist or a ge-
ologist. I like the solidity of the planet. How it's
been here for century after century." He gave a
small shake of his head. "Does that even make
sense?"

"Yes. We like the earth for different reasons. Or
perhaps our reasons aren't so different."

He nodded, a small smile on his lips, tilting one
corner of his mouth. She noticed the scar on his
jaw once more. She lifted her hand, but couldn't
quite reach his face.

"Declan, how did you get this?"

His features went absolutely dark instantly, his
eyes shuttered. He shook his head, running his
hand back over his hair as he looked away. "We
need to talk about something else."

"If you like. I'm sorry, Declan."

He shrugged.

"I see pain in you. I hope someday you can
share it with me. Sharing it can take some of it

away. I have discovered this in talking with you, and with Ruth Hehewuti. I'm happy I'll be talking with her again."

"I'm not really the sharing type," he muttered.

"Perhaps that's why you hold so much pain."

He looked at her then. His eyes were a blaze of blue, his lips a tight line. "Maybe."

They had that in common; so much hurt. But she was ready to let go of hers. Declan wasn't. If only he would let her help him, the way he was helping her. But she knew waiting. Knew patience. That's what her whole life had been. She had waited for years to fulfill her purpose. Had waited for phases of the moon, dreading the coming rituals. Had waited on The Grandmother's moods…

Her mind clouded, her vision dimming as though she were underwater. Everything was a watercolor blur. She blinked, hard, then again, and it became crystal clear.

She was tied down onto the cold concrete floor of the basement, the ropes that were tied to the iron stakes sunk in the concrete were biting into her wrists and ankles. She hated it. She preferred the earth against her bare back. But it was winter and too rainy to go outside. Bad for The Grandmother's arthritis. She could smell the melted candle wax, acrid in her nostrils. The harsher odor of burning herbs. The scorching scent of her own dread.

The Grandmother stood over her. She was alone, chanting, her body swaying. She was not well.

She didn't like it when The Grandmother was having one of her bad spells. She used the knife then. Cut into her flesh. Never a deep wound. But she sometimes forgot to give her the dreaming herbs, so it was harder to take.

She could almost smell the metallic scent of the blade before The Grandmother knelt and bent over her to pierce her flesh. Just a small cut on her thigh, then the scent of her own blood. The smell was as metallic as the knife itself. It hurt, but not too badly. She had borne worse. Worse was the pain of knowing The Grandmother hurt her on purpose, perhaps to release her own pain.

The Grandmother cut her leg again, deeper this time, and she flinched, biting her lip to keep from crying out. The pain was harder this time, making her dizzy.

The blood was pooling between her thighs, growing sticky as The Grandmother chanted. It seemed to go on forever. Finally, The Grandmother stood, swayed. She saw the old woman's beady black eyes roll up in her head before she fell to the floor.

Fear rose, turned into panic. She was tied down, and The Grandmother was sick. No one would come. No one ever did. There was nothing she could do. For either of them.

She tried to call Asmodeus to her, but awake and without the drugs, he was too far away.

Alone, helpless, she wept.

CHAPTER SIX

"A<small>NGEL</small>!"

He caught her as she fell. Her cheeks were pale, her eyelids fluttering. Was she having some sort of seizure?

He carried her to the sofa and laid her down, keeping one hand behind her head.

"Angel." Her eyes opened, that stunning blue. "Are you okay?"

"Yes. I'm better now."

"What the hell happened?"

"I don't know. We were talking about books, I think."

Liam wedged his way in between Declan and the sofa and nudged Angel's hand. She stroked his big head.

"We'd kind of gotten off the subject," he told her.

He was watching her face carefully, looking for…hell, he didn't know what. He just wanted to be sure she was really all right. His heart was still hammering. If anything happened to her…

"Oh, yes," she murmured, her gaze wandering. Her hand went to his arm, her fingers resting there, playing with his watchband.

"Do you really feel okay? I can take you to the hospital."

"There's no need. I was just…remembering."

"Remembering?"

"Things that were…unpleasant."

She moved her hand to her left thigh, rubbed it.

"Are you hurt, Angel?"

"Not now. But I was. It was as if I was dreaming about it, more than remembering. I don't understand what happened. But I'm fine now."

"Your body's been through a lot. Maybe it's the drugs working their way out. Or some sort of delayed shock reaction. Maybe I should take you over to the hospital to have you checked out."

"I truly am fine, I promise. Don't take me anywhere, Declan. Please."

He looked at her closely. Her cheeks had color once more, her eyes were clear now. "Okay. But if this happens again, we're going straight to the hospital. Maybe we need to get some food in you. Are you hungry?"

"A little."

He nodded. "Will you be okay here by yourself for a few minutes?"

"I've lived most of my life by myself."

He wasn't sure what else to say to that, so he

got up and went into the kitchen. He noticed Liam stayed behind, his head in Angel's lap now. He felt better with the dog standing by her. Liam would let him know if anything happened to her.

Christ, he was like some mother hen, worrying over her. When was the last time he'd worried about anyone but himself? Too long ago. Maybe it was time to think about that.

Not Abby. Don't want to think about Abby.

No, but maybe time to think about how he'd gotten to be such a selfish bastard.

He opened a can of chicken-vegetable soup and emptied it into a small saucepan, put it on the stove to heat. He went to the refrigerator and poured a glass of apple juice for her. Then he reached into a cabinet and poured himself a finger of Scotch without even really thinking about it.

He tossed it back, enjoying the burn as it went down his throat.

He wasn't much of a drinker. But he was so damn tense. Questioning himself. Angel made him question himself. He didn't like it. Knew he probably needed it.

The soup heated quickly. He spooned some into a bowl, brought it and the juice and a paper towel back into the living room and set everything on the side table next to the sofa.

"Can you sit up to eat?"

"Yes."

Angel shifted, wincing as she leaned her back against one arm of the sofa.

"Here, let me get you a pillow."

She leaned forward, let him place a couple of throw pillows behind her. She settled back carefully.

"Okay?" he asked her.

"Yes, much better now. Thank you. May I have the soup, Declan?"

"What? Sure." He handed her the ceramic bowl, then sat in the leather chair.

"You made this?" she asked, raising the bowl to her face, the steam rising against her skin.

"Sort of. It's from a can."

"A can?"

"You didn't have canned food?"

"We canned food for the winter. Peaches and tomatoes. And I made jam for The Grandmother. That was her favorite. But in jars, not cans. And not soup. It smells wonderful."

"I don't know if I'll ever get used to how many things I take for granted that you're totally unfamiliar with."

"I'm not sure I will, either." She tasted the soup, smiled. "This is very good. Are you not having any?"

"Maybe later."

Outside, an owl hooted. Liam's ears lifted, but he was used to the soft nighttime sounds. He was more focused on Angel's soup, watching every motion of her spoon hopefully.

Angel picked a small piece of chicken from her bowl, paused. "May I give this to Liam? He looks hungry."

"He always looks hungry. But sure, you can give it to him."

She held the tiny bit out for the dog, who took it delicately from her fingers in his enormous teeth.

"Good boy," she told Liam, who wagged his tail stump.

"He'll be devoted to you forever, now," Declan told her. "Actually, I think he was the minute he saw you."

So was he. But he wasn't going to admit that out loud. Hell, he didn't want to admit it to himself.

"Declan? Will you tell me about some things?"

"What kind of things?"

"About the world. About your life. I don't know what anyone else's experiences have been, but I've gathered from books and from people at the hospital that my existence has been unusual."

"That's for sure."

"So tell me. Tell me about a normal life."

"I don't know if mine was 'normal.' I guess that's a subjective thing."

"Tell me about growing up. With a mother and a father."

Her eyes were shining. He could see she was

on the verge of tears. He didn't want to talk about his parents. But he wasn't going to deny her anything, with her looking at him this way.

"You've wondered about that for a long time, haven't you?" he asked her quietly.

"Always. But there was no one to ask. The Grandmother did not encourage questions that had nothing to do with my education. And this particular question I always sensed would make her angry. Please tell me."

He leaned forward, resting his elbows on his knees. "Okay. Okay."

Angel turned to set the bowl on the table, then settled herself onto the throw pillows, her blue gaze focused on him. She had a strange way of doing that—focusing on one thing so purely he didn't think she noticed anything else.

"So…" he started. "I grew up around here, in Mendocino. My dad, Oran, was a forest ranger. That's probably why I became one myself."

"In the hospital Liz explained your job to me, how you watch over the forest."

"It's not as grand as it sounds."

"It sounds important to me. Will they miss you from your job if you're here taking care of me? Liz wanted to take a day away from the hospital and they wouldn't allow her to. I heard her talking to another nurse about it."

"I took a leave of absence." When she looked

confused he explained, "I let them know I needed to be away for a while. It's not a problem."

"I want to know more, what you do when you work each day. But right now I need to know what it is to have a family. To have a mother. Tell me about your mother, Declan."

Small stab of pain in his chest. But he could talk about her, couldn't he? He'd loved her. He just wasn't used to it. Who would he have talked to about her? There'd been no one since Abby. But it was too much to think about right now. Abby. His mom.

Focus. One thing at a time.

He pulled in a breath, blew it out.

It was his mom Angel wanted to hear about, and there was as much love for her as there was pain. He couldn't feel one without the other, but maybe for a few minutes he could focus on the love.

"Her name was Mary. She and my dad met when they were teenagers. He always said there was no other woman for him." He had to pause and pull in another long breath. "Anyway, she was totally devoted to him. And to me. She was a good mother."

"Do you look like her?"

"I get my blue eyes from her. But her hair was a lighter brown. She had pale skin, like yours. She was a tiny thing, like some sort of fairy. I could pick her up by the time I was thirteen or so. It made her laugh."

Another small stab, like the twisting of a knife. Still, after all these years.

"And do you have siblings? Brothers and sisters?"

"I… No."

"Declan?"

He didn't talk about this. Ever. He didn't think he'd said a single word to anyone in his entire fucking life. But he was going to tell Angel. He didn't know why.

"When I was five years old, my mother had a baby. Her name was Erin. I remember how I was told that I had to be a good big brother to her. I don't remember being jealous. I know some kids are. But Mom was so happy about the baby. I'm not sure how old Erin was, but I don't think we had her very long. A few months, maybe. She died of SIDS, I guess, although I didn't understand it until I was older. No one ever talked about it. She was just…gone."

"SIDS?"

"Sudden infant death syndrome. Babies just… die sometimes. No one knows why."

"And you felt you'd failed as her big brother."

He looked up at Angel. "Yeah."

"I'm sorry, Declan."

"It's okay." He shrugged, even though there

was no sincerity in it. It fucking wasn't okay, was it? Which was why he never thought about Erin. Never talked about her. Easier not to think about it.

"What was your family like after that?" Angel asked.

"Everything just went on. Everyone accepted it. Mom was sad for a while, but not forever."

"And your father?"

"I don't know. I don't remember anything about how he reacted to it."

"You seem very distanced from the death of your sister, Declan."

No apologies. Just forthright honesty from her.

"Maybe I am. No, you're right. I always have been. Shit." He twisted his hands together. "You're right."

"And do you really think everyone simply went on without her? I don't see how that's possible. Even when one of The Grandmother's dogs died, or I found a bird still and lifeless in the garden, I mourned."

He unclasped his hands, ran one through his hair. Why did it feel as if his breath had left his body? He didn't want to ask himself what Angel was asking him. And how did she sense these things? How did she have this kind of insight into situations she'd never really experienced?

He took in a long breath, blew it out. "Maybe.

You probably have a point. I don't like to think about it."

She said, her voice soft, "Sometimes I think when something bad happens to a child, they develop a perception of the event that has nothing to do with what actually happened. We make something up that's easier to bear. And we carry those ideas into our adult life."

He nodded, his mind racing. It was too much to take in all at once. "Yeah. You're right. I think that's exactly what I've done. But at this point I have no idea how to separate what really happened from my five-year-old ideas about it."

"Maybe we don't have to. I'm not sure. I have to think about it some more. I didn't mean to upset you, Declan."

"No, it's fine. I don't mind talking about it with you so much."

She smiled at him, warming him. And making his stomach tighten with need. The need to just kiss her. Hold her.

Don't think about it now.

"Do you have photographs of your family?" she asked him.

"You know photographs?"

"There were photographs in the hospital, at the nurses' station. Photographs of their children, mostly."

"I have a box somewhere. But this is my mom."

He got up, took a framed picture from the bookshelf and brought it to Angel.

"She's pretty. She looks like a happy person. And you do have her eyes. Does she live nearby?"

He took the frame from Angel's hand, carefully set it back on the shelf. With his back turned to her, he said, "She died."

"Ah, Declan. I'm very sorry."

"Please don't."

"Don't be sorry? But I am. You have lost much."

"Don't pity me," he said, his tone harsher than he meant it to be.

Angel was quiet for several moments, while he stood there feeling like an asshole.

Have to get it together.

He turned back to face her. Her brows were drawn together, worry etched on her face.

"Angel, I'm sorry. It was a long time ago. I don't know why I'm being like this."

"There is a difference between empathy and pity."

"Yes. You're right."

"I don't feel pity for you."

He nodded. "I know."

He did know. His shoulders loosened a little.

"We don't have to talk about it anymore. Thank you for sharing your family with me."

"Sure."

The gears in his head were shifting. This brief

conversation was some sort of emotional roller coaster for him. Not the kind of discussion he usually had with anyone. Maybe that's why it was so damn confusing. He needed to calm down, take another breath and just calm down.

"All done with your soup?" he asked her. He couldn't talk anymore.

"Yes. Thank you."

"Maybe we should get you back into bed. I'm taking you into town to see Ruth Hehewuti tomorrow."

"I will be glad to see her."

He wouldn't. But he knew Angel needed it.

"Come on. Let's get you up."

Once he had her settled in her room he sat down at his desk. The computer screen was a pale, blue glow. He should probably get on there, do some more research, see if he could find out who Angel was, what had happened to her. But he was distracted by their conversation tonight.

He still could not believe he'd told her about Erin. And his mother. There was some weird sort of purity about Angel—he didn't know what else to call it—that made him want to open up with her. She was completely without judgment. He'd never met anyone like her.

He didn't get how he could be talking to her about these intensely private, loaded issues and still be so distracted by the way she looked. By his overwhelming desire for her.

Nothing made much sense when it came to Angel. It was as if the normal rules of the world didn't apply. Or maybe that was just something he was making up to excuse what he was feeling for her. Because *that* made no fucking sense at all.

He had known this woman for just over two weeks. And she'd been unconscious the first few days.

Crazy.

And yet here he was. She was in his home. He was telling her things he'd never told anyone else. And if he didn't have her, he was going to lose his goddamn mind.

But that was completely off-limits.

He pushed back from the desk. He had better put himself to bed, or have a few more shots—or both—or he was going to drive himself insane thinking about this stuff. Thinking about her.

Angel.

He shook his head. Another shot of Scotch would only weaken his resolve, rather than help the situation any. And Lord knew he was weak enough already. He heaved himself out of the chair and shut off the lights.

Better just to crash for the night, sleep off the confusion, the doubts. His craving for Angel.

Not that he thought that would work. But it was

better than waking up with a hangover and a load of regret in the morning.

He called to Liam and headed for bed.

SHE WAS TRYING TO SLEEP, but her mind wouldn't still. She couldn't stop thinking about her talk with Declan. She'd been lying there for hours, the sheets too hot on her skin, until she'd had to throw them off. The cast was unbearably warm and heavy, constricting, but there was nothing she could do about that. If only her body wasn't so heated. If only she could stop picturing his face, his long and beautiful hands.

Declan.

He was such a good person. Better than he knew, she suspected. She could see his guilt, guilt that didn't belong to him. If only he understood that.

She wished she could comfort him, but she sensed it was too soon for that. She would have to take that connection slowly. It was something he was afraid of. Tonight had been a start, though.

She had been told all her life that the most effective way to reach a male was through sex. It made sense to her. Sex was the most intimate and beautiful of acts. And she wanted him. Her body never stopped yearning for his. For the touch of his hands. Even for his gaze on her face. But how much better to touch him, to feel his body against her own?

She moaned, shifted in her bed, felt how very empty it was.

She would rather be in his bed. She wanted to offer herself to him. But she was unsure as to how—and when—to go about it. Nothing, not all of her training, had prepared her to deal with this. A man, rather than a god or a demon. Such a simpler being, yet infinitely more complex at the same time. But this much she knew: all males had that same drive, the same physical needs, man or god or animal. And *that* she knew what to do with.

Go to him.

Her body surged with wanting simply thinking about it. She knew what she had to do.

Sitting up, she found her crutches in the dark, and made her way to his door. It was closed, but not all the way; it was easy to push it open with one crutch. Liam made a small, sleepy sigh from where he was curled up on the floor, an enormous black lump she could barely make out. The only light was the half moon shining pale silver through the curtains, but it was enough as her eyes adjusted to the dark.

She could see his still form in the bed. He was lying on his back, the blankets bunched around his waist, and she saw for the first time his bare chest. He was beautifully formed, strong. She could tell that much even in the shadow of his silhouette. Her body heated even more.

Need to touch him...

She hobbled to the bedside, set her crutches on the floor, and sat on the edge of the mattress. It gave way under her weight, but he didn't stir. Watching him, wishing he would wake up, see her, *want* her, she pulled her thin cotton nightgown over her head and dropped it next to the crutches.

The night air was cool on her skin, her nipples peaking. From the air, from being this close to him, naked. From the earthy scent of his body.

She slipped under the covers with him.

Declan...

Her breath caught in her throat as her arm brushed his shoulder. Lust kicked hard, shimmering over her skin, her sex tightening.

Need you, please, Declan...

She held her palm over his chest, let it hover there, waiting. Teasing herself. Then she lowered it, barely daring to let her fingertips brush his body.

His skin was soft, which surprised her. Soft skin, soft, silky hairs around the flat nipples. But beneath the smooth skin was hard, solid muscle. So different from her own body. Beautifully different.

He sighed in his sleep as her palm slipped over his flesh, and she answered with a quiet moan as her fingertips met his nipple. It was smaller than her own, flatter. Harder. Her sex went wet, her breasts aching. She squeezed her thighs together, but it only made her need worse.

"Declan," she whispered, but he huffed out a breath and remained asleep.

She moved her hand down, explored the tight wall of his stomach. Such hard muscle there, rather than the curving, soft flesh of her belly. Below it would be his cock.

She wanted to touch him there. To touch a cock for the first time. To take it in her mouth, to taste his desire on her tongue. To bring him the pleasure she had been raised to bring.

Yes.

She was soaking wet, her thighs rubbing together. It wasn't enough.

If only he would wake. Want her. Touch her. Fuck her. She was so ready. This was what she had been prepared for her entire life. And to give herself to this man, *this* man, who she had come to care for. To love. And who treasured her in a way she'd never dreamed of. He didn't have to tell her so. It showed in everything he'd done for her, everything he continued to do.

Her heart surged, her body trembled.

Need you, Declan.

She moved her hand lower, let her fingertips feather over the velvet head of his swelling flesh, felt his body shiver, felt hers do the same.

She moaned. He groaned. And tensed all over.

"Angel? What…?" He sat up, knocking her hand aside. "Jesus Christ. What are you doing here? What are you *doing?*"

"I am here for you. I need you, Declan. And you need me."

"What? I… No."

"You do not want me?"

"Angel, we talked about this." He ran a hand over his hair, scrubbed at his face. "Jesus." He looked at her, and she could just make out the dark gleam of his eyes. "You have to go."

"I want to stay here with you."

There was a small edge of panic in his tone. "You can't stay in here."

"Declan, I want you. To give myself to you. This is right."

"It's *not* right. It's all wrong."

"How can this be wrong? It feels right to me. It feels perfect." Tears were gathering in her throat, making it hard to talk. If only he would listen to her. "Declan, please. Have me."

He swung his legs over the side of the bed, started to pace, seemingly unaware that he was naked, still hard.

"Angel, this is crazy. We can't do this. *I* can't do this. I have a responsibility here. I explained that to you. This is impossible. You have to go back to your own bed. And you have to stay there. This is *not* happening." He came back to the bed, put his hands on her shoulders, holding on tight. "Do you understand? This will not happen. Not now. Not ever."

The tears flooded her throat, her eyes. A sob escaped her. She couldn't speak.

"Aw, shit. I'm sorry, Angel. Don't cry. It's not that I don't want you. You have to know that. I just don't see how this is possible. I'm supposed to watch out for you. Take care of you. Not take advantage of your gratitude."

"It's more than gratitude."

"Maybe you think so now. That might change. I'm pretty sure it will. You'll recover and become more used to the world. See more of it. And everything will change for you."

"I won't change my mind about you," she said quietly, wiping at her eyes.

"I think you should talk this over with Ruth. Okay? She'll help you to understand."

"I understand, Declan. I understand that we are meant to be together. Why else would you have been the one to find me? Why else would you have brought me to your home?"

"It was some weird fluke that I found you. It was coincidence. I happened to be on the beach that morning, that's all. And I brought you here because...I had to. No one else was going to take care of you."

"You see? That's what I mean."

"Don't, Angel. You're twisting this around."

"Declan, I would never do that."

He sighed. "Not on purpose. I know that. Just talk to Ruth, okay? And let me take you back to your room."

She was glad he was calming down. She pulled a long breath in, forcing herself to calm, too. This would perhaps take more time than she'd thought.

"And if Ruth tells me I'm right?" she asked him.

There was a long pause. "We'll deal with it then."

"You seem very certain she will agree with you."

"Can we just get you back to bed? And, Jesus, where's your nightgown? Here, put it back on."

He handed her the bit of cotton and she obediently slipped it over her head as he pulled a pair of pajama bottoms from beneath his pillow, where they'd been bunched up.

"I'll go back to bed. And I will talk with Ruth tomorrow."

"Good. That's good."

She would do as he asked. For now. But she had felt his unconscious response to her merest touch. That had told her all she needed to know about his desire for her. He needed some time to accept it. To come to accept that she was right.

They were meant to be together. And they would be. That was the only thing in her life she was sure of.

CHAPTER SEVEN

DECLAN DRUMMED HIS FINGERS on the wooden arm of the olive-green chair in Ruth Hehewuti's waiting room. It was a small space with only two other chairs, a table with a lamp and the requisite pile of magazines. A few Hopi artifacts, reflecting her cultural heritage, hung on the walls: coiled plaques made of woven sumac and willow, and a sepia-toned print of a Hopi woman in front of a pueblo.

It felt stuffy. Or maybe it was that he didn't like waiting.

He realized how much noise his fingers were making, so he stopped the drumming, stood and shoved his hands in his pockets. The room seemed even smaller with him standing up.

To his relief the door opened and Angel stepped through.

"I'm all done, Declan."

She smiled at him, and he went a little loose all over. A nice sensation.

"Hi, Declan. It's nice to see you," Ruth said.

She held out her hand to him, but it was a moment before he could make himself respond.

She was tiny, which always surprised him for some reason. She had dark eyes, nearly as black as her hair, which had a little silver running through it. It was pulled back into a tight bun, but her face was too softly featured for it to make her look severe. Long turquoise-and-silver earrings hung from her ears. She had a kind face, he realized. Maybe he was able to see that only in this context, where she was taking care of Angel. Being something other than his father's girlfriend.

"Hi. Nice to see you, too." He shook her offered hand.

"Shall we go talk for a bit?"

"Uh, sure. Angel, you don't mind waiting?"

"Of course not."

Everything was that simple with her. He liked that.

"Okay. I won't be long."

He helped her into the chair, realizing as he did that she was perfectly able to seat herself. He felt a little foolish doing this in front of Ruth—catering to Angel's needs. But fuck it. Why shouldn't he do whatever he thought was best for Angel, no matter who was watching? Ruth was Oran's girlfriend, not someone who was here to judge him.

Not the way he was judging her.

He sighed inwardly as he straightened up. Ruth

stood back to let him pass through the door into her office.

It was a comfortable room with a large, over-stuffed sofa strewn with colorful pillows. A hand-woven rug covered the floor, and there was a shelf filled with Hopi pottery in intricate red-and-black designs, and a small collection of kachina dolls tucked between the rows of books. Ruth gestured to the sofa and sat in a matching chair across from him. The sofa was soft, but he felt better sitting straight up, leaning forward a little, his hands on his knees. More in control.

"So," she said, still smiling, "first I want to make sure you know that Angel has given permission for me to discuss with you the things she tells me in session. And that as her guardian I feel it can be useful."

"I'm not her guardian." His fingers flexed, digging into the knees of his jeans.

"Not legally, no, but in every sense of the word, yes? You've given her a place to live, you take care of her. You're the one helping to reintroduce her to the world."

He rubbed his palms over his thighs, trying to rub out some of the tightness in his shoulders, his jaw, his chest. "I guess that makes sense."

He still didn't know why being called Angel's "guardian" made him so uncomfortable. It wasn't that he didn't want to be responsible for her well-being. He'd chosen to do it. And not because there was no one else around who was willing to help her. He *wanted* to. Enough that even if there had been someone else willing to step in and care for Angel, he probably would have fought them on it. Maybe he didn't like being reminded about his sense of responsibility toward her because it made his intense attraction to her seem more wrong. Not that he was going to do anything about that.

"She trusts you," Ruth went on, "which is the most important issue here, in allowing me to speak to you about what goes on in my sessions with her. But I also want to be clear that after the three sessions we've had, once while she was still in the hospital and twice here in my office, I feel she's able and competent to make that decision. There is no breach of doctor-patient confidentiality."

"I understand." He glanced at the window, then looked back at Ruth. She was watching him, her face placid, as if she would wait forever for him to talk with her. "That's been a question for me— Angel being capable of making decisions for herself. About continuing to live with me. About her future. About her work with you. So I'm relieved to hear it."

"But you're not entirely comfortable here?"

"Not entirely."

"Do you feel there's a conflict of interest because of my relationship with your father?"

He shifted, pressed his palms onto his thighs. Jesus. He really did not want to have to talk to this woman about his father. Didn't want to be faced with the fact of their relationship. Better to avoid it, to talk about Angel. Wasn't that what he was here for?

"That had occurred to me. I'll be honest about that. But Stephen—Dr. Kane—assured me you're the best person for the job so...Angel's well-being is the priority. I can definitely work around any discomfort on my part."

"I'm glad to hear it. She really does trust you implicitly, you know. I think it's important for her to trust someone right now."

He nodded. He wasn't sure what to say. "So, what am I here to talk about, exactly?"

"I want to touch base with you about Angel's progress from time to time. To let you know if anything important comes up. To give the benefit of my professional opinion as to how we can both best help her. And to hear your ideas."

"I'm hardly any kind of professional. I don't know if I'd have any ideas that would be useful."

"You interact with her every day. I'm sure you observe things about her she would never think to tell me. About her day-to-day state of mind. Her emotional arc."

"Are you concerned about her being depressed?" he asked.

"Are you?"

"I've thought about it. That someone coming out of her situation has to have some post-traumatic stress issues."

"I understand you're familiar enough with the term to know what that might mean."

He glanced up, his eyes narrowing, his system kicking into high alert. "And by 'understand' you mean my dad's been telling you my business."

"Declan, I'm only addressing it because I believe it's useful, helpful, for you to be able to recognize the signs. Because for many people that would be the case. But I believe Angel is different."

"What do you mean?"

She clasped her hands on her lap, a small smile on her lips, her dark eyes crinkling. There was something about her that made him want to relax with her, even though he was fighting it, that made him lower his defenses.

"Among certain cultures, my own being one of them, there is a belief that some people come into this life as innocent souls. Pure souls. They can't be corrupted. No matter what happens to them, they remain virtually untouched. It's my belief that Angel is one of these people."

"I don't mean to insult you, Dr. Hehewuti, but that sounds a little far-fetched."

"Please, call me Ruth. And yes, I'm sure it

does." She leaned forward in her chair. "I'm sure you've noticed her sunny personality. I truly don't think there's anything darker hiding beneath the surface. I don't think she realizes the enormity of what she's been through."

"Are you saying it's some idiot savant thing?"

"No, absolutely not. Angel is highly intelligent, and oddly well-educated for someone who's spent most of her life isolated from the world."

He nodded. "I think so, too. I can't figure her out. How it's possible that she's come through this so intact."

"I don't think she's been as traumatized by her experiences as one would usually expect. She has a tendency to simply accept everything at face value. I don't feel it's a defect in her mental or emotional capacities. I see it as a gift. And she has others."

Ruth stood and went to the bookshelf, pulled from it a large pad of paper, flipped it open and handed it to him. On it was a drawing of a wood-pecker, done in crayon, but in exquisite detail.

He looked up at Ruth. "What is this?"

"Angel drew it today."

"What?"

"And this one the other day." She flipped to another page and on it was a pencil drawing of a sparrow. Again, every tiny detail was flawlessly done.

"These are amazing. I had no idea she could

draw like this. I think she mentioned she liked drawing, but I never thought she'd have this kind of talent."

"When she told me she liked to draw I thought she might draw something that would lead me into her past. It's something therapists use sometimes, to bring out suppressed memories in a patient."

"And instead you got this." He shook his head. "These are incredible."

"She's very talented. You should see these, too."

She gestured for him to flip the pages. The first one was an image of Liam done in crayon, his big head, the sad brown eyes. His expression was perfect, the shading on the folds of dark fur incredibly realistic. He moved to the next page and was surprised to find a drawing of himself. His face, the expression wary. God, did he really look like that to her? But he supposed he did. He *was* wary. But again, the work was really something.

"I can't believe this."

"I thought it might be good if you could get her some paper and perhaps some charcoals to use at home," Ruth suggested.

"Sure. Of course." He closed the drawing tablet and handed it back to Ruth, who sat in her chair once more. "Is there anything else I should know?"

"Angel mentioned she's talked with you, but I don't know if her ideas about whether or not she's actually given you useful information are accurate.

You know about the woman who raised her? The one she calls 'The Grandmother'?"

"Yeah. She talks about her a lot. She seems attached to her. I don't get it. The woman obviously did some awful things to her. Things I can barely stand to imagine."

Ruth nodded. "She was the source of the ritual abuse Angel suffered. The one who gave her the drugs, although there were others in that compound. I believe this woman is one of those charismatic leaders. There are clearly mental issues, possibly she's bipolar or psychotic. Obviously I can't make any sort of conclusive diagnosis, but she definitely is—or was—a dangerous person. Yet someone others would follow. Highly intelligent, from what Angel has said. Able to charm. She's taken this Christian-based devil worship to an extreme. Twisted it and made it her own, created her own rules. Although Angel's memories still aren't clear, and it seems there was a group of other people involved that night, I absolutely believe that she was the one responsible for the attempt on Angel's life. Angel told me today that The Grandmother was the one who put those cuts on her shoulder blades."

"Yeah, those are crazy. What do you think those are about?" Declan asked her. "I have some ideas."

"It appears—and what I know about this Grand-

mother woman's beliefs make it more apparent—
that they were to make room for wings to sprout."

"Jesus. The woman is really sick."

"Yes. But you also have to understand that she
taught Angel, provided her with a home, and tasks
that gave her a sense of purpose. Many parents
don't offer their own children more."

"I guess so. But it all seems insane to me. Can
she really love the woman? Or is it some unhealthy
attachment Angel needs to learn to let go of?"

"Both, perhaps. Love is love, Declan. It doesn't
simply go away, no matter the source."

"Doesn't it?"

Why did he feel angry? Defensive, suddenly.

Ruth was watching him, her dark gaze on his
face. She said very carefully, "No, I don't think
it does."

They were both quiet for several moments. He
knew she was thinking of his relationship with his
father. He *was*. But he was not going to discuss
that with her.

He clenched and unclenched his fists in his lap.
When Ruth's gaze flicked to his hands he stopped
doing it.

"Are we done?" he asked. Demanded.

He didn't mean to sound so harsh. Rude. But
he had to get out of there.

Ruth maintained her serene expression. "Yes,
for today. I hope you'll come back and talk with

me. I'd like to see you once each month, if that's possible."

"Yeah, sure. That's fine," he said. "Look, I don't want to leave Angel waiting."

Partially true, but a lousy excuse for his shitty behavior. Still, it would have to do for now.

He stood. So did Ruth.

"You're going back to work soon?" she asked him.

"On Tuesday. I have Sundays and Mondays off, so I can bring Angel here to see you on Mondays. I have a medical services van scheduled to bring her here on Thursdays."

Ruth nodded. "Good."

"I figure she'll be okay at my place while I'm at work. She can get around enough to fix herself lunch."

"I think she'll be fine. She's not at all nervous about it. She tells me your dog, Liam, will be there with her, to watch over her."

"He will. He's totally in love with her already."

Why the sudden ache in his chest?

"I'll see Angel on Monday, then."

"Thanks."

She reached out to shake his hand once more, and he took it. She really was a tiny thing. Like his mother.

Don't even go there.

He opened the door and found Angel reading a magazine.

"Ready to go, Angel?"

"Yes."

Her smile was dazzling, as always, lighting up her face.

He helped her outside and into his truck, got in and pulled onto the highway.

"Hungry?" he asked her.

"I am."

"Why don't we stop somewhere for lunch? Are you up to it?"

"Stop?"

"Uh, there are places we can go for meals. Restaurants. Cafés."

"Oh, yes. I've read about such places."

"I'll take you someplace quiet, since this is your first outing." He turned to her, realization dawning. "Angel, this is your very first outing."

"Yes, Declan."

"Wow."

"I am not nervous. You will be with me."

"Nothing to be nervous about. We'll just sit and eat."

"And see people. A new place. I haven't seen many places. I'm excited."

A café was exciting? Every time something new came up for Angel, he was reminded again of how limited her life had been. It was hard to comprehend all at once.

A few minutes later he pulled into the parking lot of Bitsy's, a small breakfast and lunch place he hadn't visited in a while. But it was only eleven-thirty and should be fairly quiet.

"It looks just like a picture in a book," Angel said as he helped her from the car. "It looks friendly."

"The food is nothing fancy, but it's good."

He led her inside, held the door for her, helped her slide into one of the blue vinyl booths. Angel was a little wide-eyed, her gaze darting from the counter where several people sat drinking coffee, to the shiny register at the front, to the few occupied tables. He remained quiet, letting her soak it in.

A waitress approached. "Can I get you something to drink?"

"Angel?" he asked.

"I don't know. What can I have?"

"Anything. Whatever you want."

"Truly?"

He smiled, nodded.

She turned to the waitress. "May I have water, please?"

"That's all you want?" he asked her.

She nodded her head, and he ordered a cup of coffee.

She took a piece of her hair, twining it around her fingers, her cheeks coloring. "Declan, I do not know what *anything* means. I feel…embarrassed. This woman obviously assumed I knew what to ask for."

"Don't be embarrassed. You'll figure it all out. You don't have any cultural context for this kind of stuff, but you will, eventually. You'll build up the knowledge a little at a time. I'll help."

"Okay."

"Do you like chocolate? Maybe we should order a cup of hot chocolate for you."

"I do not know chocolate."

"Ah, you have to try it, then. I think you'll like it. It was my favorite when I was a kid."

He turned to ask the waitress for the hot chocolate, then back to her, a small smile playing at his mouth. He seemed pleased with himself.

Angel felt warmed by Declan's reassurance. This was all so new—she didn't know how to take it in, to make her brain function while it was so busy simply absorbing.

The café was pretty, with its blue bench seats— booths, she remembered having read somewhere— the shining utensils, the long white counter, where pies were lined up under glass domes.

No one seemed to think it strange that she was there, but it felt strange to her. She wrapped her sweater tighter around her body. It was one that

Liz had given her, a soft, pretty gray she thought looked nice with her pink cotton dress. She ran her fingers over the weave of the sweater, letting her fingertips help to lose herself a little in the texture.

"Are you okay, Angel?"

She glanced up to find Declan's dark blue eyes on her. "Everything is just so wide-open. But shining and clean. It'll take some time to get used to. It's like reading ten books at once. And, Declan, I wanted to ask you, what is internet? And *online?*"

He groaned. How to explain? He barely understood it himself sometimes.

"Where did you hear about it?"

"The other day I was listening to music on the radio, the way you showed me, and they said the radio station could be found on the internet. And each day I have heard of internet and *online* on commercials."

"I'm not sure I know how to tell you about it. It's a way for people all over the world to connect. To get information. I think I have to just show you."

"Okay."

"I'll show you when we get home, if you want. But be prepared. This is going to be a lot to take in, and I'm no expert."

"It sounds…inexplicable. Is it some sort of abstract concept?"

The corners of his mouth quirked, and she wasn't sure if he was happy or amused. "Sort of.

You going to ask me how the moon circles the earth next?"

"Oh, no. I've read all about astronomy. Isaac Newton, Ptolemy."

Declan grinned then, his lush lips parting over his strong white teeth. So beautiful to her, as always.

"You are a strange and amazing creature, Angel," he told her. His comment would have made her doubtful, except that he was still smiling at her, looking more pleased than ever.

The waitress returned and set down Angel's glass of water, brimming with ice, her cup of hot chocolate, which smelled wonderful, and Declan's coffee. Declan pulled a small, white container from a bowl and she was surprised to see milk pour out of it into his coffee. A drop spilled onto the edge of the cup, and he wiped it with one finger.

She shivered, remembering his hands hard on her shoulders when she'd come into his bed the other night. His hands were warm, strong...

The waitress laid down what looked like two large books, with only a few pages. They said *Lunch Menu* on the front.

"Declan?"

"Here, you read it to see what kind of food they have. This is how you choose what to eat."

She shook her head. "So many things. I don't know where to begin."

"What do you like to eat?"

"Soup?"

"You don't want something heartier than soup?"

"I don't know. What else should I have?"

"Sorry, Angel. I'm not helping enough. It's hard to remember sometimes that this is really all alien to you."

"It is hard for me, too. Will you decide for me, Declan?"

"Sure. Uh…the chicken pot pie is great. I think you'll like it."

She nodded, picked up her water glass and sipped while he told the waitress what they wanted.

The world was always a bit of a shock to her, no matter how much she enjoyed it. She'd dreamed of seeing places and people, especially when she was reading. Books had been her only tie to any world other than the one she lived in: The Grandmother's house and garden. The other places she was sometimes taken to at night. But she always had the dream herbs, then, so that was always blurred. The only other place she'd known was the darkness where she met Asmodeus.

She had not called to him for a number of days, and he had not come to her. She was trying not to think of his anger. She was trying not to think of her old desire for him. Her desire was only for Declan now.

Declan. Everything about him amazed her, gave

her pleasure. She had never known a man would be like him. Hard and soft all at the same time. The warmth of his body, of his smile. Of his protectiveness.

"Declan, thank you for all of this."

"For lunch? You're welcome."

"For that, yes. But for everything. Finding me. Saving me. Helping me find my way now."

She reached across the table and took his hand in hers, saw his cheeks flush.

"You're welcome."

"Why do you do it?"

"What?"

"Why are you willing to do these things for me?"

"Why wouldn't I be?"

"I have gathered that people are not always willing to help others. That some people come to it more naturally than others do. Why do you think you are such a person?"

He paused, shook his head, lifted his cup and drank. "You like to get right to the heart of things, don't you?"

"Yes."

He laughed a little. The second time she had heard his laughter. She liked it very much.

"Try your hot chocolate, then I'll tell you."

She smiled, lifted the steaming cup, held it to her lips and sipped.

Such goodness on her tongue, she could barely believe it.

"Oh, this is lovely. I don't know how to explain how good it is."

"I thought you'd like it."

He had a big smile on his face. She loved that they could both be happy at the same time. That *her* being happy made him happy. She sipped once more, savoring the sweet, earthy flavor on her tongue.

"Tell me now, Declan."

He nodded, sipping his coffee before setting the cup down. "I think my mother had a lot to do with it. That was just *her*. She was always doing work in the community. Volunteering at the hospital, knitting blanket squares for the military."

"I can knit, but I'm not very good at it. The Grandmother often told me I drop my stitches. What about your father?"

He shrugged. "I guess he did his share of that kind of thing, too."

"Yet it's hard for you to give him the same credit."

Declan looked down at his cup, wrapping both hands around it. "Yeah. I guess it is."

"I'm sorry, Declan. That you are angry with your father."

He raised his face to look at her. "I'm not angry." He ran a hand through his hair, his fingers sliding between the dark strands. His eyes were blazing blue. He was so beautiful. So hurt. "My father is a good person."

She nodded, even though he'd said the words through a clenched jaw.

"Look, Angel, you don't have to clam up. I don't mean to be defensive with you. But I don't talk about my dad."

"It seems there is a lot you don't talk about, Declan."

He let out a long breath of air. "You're right. I don't. I guess I haven't had anyone to talk to in a long time."

"Why have you had no one to talk to?"

"That's the million-dollar question, isn't it?" he said, more to himself than to her.

She paused, thinking. He was so alone, even though he didn't need to be. He had access to the whole world. Perhaps that idea was as daunting to him as it was to her. "I don't understand you, Declan. But I want to. I want to help, as you've helped me."

"It's okay. There's nothing to understand. I'm fine."

"Why don't I believe you?" she asked, smiling to soften her words.

He smiled back. "Because you're wise beyond your years in some strange way, Angel. It can be a little scary sometimes."

She laughed. She could tell he was teasing her.

"So, Ruth showed me some of your drawings today," he told her, changing the subject. "They're good. More than good."

"I enjoy drawing."

"I think you could really do something with it."

"Do something?" She didn't know what he meant.

"Sell them. There are a ton of small art galleries all around Mendocino. They sell stuff from local artists. We should take your work to a few of these places, see if they'll take them."

"Sell them?"

"You could make some money, I'd bet. It'd be good for you to have some income of your own. Not that I mind paying for stuff for you. But it would give you some independence."

"I'm not sure I understand. People would give me money for my drawings?"

"I think so. I like art, know a little about it. I'm not an expert, or anything. I make stuff, too. All the wood carvings around the house."

"I thought perhaps you had made those. They're very beautiful."

"I don't know about that. I just like to do it. It makes me…calm, I guess. But your stuff is amazing. It really is. It would sell."

"Declan, I don't know what to think."

"We'll figure it out. I'll help," he told her.

"So this is Angel."

She looked up to find a man standing next to the table, and knew immediately who he was. He looked just like Declan, if not quite as tall, with a thick head of silvery-gray hair and gray eyes. Kind eyes, but there was a bit of wariness in them, as well.

"Dad." Declan seemed momentarily shocked, then he stood up. "Angel, this is my father, Oran Byrne. Dad, Angel."

Oran shook her hand, smiling at her. "I'm glad to see you somewhere other than at the hospital."

"You saw me there?"

"Yep. The day you were taken in."

"Dad was with me when they first admitted you," Declan said, still seeming tense.

"It's nice to see you up and around," Oran said. "You look like you're doing well."

"I am doing very well. Declan has been helping me."

Oran nodded. "He's good at that."

"Will you eat with us, Oran?" Angel asked. She saw a brief flash of something dark and unsure in Declan's eyes. But so many small things Declan had said told her there was a rift between him and his father, one she hoped they would heal. She couldn't imagine having a real family and rejecting them.

Oran smiled, and it was Declan's same smile. "Sure. Why not?"

He slid into the booth next to his son. Angel thought she saw Declan flinch. But she believed this was the right thing to do.

Oran lifted his hand and the waitress came with a cup of coffee for him, greeting him by name. Angel noticed he used one of the small plastic containers of milk, just as Declan did.

"How are you feeling, Angel?" Oran asked her. "Is the leg hurting much?"

"Not too much. But I am anxious for the cast to be off so I can move around normally again. There are so many things I want to do that I'm unable to do now."

"You seem to be healing pretty fast. I'm sure it won't be long," Oran assured her. "You look great."

"Thank you. I feel good."

"Liam keeping you company?"

"Oh, yes. He's always with me. When I have napped he stays on the floor right by my bed. And if I go onto the porch, he follows me. He's the most beautiful dog."

Oran smiled. "He is pretty good-looking. And smart. I found that out when you were in the hospital and he stayed at my place. Makes me think maybe it's time for me to have a dog again."

"Then Liam would have another dog to play

with and bond with. It would be good for him. And for you. Being too much alone is not a good thing."

"No, it's not. I was alone for a very long time."

She caught a shadow crossing Declan's features. He was fidgeting with his spoon, turning it over in his hand, rubbing the bowl of it between his fingers. Looking as though he wasn't listening to the conversation, even though it was apparent to her that he was listening very closely.

"I'm sorry, Oran," she told him.

"Ah, it's all right. I've been less alone recently."

Angel smiled. "Because you are with Ruth."

"Yeah." Oran grinned, just a small quirking at the corners of his mouth as he glanced sideways at Declan. "How did you know about Ruth and me?"

"There is a photograph of the two of you in her office. She explained it to me when she was talking about confidentiality and conflict of interest. I do not see it as a conflict."

Declan shifted, looked out the window.

"Dec? Do you have a problem with Angel seeing Ruth?"

"No, of course not." Declan shrugged. "Seems she's the most qualified."

"That wasn't what I was asking, son."

Declan turned to his father. They looked almost like mirror images of each other in profile, other than the color of their hair, and the texture of Oran's skin was a little rougher with age.

"Yeah, I know."

There was bitterness in his tone, which surprised her. Oran had caught it, too. The two men were staring at each other, each with eyes that had narrowed a little. She sensed there was some sort of power struggle she couldn't quite understand going on between them.

"So?" Oran asked. "Is it okay or isn't it?"

Another pause before Declan finally answered, "Yeah, it's fine. Fine."

"Okay. It's good to air this stuff. Ruth has been teaching me that."

Declan nodded, picked up his coffee cup, his gaze going to the window once more.

Declan had healing to do, just as she did. And just as he was helping her, perhaps she could help him. His obviously damaged relationship with his father might be a good place to start. She would do what she could to encourage him in that direction. It would feel good to help Declan. And Oran.

She liked Declan's father. He was a good man; she knew that much right away. She understood he was part of the reason Declan had grown to be such a wonderful man, whether Declan wanted to admit it or not.

She also understood love was not always unconditional. That was something she had come to on her own. A decision she had made very early in life: to love those she had in her life, no matter who or what they were. Even in the books she read, she had come to see that in each person was some kernel of something to love. Even when they did things that were hurtful, it was still possible to love them.

She could teach that to Declan. She wanted to.

She had found a great deal in him to love already. And she would discover more, day by day. It didn't have to take away from her love for The Grandmother. For Asmodeus. Love was something that multiplied. Love was limitless. She believed that in her very soul.

The idea struck her that perhaps this meant she didn't have to give up Asmodeus. That she could love him and Declan equally, without measure or a need to balance or choose.

She had so much to give. She felt as if her heart was an overflowing well she'd never had an outlet for. But she did now. Liam helped with that; he accepted her affection easily, and loved her back. But people were more complicated than dogs.

If only Declan would accept her love. If only he would return it.

And meanwhile, tonight, when she was alone in her bed in the dark, she would call to Asmodeus. She would give him her pleasure once more, since Declan would not take it. Perhaps Asmodeus would teach her what she needed to know to please Declan so that he would no longer refuse her.

Yes, she would call her demon lover to her, her lord of lust. She would seduce him with her body, her beauty, her words. And someday, she would seduce Declan, as well.

CHAPTER EIGHT

DECLAN HAD BEEN QUIET ever since seeing his father
at lunch, and Angel hadn't tried to get him to talk.
They'd come back to the house, and he'd gone for
a long walk, leaving Liam with her. She'd spent
her time reading through an old book of poetry—
lovely, silly pieces by Edward Lear. The pages
were yellow with age, fragile, and the leather cover
was worn. In the front of the book was a bookplate:
Mary O'Connell. Declan's mother, she guessed,
and when Declan returned from his walk, he told
her that had been his mother's name before she'd
married, but it had been obvious he hadn't wanted
to talk more.

He was still a little withdrawn after his walk,
if not as much so. The walk had healed him, at
least in part. She understood the power of solitude,
and was happy enough to let him be. They'd had
a quiet dinner, then had listened to an opera together, Declan explaining the story. She had found
the tale of Lakmé, a tragic fable of forbidden love,

sad and sweet, the music itself exotic and beautiful. Exquisite.

Declan had claimed to be tired and gone to bed
early, and she'd followed suit. Now she lay in her
bed, naked and ready for Asmodeus, should he
come to her tonight.

But sleep would not come. She was too anxious to see him, her body melting, ready. In need
of both her demon lover and the man who slept in
the next room. Asmodeus as a conduit, perhaps,
to reaching Declan. Or so she hoped.

She got up, hobbled to the window and opened
it, letting the night air in to calm her. The crickets
hummed in the night shadows. The moon was a
sliver in the sky, casting pale, silver light onto the
tips of the trees and across her bed.

What was it about the moonlight that made her
yearn for Declan even more?

She lay down on the bed once more, willing her
mind to release its thoughts, her body to still. And
with the song of the crickets to soothe her, she finally drifted off.

She knew the dream place. She was falling
into the warm, womblike darkness. It was familiar, that strange plane where she found Asmodeus.
She called to him.

"Asmodeus!"

She fell, alone, the wind making serpentine
coils of her hair around her naked form.

She called again.

"Asmodeus. Come to me."

He was there, just out of reach. She felt his heat, but he did not reveal himself. She knew he was toying with her. They were still falling through the dark.

"Come to me, Asmodeus, and let us be as we were before. I need you."

"Ah, you need me now, do you, little one?"

He stood before her, then, radiant. His hard, naked body golden and sleek, his coal-black eyes burning. Beautiful. Full of danger.

Desire swarmed her system.

"Yes." She knew it would do no good to make excuses for her absence. "I've missed you."

"Have you? Not always, I think. You have other diversions, now that you are no longer The Gift."

"I have a name now." There was a certain pride in that. She didn't quite understand it. "I am called Angel."

It was the first time she had thought of her name—her identity—in her own head. It was a strange and lovely sensation.

Powerful.

"You are different, little one."

"Yes."

"He has made you different."

"Yes, in part. But some of it is simply my freedom."

"But are you truly free? Are you not still ruled by your desires?"

It was true. But not in the black-and-white way her demon lover presented it. "I'm free to choose whether or not—and how—I act on those desires, Asmodeus. It's different. I am…a person. My *own* person. I belong to no one but myself. The first possession that has ever truly been mine."

She felt a surge of power as the truth of the idea hit her. They had stopped their fall, suspended now in the heat and the darkness, the demon's body giving off a golden glow, illuminating the empty space around them.

"I am not certain I like these differences," Asmodeus said, his dark, perfect brows drawing together over his glittering eyes.

"You do not like that I have any sort of independence."

"On the contrary, I have always enjoyed your sense of independence. That you never simply bowed to my instructions, to the plan for you. I have loved that tiny, fierce spark."

"Yet that was my downfall in fulfilling my duties."

"Yes."

"And you never told me."

"Had the Dark One accepted you, we would never have seen one another again. You would have been entirely his."

What was he telling her? That he had manipulated her for his own ends? Or was it something else, something less malevolent?

"Is this some sign of…affection for me, Asmodeus?"

"I have told you I love you, little one."

"In the way you are able. I expect no more from a creature such as yourself. But I need more," she informed him, watching his face very closely, seeing the shadows crossing his flawless, stony features.

"You believe this man can give you more?"

"He does." She paused. "In his own way."

"You cannot be fulfilled entirely by either of us alone. This is why you still come to me."

She held her chin high. She saw no shame in doing what she needed to do. And he was a demon; he could not be truly hurt by her actions. "I need your help, Asmodeus."

He smiled then, a flash of white teeth that was almost a gnashing snarl.

"I am here to serve," he said.

She ignored the sarcasm in his tone. That was simply his way. She could see from his naked, hardening flesh that he would happily do as she asked, if she asked in the right way.

"Asmodeus, you are the demon of all things carnal, a prince of lust. You have taught me so much. But I know there is more you can show me. I ask you to make me a siren whose call is irresistible. To complete the task you set out to do when you first became my mentor."

"And if, in doing so, I can convince you to stay with me, rather than giving yourself to him?"

"I don't believe that will happen."

"You are honest about your intentions, at least," he said. "You are enjoying the world too much. You want to explore it. You want to be loved on human terms. But the world is a complicated place, little one."

"I'll take it on those terms. Yet, I still think of you, and yearn for you. And know you are the only one who can teach me what I need to know."

"You flatter me."

"It is not empty flattery, Asmodeus."

His smile widened, making her think of the fairy story she had read many times.

The better to eat you with.

She shivered, longing coursing through her body. If only she could *touch* him.

She shifted, trying to move toward him but there was no gravity where they were. He did nothing to move closer himself.

"Do you not still want me, Asmodeus?" She ran her hands over her bare breasts, cupping them.

His hand went to his erection, began to stroke.

"I never cease to want. It is intrinsic to my very existence."

She smiled at him, squeezing her stiffening nipples between her fingertips. Pleasure surged, a warm, piercing sensation, arrowing through her breasts, into her sex.

"You will come for me," Asmodeus said, his voice thick with need.

"As always," she answered, one hand slipping in between her thighs to find her damp cleft. "Tell me how best to please a man, Asmodeus."

His stroking fingers paused, his brows lowering. "You ask me to help you seduce this man?"

"Yes. I beg it of you, Asmodeus."

She spread her thighs, slipped one finger between the swollen lips of her sex, pulled it out wet with her juices.

"Ah, you torture me, little one," Asmodeus groaned. "Tell me, would your flavor be as sweet as you are?"

"Sweet and full of salt. Full of desire. For you, Asmodeus."

"Tell me what you desire," he demanded.

"To see you watching me, growing harder and harder as I caress my breasts, my sex."

She stroked the swollen lips, letting her fingertip delve inside once more. "Young and virgin and tight."

"Ah…" he moaned. "Tell me more."

"My body is like velvet inside. Hot and soft." She pulled in a gasping breath, pleasure making her warm and loose all over. "I want to feel you slide into my body. To feel that first painful piercing of my maidenhead. To grasp your hard flesh within me."

She was growing wetter as she spoke, her own words bringing desire, hot and stinging, like a current in her veins.

"Yes. I want you, little one. To slide into your body, to push inside, to feel the warmth of your innocent virgin blood on the perfection that is my fallen flesh."

He strummed his fingers up and down the rigid shaft.

"Is that how I would touch you, Asmodeus?"

"Yes…" He let his head fall back, ecstasy on his hard features. "Teasing at first. Tempting. Merciless." His fingers stroked lightly up, then down, and she mimicked his movements with her own hand between her thighs. "Then you would grasp my hard and blood-filled member, and squeeze."

He did so, his fingers tightening, until the head was a dark copper.

Pleasure stabbed into her at the sight. So beautiful. Her fingers pressed onto her clitoris, plucked at the swollen nub.

"Spread your legs wider, little one, and tilt your hips. Let me see the pink flesh there. Ah, yes…"

She did as he asked, and as he lifted his head to gaze hard at her open sex, she felt the heat of her fluids trickling down one thigh. Her sex ached, a hard pulse-beat of need.

"And how would I please you most, Asmodeus? With my hands? With my mouth? With my tender, open sex?"

"With all three. First with your pretty hands, then with your hot, wet mouth. You would suck me in, your tongue twining around the tip."

She dipped her fingers into her opening, heard with pleasure his long sighing breath.

"What else, Asmodeus?" she asked breathlessly.

"You would open your mouth wider and take me in, sucking hard and deep, opening your throat for me."

He was hard and golden, perfect, swelling even more. She loved the sight of it. Loved to see his pleasure.

"I would pump into you, girl. Hard strokes that showed no mercy, feeling your lovely body clasp around me. Soft and tight and…just…like this…"

His hips arched, and he came, spilling out into the darkness. And she came with him, her body tensing, pleasure pouring through her as she shook with it.

"Asmodeus…yes!"

She shivered as her orgasm went on, pounding through her system like thunder. She was left panting, weak.

She looked up to find her demon lover staring at her.

"That, my little beauty, is how you will seduce this man you want so badly. With the innocent desires of your body. It is beautiful, always. Pure. Do you understand?"

She nodded, still too breathless to say more than "Yes."

"Do not forget that it was I who taught you these things."

She shook her head. "I will never forget."

"Ah, but someday you will."

The wind had come up again, warm and gentle against her damp, naked flesh. Asmodeus's eyes burned black as hot coals. His long hair, so pale it was nearly translucent, whipped in the wind, lashing at his golden cheeks. There was a small frown on his otherwise perfect face.

She realized the truth of what he said: that someday she might forget him. Not forget him, but cease to need him, perhaps. And she felt herself float away from him, bit by bit.

DECLAN DIDN'T GET AS keyed up anymore, walking into Ruth Hehewuti's office. Angel always told him how wonderful Ruth was to her, which scored points for the woman, in his mind. He still didn't like being faced with her relationship with his father, but it was Oran he was pissed at, not Ruth.

She smiled as she waved him in. They both sat down, Ruth across from him in the big chair.

"Declan, it's nice to see you. How have things been going? It's been two weeks since we last spoke. And Angel has been with you how long now? Two months?"

"About that, yeah. She's changed a lot. Well, maybe not a lot. She's basically the same. Cheerful, curious about the world. Incredibly intelligent. Eager to know everything, and she picks up information and absorbs it at an amazing rate. She's definitely more confident than she was even a month ago. More relaxed."

"She seems so to me when she's here. I'm glad that's translating to her behavior at home, as well."

"It is. She's getting around a lot better with the cast off. Maybe that makes her feel more independent."

"I'm sure that's helpful. She's been drawing a lot of pictures of your house when she's here. That tells me she feels at home."

"You still have her draw here?"

"It's useful in therapy, as I mentioned before. It tells me a lot about how she sees the world. There are also pictures of Bitsy's café, one of the waitresses there I gather she's become friendly with. *Life,* as opposed to simply pretty things. It's a sign of growth. But there's more. She's drawn The Grandmother—several pictures of her."

"Jesus." His hands curled into fists. "I don't know if I even want to see that."

"I understand. But I should tell you that Angel has given me permission to send the drawings to the state police, as well as copies to some of the people Oran knows."

He nodded, his pulse accelerating. "The pictures could help find her, maybe."

"Yes, it's possible."

"That's good." He pressed his hands onto the tops of his thighs, rubbed at the denim. "That's really good. Are they… When I think of that woman's face, I see the old witch from *Snow White,* from when I was a kid. A nightmare."

"They are all part monster, part mother, which doesn't surprise me."

He shook his head. He was having a hell of a hard time with the "mother" part.

"So, tell me, how are you doing with all of this?" Ruth asked.

"Me? I'm fine."

Ruth smiled. "Can you expand on that a little?"

He shoved his hands in his jacket pockets, then, feeling foolish, pulled them out again. "I'm not sure what you want me to say."

"Whatever is relevant. How are you feeling about having taken on this enormous responsibility? Do you ever feel overwhelmed? Unsure?"

He shrugged. "I understand it's a big responsibility, but it doesn't *feel* like it, if that makes sense."

"It does."

"I guess I get… Sometimes I'm not sure what I'm doing is the right thing for her," he admitted. "I don't know exactly how much I'm supposed to be doing, other than providing a home for her, making sure she's fed, that she gets medical care. I feel like I have to help her get to know the world. I've been taking it a little at a time. I feel bad about having to go back to work, even though I know she's fine at the house on her own. She seems to find ways to keep herself occupied. I've given her free rein over my bookshelf, brought her more books from the library—whatever she asks for, or that I think would interest her. She reads all the time. I've shown her television because she asked. I'm not big on it myself. But I think she needs to start having some sort of cultural context if she's ever going to be able to function."

"Absolutely," Ruth agreed. "Angel told me about you taking her to the grocery store, and out to Bitsy's for dinner. That you've taken her to a few of the local galleries and discussed talking to them about selling her art when she's ready. She likes being out, meeting people. She's eager. And it's good for her to get out. I also think it's good that you've been taking things slowly, but she may be ready for a little more exposure to the world."

"I agree that it's good for her. So, what am I missing?"

"I don't know that you're missing anything. From what Angel says, you've been wonderful with her. I don't think you need to doubt yourself, Declan. There isn't any set protocol for this sort of thing. Her situation is pretty unusual, and there's a lot you'll have to play by ear."

"There's nothing that's really startled her so far. She's incredibly adaptable." He was always amazed by her.

"I wouldn't have expected her to make this kind of progress, knowing what her life has been," Ruth said, "but she seems to be adjusting. She's developing normal relationships, which is often a concern with a history of this sort of ritualized trauma. She's told me she talks with Georgia, the waitress at Bitsy's, and she has a favorite checker at the market. And then there's you." Ruth paused for a moment before leaning forward, folding her hands over her knees. "Have you two discussed sex since the night she climbed into your bed?"

"Jesus. She told you about that?"

His face was steaming hot. This was not a conversation he wanted to have with anyone. Especially his father's girlfriend.

"I'm sorry, Declan. I know this can be uncomfortable. But Angel feels very attached to you, and I believe that needs to be addressed."

His fingers flexed, his fists balling up. But she was right. He forced his hands, his jaw, to relax. "Okay. Okay."

This was worse than having "the talk" with his father when he was twelve. Not that he was prudish, by any means. He'd had plenty of sex with plenty of women. But this was different. Most of the sex he'd had had been fairly meaningless. He'd pretty decisively never developed a real connection to any of the women he'd dated or slept with. But Angel…he was becoming attached to her, too. More than attached. He didn't want to think too much about it.

"Angel has an extraordinary view on sex," Ruth went on. "Her perspective is completely pure. I mean that she hasn't been contaminated by being told it's something dirty, or to be ashamed of. She sees sex and desire as something beautiful, even precious. A gift she wants to share with you, specifically."

He shook his head. Were they really having this conversation? "Look, I'm not some kind of pervert."

"Angel doesn't think so. Neither do I."

"You keep talking about how innocent she is."

Ruth nodded. "In certain ways. But by *innocent* I don't necessarily mean childlike. You've lived with her in your home for over two months. You've talked with her. You know how bright she is. How sharp her instincts are, her insights."

"What are you trying to say?"

"That you can have an adult conversation with her about it. That discussing these things with her might be more constructive and conducive to her growth than ignoring the topic, or treating her as though there's something intrinsically wrong with her desires."

He ran a hand through his hair. "I don't mean to make her feel bad."

"And I don't mean to make *you* feel bad. This isn't about rubbing your nose in anything. I don't operate that way. Just be open to talking with her, Declan. You're both adults. We have to treat her as an adult if she's to find her place in the world."

"That makes sense, I guess. It does."

Why did he feel as though Ruth was trying to give him permission to be with Angel? It was too weird.

He *did* want to be with her. No question about it. But that didn't mean he had to do more than recognize it. He didn't have to act on it. Angel may be an adult, physically, but she was still an innocent young woman who'd been isolated from the world. A virgin, for God's sake. Could she have the maturity to make intelligent decisions about her own life? Wasn't that why she was still basically under his care?

It wouldn't be forever. Eventually Angel would be capable of caring for herself. She would move on, make a life for herself.

He didn't want it to be without him.

But wanting to be with her was crazy. Wasn't it? Or was it?

He still didn't know what to think. What to feel. If he should allow himself to feel anything.

Too damn late for that.

That was the truth. He cared for Angel. More than cared. He wasn't ready to look at how deep those feelings ran. He never had, not since Abby. But it had been over six years. How long was he going to carry that shit around with him? The bitterness. The loss. The need to remain completely shut down, a wall between him and every other person on the fucking planet.

Angel had broken through that wall already.

He was right. It was too damn late.

DECLAN STOOD ON THE PORCH, throwing an old tennis ball for Liam, trying to work on a small carving of a trout between throws. The dog never tired of this game. He'd probably chase the ball until he dropped, if Declan's arm didn't wear out first. But it kept Liam happy, and it created a sort of meditative state for him, too. He'd been playing with the dog for a good half hour. Angel was inside now, cleaning up from dinner. She'd insisted, even though she'd been the one to cook. She was a good cook. It was nice to come home to a hot meal.

And Christ, was he really that guy? The kind that goes to work all day and comes home to dinner and a beautiful woman? Had he ever wanted to be that guy? Had he ever thought he could?

Having Angel around was making him question himself too much for comfort. But he liked having her there. Too much for comfort.

He lifted his arm, ball in hand, and Liam watched him with absolute concentration, his body tensed for the throw. Declan pitched the ball and Liam raced after it, his big, pink tongue lolling. He went back to the piece of wood in his hand, shaping the tiny scales, while Liam ran for the ball and came loping back.

He'd spent the week trying not to think about his conversation in Ruth's office, but of course, it was all he could think about. He couldn't escape the realizations he'd had that day. About Angel. About himself. No matter how practiced he was at keeping a lid on his emotions it kept coming up.

Liam nudged the ball with his big nose, and Declan rolled it under his booted foot, holding it there.

"That's enough, boy. You're gonna wear us both out."

Liam watched the ball longingly for a few moments, then sat down at the bottom of the stairs, wagging his stumpy tail. Declan let his gaze rest on the trees, highlighted by the lowering sun. The air was getting misty with the first of the evening fog, bringing the rich, loamy scent of the woods to life. He took a deep breath, held the cool air in his lungs.

The issue of sex kept coming up, too. Not that Angel had tried to get back into his bed again. Not that it was anything new. But he thought of her constantly: while he was at work, when he was with her, when he was alone in his bed or in the shower. He'd stopped resisting that pull, figuring it was better to work it out of his system. Not that it ever seemed to help for more than a few minutes.

He groaned. He had to stop this physical obsession he had with her. Somehow.

He rubbed his fingers over the wood, letting the rough texture bite into his skin. Why couldn't he calm down? It hadn't gotten any better. If anything, it was more intense as he and Angel got to know each other. They were comfortable together now, despite the hot zing of chemistry between them. Despite how much energy it took for him to resist the absolute driving fucking *need* to touch her. Be with her. Some days he didn't know how much longer he was capable of resisting. Not that he'd jump on her out of the blue. But if she came into his bed again…

Liam jumped up and Declan knew Angel had come out onto the porch.

"Declan, may Liam have a little beef stew? I saved some of the meat for him."

"Sure."

She came to sit next to him on the porch steps. He did his best to ignore the heat emanating from her body. The smell of her hair. The tightening in his groin.

"Dinner was great. Thanks, Angel."

"You're very welcome. I like to cook for you."

"Liam likes it, too." He patted the dog's head, who only had eyes for Angel, hoping for another bit of meat.

She was in one of the sundresses she'd taken to wearing. She loved anything with flowers on it, and he'd taken her shopping at a local boutique recommended by Georgia and bought her a good dozen. The shopping had overwhelmed her, but she'd loved it.

All too aware of the rise of her full breasts above the edge of floral cotton, he realized he'd never thought to suggest she buy a bra. Not that he minded.

"I brought a paper towel for you, Declan. I know how slobbery Liam's toys get."

"Thanks."

He set his unfinished carving down on the stair, took the paper towel, wiped his hands. They sat quietly together then, listening to the sounds of the forest settling in for the night: the soft chirping of the birds, the quiet sigh of the wind in the leaves. They did this often, both of them content in the still evening air.

"What are you working on?" she asked him, picking up the half-finished piece.

"It's a trout. A steelhead, like the ones my dad and I used to catch."

"Is this for him?"

"What? No. I don't know." He took it from her, rubbed his thumb over the grooves in the wood.

"Oran would like it, I think."

"Yeah. Maybe."

He looked up and Angel's blue gaze was soft on his. She rubbed her arms, pulled her hair around her shoulders. Even in the dying light, it still looked like spun silk. Golden. Shining.

"Are you cold, Angel?"

"No. I'm warm enough. I don't want to go in until the sun is done setting. I don't want to miss it. I've always loved the sunset."

"Do you miss it?" he asked her, not even certain why he felt a need to bring it up. "Do you miss your old life, Angel?"

"Sometimes. I still miss my garden, but my leg is so much better, I hope to plant here soon. A new garden will soothe me."

"But you need soothing."

He looked at her closely. Her face wore her usual sweet expression, but her sky-blue eyes were serious, and there was a small frown on her lovely mouth. Her hands twisted together in her lap.

"Yes. I miss The Grandmother. I know you think it's strange. But I do. She was all I knew my entire life."

"For most of it, anyway. Do you remember anything before that yet?"

"Small flashes sometimes." Her golden brows furrowed. "I sometimes see things just as I'm falling asleep. A woman with hair the same color as mine, and my eyes. She has warm hands. But when she talks to me I can't understand what she's saying. And then it goes away."

"Your mother, maybe?"

"Maybe. How would I know?"

He nodded. He still had only the faintest grasp on what it was like to be her. Someone with a lost past. A lost family.

"There had to be good times in your life, Angel." He wanted there to be. He couldn't stand to think of her in some constant, utterly miserable existence. Fucking awful to think of her like that.

"There *were* good times. When The Grandmother felt well we would talk in the evenings about what I had read that day." She took the ends of her long hair, twisted them between her fingers, her gaze going distant. "She knows so much. I loved when she taught me about the ways of herbs, the ways of the birds and the earth. And when she was ill, I liked to care for her...not that she was sick, of course, but the taking-care-of-her part. Is that odd?"

"I don't think so. In my mind it means you're empathetic. It's a good trait."

Angel smiled, that lovely, brilliant smile, and then it dimmed. "It wasn't all good, Declan."

"I know."

"There are many things I haven't told you. I've talked to Ruth. I know you have some bits and pieces, but there's more."

"You don't have to tell me anything you don't want to."

"But I do. I want you to know. Is that all right?"

"Yeah. Of course."

She reached out and took his hand in hers. Her fingers were warm. The heat of her was there, but he pushed those thoughts aside to listen. His stomach was pulled tight. He knew whatever she had to tell him was going to be hard as hell to hear. Hard to have her looking right at him while she told him this awful shit, but he wasn't going to turn away from her.

"You know I was with her from a very young age. Ruth and I have figured that I was about five years old. I remember being afraid of her, The Grandmother. Well, I was always afraid of her, but at first there was nothing but the fear. She did some…terrible things to me." Angel stopped, her grip tightening on his hand. "She started giving me the herbs—the drugs—even then. She would drug me and sit me on her lap by the fire and tell me things. I suppose she was teaching me her ways, her beliefs. That was how it started. I didn't even know at first there were other people. The compound. She kept me to herself for a while. Maybe as long as a year. Maybe more."

Her face was tightening up a little at a time, turning into a rigid mask. He'd never seen her like this and it scared the shit out of him. But he didn't want to interrupt her.

"Things got harder," she went on. "She started to take me outside at night, into the forest. The others came, then. I never saw their faces. They wore hoods. I only heard their chanting voices, and sometimes they would whisper to each other, but I rarely understood what they were saying. When I was little I thought they were ghosts in the dark. As I got older I would see their shoes when I was tied to the ground, and I understood they were real people."

"Jesus," he whispered. It slipped out, he couldn't help it. But it was as though she hadn't heard him.

"They staked me to the ground and spread rock salt around me in a circle. I was always naked. I don't mind being naked, but sometimes it was cold.

And the ground was hard, even with the dreaming herbs. And I remember when they tattooed my palms…"

She let go of his hand, held both of hers faceup, looking down at the red pentagrams there, then curled her fingers closed. It hurt him to see those marks in her skin, to think of what she'd been through. Too fucking awful. But he was going to sit there and listen as long as she needed to talk about it.

Her voice was fading, but she was still talking. "The Grandmother was always in charge. No one dared to speak against her, to argue with her. Everyone did her bidding. I came to understand that very early on. They worshipped her, I think, almost as much as they did the Dark God."

He swallowed hard, trying to keep quiet, to let her speak no matter how awful it was.

"Sometimes they cut me…" Her voice was a whisper and he had to strain to hear her. "They used a hunting knife. It was different from The Grandmother's ritual knife. Hers has a handle made from hazelwood. The others would make just small cuts to gather my blood. They marked me in my own blood. More pentagrams, other symbols. And then I would go to the dream place." She took a quick breath, exhaled. "There is a place, another plane—I've told you a little about it before."

"Yeah." He didn't like to think about what went on there. That whole demon thing. She hadn't brought it up for a while. "As long as you understand it's just a dream."

She wrapped her arms around herself, seemed to come out of the daze she'd been in while talking, looked right at him. "I don't want to tell more just now, Declan."

"Sure. Whatever you want. I understand."

"Do you?" She was watching him very closely, as if the answer were crucial.

"What do you mean?"

"A life is made up of both good and bad. Can you know someone if you don't know both?"

He wasn't sure he liked where this conversation was going. But it was true. He shrugged. "You're right, I guess."

"I want us to know each other."

"So do I." More than he liked to think about.

"Declan, I've told you some of my bad. Will you tell me about yours?" He started to shake his head, but she insisted. "Please tell me. Share that part of yourself with me. Please, Declan."

How could he deny her? He didn't want to talk about this stuff. But she was right. And some part of him was actually eager to get it out. To let her know him. And who else could he talk to about it? There was no one but Angel. There never had been.

"Okay. I'll tell you. I'll tell you the things I never talk to anyone about."

CHAPTER NINE

THE SUN WAS SINKING BEYOND the veil of trees, their branches making dark silhouettes against the sky. The mist was coming in, giving Angel tiny goose bumps over her arms and shoulders, but she didn't want to go inside to get a sweater. Declan was ready to talk to her about his pain, and she didn't want to risk doing anything that might undermine the shaky trust he had in her at this moment.

Declan rubbed a hand over his jaw, at the scar that ran along it, then ran his fingers through his hair. He wouldn't look at her. But that was all right. The important thing was that he talk to her.

"I don't know where to start. There's my mom… and Abby. And my father."

"Ruth always tells me to start at the beginning."

"Okay. Okay." He sat a few more moments, staring off into the trees, while all around them the forest grew darker, quieter. "So…my mother got sick. I was about twenty, away at college in San Francisco. I came home right away. Do you know about cancer, Angel?"

He looked at her, his eyes gleaming in the pale light coming through the windows from the one lamp she'd lit in the living room. They were a deep, midnight-blue. Full of banked emotion.

"Yes. One of The Grandmother's dogs had cancer when he got old. I read about it. I wanted to help his pain, but it was hard—he hurt no matter what I did. I'm sorry, Declan."

He turned away once more, and she thought perhaps it was easier for him to talk that way.

"Everything happened really fast." He shook his head. "Actually, it took months. But I felt… shocked the whole time. Anyway…she had a round of chemotherapy, and it worked at first. Then it stopped working. She got sicker and sicker. They offered another treatment, more chemo, something new. They said it would give her more time."

He stopped, and she watched the tight line of his shoulders, his mouth. She could hear his strained breath. She wanted to reach out, to touch him, soothe him. But she understood he wouldn't want that right now. He was too involved in the old pain that still hurt him so much.

"So," he continued after a long pause, "she decided she didn't want it. I asked my dad to talk her into it. He refused. Said she could make her own decisions. But goddamn it, she was too sick." His voice was a low growl, but she could hear the fury there as easily as if he were yelling. "He should have done it. He should have made the decision for her, taken it out of her hands."

He went quiet and Angel let him sit for a few moments. "Declan, she may have simply been ready."

His head whipped up at that, his stare hard on her face. "Ready to die?"

Oh, yes, he was angry. But she knew it wasn't really directed at her.

"Yes. She may have had enough suffering. And chemotherapy is terribly hard on a person's body, isn't it? I read about it in the books."

"It was fucking torture for her. Five months of it."

"I know you wanted her to stay with you. But you can't ask that she choose to suffer more in order to do that."

"It would have extended her life. It wasn't just for me," he insisted.

"Wasn't it?"

His eyes narrowed and she could feel the anger and the grief radiating from him like a wave of heat. Except that everything about him was icy cold. She shivered. But she wasn't going to let this go. She knew she was right.

"I don't mean to be cruel, Declan. But if she didn't want to live any longer, and your father— her husband and life mate—accepted that decision, then it wasn't up to anyone else to make. Not even her child. That's the only way I can see it, and perhaps I'm wrong. But I think the earth was ready to receive her, Declan, and she was ready to go. This is part of the cycle. We must all accept. When we don't, the pain and the fear and the grief build up until we drown in it."

He rubbed his palms on his jeans, his mouth loosening a little. "Maybe." He pulled in a deep breath, blew it out. "I don't know. I've been so used to carrying this around with me. Being pissed off because it's easier, maybe."

"Is it really easier? After all these years, don't you want to simply feel better?" Angel asked.

"Maybe part of me doesn't want to feel better. There's some sick security in hanging on to it. And I am fucking pissed at my dad. He should have done more. He should have at least had one conversation with her. How hard would that have been? I can't let that go. That he wasn't willing to let her have one more chance at getting better. That he wasn't willing to give us one more chance at being a family."

She shook her head. "I don't think it's sick. I believe it's human nature to stay with what is familiar. Safe. But I also believe we can aspire to more. If I didn't truly believe that, I would never be anyone but that girl who was completely controlled by The Grandmother. I would never be able to survive being away from that control. And yet, here I am, learning to live a different life."

"Maybe you're braver than I am," he muttered, half under his breath.

"Tell me about Abby, Declan."

He started to shake his head, but he began to talk anyway, his gaze firmly fixed on the dark ground in front of him. She could see even in the dim light the vein pulsing in his temple, how tightly his jaw was clenched, and her heart hurt for him.

"God. That was…maybe even worse. About six months after my mom died I joined the military. Do you know what that is?"

"Yes, I know."

"I had to get away, you know? I had to *do* something. I couldn't handle going back to San Francisco, back to school. I didn't feel like I could just get back to my old life because it *wasn't* my old life. Nothing felt the same. Like it would be too weird to pretend it was. So…they sent me to the Middle East. To Bahrain."

He paused, rubbed at his scar. "It was my job to guard the family of a diplomat—an important American official. Abby was their daughter. She was sweet. Pretty. Forbidden. I fell for her the minute I saw her. We developed a relationship, of sorts. We'd talk sometimes, in the evenings. I was always careful not to overstep the boundaries with her.

That was a part of my duty. It would have meant a discharge for me. The situation was impossible. I'd been thinking for weeks about a transfer. It would have been the smart thing to do. But I couldn't do it. Maybe I wasn't smart enough."

Again, he stopped, and she let him just sit and breathe. He was quiet for so long she wasn't sure he'd tell her more. But then he started talking again, both palms rubbing slowly over his denim-clad thighs.

"We were in the marketplace. I don't know if you've ever seen pictures of these places in the Middle East. Even now it's more like the bazaars a few hundred years ago, right there in the middle of a city. Tents and crowds and noise. I should have been more alert. But I was always so distracted by her…but that was no excuse. I had a job. Fuck."

She reached out then, laying her hand on his arm. He flinched at first, but she held fast. "Declan, it's okay. Just tell me."

He turned to face her once more. His features were absolutely rigid, half his face caught in shadow. There was so much pain there. So much tension. She slipped her fingers down until she found his hand, was happy when he grasped hers, held on.

"They snuck up on us," he said, his voice low and tight. "Thieves. Just common street thieves. I had a fucking gun, but they were so sly and fast.

They managed to slit her throat before I could do anything. All for their fucking purses! Hers and her mother's. Then they ran off, into the crowd. And Abby was bleeding and bleeding everywhere. Her mother was screaming. I didn't know what to do, if I should go after them or stay with Abby. I wasn't going to leave her. But there was nothing… there wasn't a goddamn thing I could do."

His hand was so tight around hers it hurt, but she held on. "Declan, I'm so sorry."

He shook his head, but his gaze never left hers. He didn't pull his hand away. "She bled to death in minutes. Fucking minutes."

"Such a terrible loss," she soothed. She reached up, stroked his hair, and he was staring at her as if he'd never been touched before. "Declan, you cannot blame yourself for this. There are terrible people in the world."

"I let them get away. I let them hurt her. *I'm* the terrible person."

"How can you say that? Do you really believe that about yourself?"

"I don't know. I know that I failed her."

"I have come to realize that each of us only has so much control over the universe," she told him. "What happens to us here on this earth. Sometimes there are other forces that are more powerful than we are. Sometimes we really are helpless. And one of those things is death. The death of animals or

people. Our own death. If we are supposed to survive, then we will. I believe I have some purpose
on this earth, and that is why I lived. I don't know
what it is yet. But I'm here."

His face softened a little. "I'm glad you're here."

His grip on her loosened, and he rubbed the
back of her hand with his thumb. The chemistry
was still there, his touch lighting her body up with
need. But the need was just as heavy and insistent
in her chest. In her heart.

"Perhaps we are both here to help heal each
other," she told him. "You've helped me so much.
I know that doesn't make up for what you've lost.
But I understand it. I understand because I've lost
my whole life."

"Jesus. I'm such an asshole. Feeling sorry for
myself after what you've been through."

"It has nothing to do with making comparisons.
Your pain is your own. But, Declan, you cannot
continue to blame yourself for what happened to
Abby. And you can't blame your father for what
happened to your mother."

He said, "I don't blame him for her getting sick.
I blame him for what he didn't do for her. Maybe
she would have died anyway. I know that. But the
chance..."

She knew she was right about this. "I hope
you'll forgive me for saying this, but I think some

of your anger at your father is nothing more than an old habit you haven't let go of."

"Pretty damn hard to let go of," he muttered.

"Your father is a good man. And *you* are a good man, Declan. You've been so good to me."

He didn't say anything then, just stared at her, his gaze on hers. He kept rubbing her hand with his thumb, and after several moments he leaned in closer. She could feel the warmth of his body, could smell the scent of the woods that was *him*. Her body responded, desire shivering over her skin. She wanted to move closer. Wanted desperately for him to touch her. Everywhere.

"Declan," she whispered, not knowing what it was she could ask for, even though she knew exactly what she wanted. Craved.

His mouth went loose, his eyes softened. She could see it even in the dark of the night. Could hear the rough intake and exhale of his breath. He came closer, his head ducking down until he was only inches from her. She licked her lips, watching him, her pulse a hot, thready skidding in her veins. Then he took in another breath, shook his head a little and pulled away, releasing her hand.

"Thanks for letting me talk, Angel."

It felt as though a weight had been dropped into her stomach. Yet at the same time her body was humming with desire, her sex damp, her breasts aching. She didn't know what to do. If she should dare to reach for him. If she should run inside, lock herself in her room and try to bring herself some relief. To dream of Asmodeus.

But it wasn't Asmodeus she wanted. It was Declan.

She wanted to cry. For his pain. For her absolute and stunning *need* for him.

He stood suddenly. "I'm going in. I need to check my email. And I thought I'd do some reading tonight. Do you have something to keep you entertained?"

"Oh. Yes. I have a lot of books."

"Okay. Good. Well…"

She got to her feet, and for once he didn't offer his hand to help her. Instead, he turned and went into the house. She stayed on the porch for several moments, Liam standing at the bottom of the stairs, waiting for her to decide what she was going to do.

If only she knew.

Declan had to accept her as a woman eventually. He still treated her sometimes as though she were a child. An invalid. And she was nearly healed. The scars on her shoulders remained, on her leg, her ribs. The smaller ones all over, from where she had been cut all her life. But inside she felt cleansed. Solid. Ready for her new life.

She wanted nothing more than for Declan to be a part of it. To be by her side, rather than holding her at a distance. She'd had such a lovely glimpse of that tonight. Not that what he'd told her had been lovely. But he'd trusted her. She'd felt connected to him.

She wanted that. Wanted him. And the wanting felt like some emptiness inside her she knew no way to fill.

Sighing, she motioned to Liam, opened the screen door and went inside to spend the evening in her room with her books. And the insistent need that beat in her veins like another heart.

She passed him in the living room, his back turned to her as he sat at his computer. The cotton of his white T-shirt pulled taut across the muscles of his strong back. She wanted to touch him, to stroke the dark hair curling at the back of his neck. Her fingers twitched, and she pulled them into tight fists at her sides.

She would have to *make* him see her. Make him see her as a woman. She couldn't go on like this much longer.

HE KNEW HE WAS DREAMING. Understood that the silky little hands on his chest weren't really there. A figment of his lust-addled imagination, fueled by desire he hadn't allowed himself to meet. If he didn't open his eyes it would be okay. As long as he was dreaming, he could let himself feel her hands on his body. That gentle stroking that was driving him crazy. Making him rock-hard already.

Her fingertips were making long, slow circles around his nipples, then brushing over them, making them harden. Almost as hard as the flesh rising between his thighs.

Was she whispering his name, her voice sweet and soft? Her voice drove him crazy, made him want her even more. Just her voice...

Ah, but her hands were even better as they made their way over his stomach, then lower. And when she brushed that swollen flesh, lightly, teasing, he went impossibly harder, his hips jerking.

She took him between her palms, her skin like warm satin, enveloping him, and she began to stroke, up, then down. Her hands were like a sheath around his swollen shaft, sending long shivers of pleasure spiraling into his belly.

He drew a breath in, blew it out, pumping his hips into her palms. Too good, but he never wanted her to stop. He wanted to stay in this dream with her forever.

He wanted to feel more than her hands. He wanted to feel her lush body crushed beneath him. To fill his hands with her gorgeous breasts, to take her nipples into his mouth, making them hard and long, grazing them with his teeth. He wanted to slip inside her, to feel that wet heat. To *have* her. Make her his.

Angel...

Her hands grasped him tighter, squeezed, then released him and he moaned in a flurry of sensation: pleasure and aching and *need*.

Need you, Angel...

She whispered his name again; he could swear he heard her. He wanted to figure it out, where it was coming from. But he felt her breath warm on his skin, then her sweet mouth taking him in. He was lost.

His climax hit so hard and fast, he was dazed by it. Blinded, as pleasure poured through his system like the ocean: that pure, that powerful. He arched up into her hot, seeking mouth, pressing again and again between her lips. Her tongue swirled against him, drawing his climax out endlessly. Finally, she pulled away, leaving him empty. Cold.

He needed her.

"Angel…"

"Declan."

"What?"

He sat up. They were in his bed, the moonlight shimmering through the curtains, striping the room in light and shadow. But he could see her clearly, her naked body kneeling next to his, her long hair like a veil around her shoulders, flowing over the curve of her breasts.

He was still pulsing with his orgasm, his cock thrumming, his body hot. And she was really there. In his bed, wiping her lips with the back of her hand.

He was shaking. What the hell had just happened? What had he let happen?

"Angel. What's going on? What are you doing here?"

"I'm here to make you happy. To show you there is no reason to deny your desires. Or mine. Have I not made you happy? Your body is happy. But I still need you, Declan. I need you to touch me."

"Jesus, Angel. I can't believe this."

"I'm real. I'm a woman, Declan, not a child. And I want you."

She took his hand, and before he knew what she was going to do, she held his palm to her breast.

Her flesh was warm, her nipple going hard beneath his fingers. He couldn't force himself to pull away for a moment. When he finally tried to, she held on tighter.

"Please, Declan. Please don't send me away again. I need you. And you need me. You cannot tell me you don't."

It was nearly impossible to think, his brain still half-dazed from coming. But he had to say something. Had to *do* something.

"Angel, this isn't right. I can't do this. *We* can't do this."

"We already have, Declan. And it was beautiful, as I knew it would be."

He swore he could feel her pulse beating in the full flesh of her breast as she leaned into his touch.

"I'm here for you. For *you,* Declan. This is where I am supposed to be. You can't tell me this is wrong. I won't believe it. I love you, Declan."

Love.

Jesus. Why did hearing her say that to him make his heart pound right out of his chest? His mind was going a hundred miles an hour. "You don't know what you're saying, Angel."

"You cannot deny you feel something for me."

He couldn't.

Goddamn it.

"Of course I do! But this is…I don't know anymore."

"Feel this, Declan." She held his hand closer, crushing her breast beneath their twined fingers. "Feel how my body heats for you. Feel my desire."

She moved his hand down, over the soft cushion of her stomach. Lower still, in between her thighs. He was helpless to stop her. And when she slipped his fingers into her sweet, wet cleft, he was paralyzed.

"Ah, God…"

She sighed quietly, her breath coming out in a warm puff of air that grazed his cheek like a kiss.

"You are the first man to touch me, Declan. And it is better than anything I could have imagined.

Your hand feels so different than mine. Larger. Stronger. And *yours*."

She held him there, pressed against her mound. His heart was beating wildly. Totally out of control. *He* was out of control. Fucking helpless.

"I need you," she said again. "I need you to touch me, Declan. I need you to quench this thirst. I feel as if I'll die of it."

Holding on to his hand with both of hers now, she slid it back and forth, over her cleft. Her flesh was soaking wet, slippery. And all he wanted was to touch her, taste her. *Have* her.

He knew in his head it was wrong. But his body felt right.

He couldn't resist any longer. He could not do it.

"Declan, please have me. I will beg you until you do."

Her hips were undulating against his hand, and he moved then of his own accord, sliding his fingers into her wet heat.

"Oh…" Her voice came out on a soft, whispered sigh.

"Angel." His voice was gruff, thick with desire in his own ears.

"Yes…"

"I want you."

"Yes, Declan. Now."

He came up onto his knees and pulled her close so that they were kneeling face-to-face. She couldn't begin to describe, even in her own dazed head, what his body felt like against hers. Hot, naked skin, the hard planes of his chest. His hands strong around her waist.

"Closer, Declan. Hold me closer."

He did, his arms nearly crushing her. She loved it. Craved it. Couldn't get close enough.

He breathed into her hair and she inhaled his scent—the forest, as always, but darker this time. This time she could smell his desire. She wanted to take him in her mouth once more. She wanted to do everything, every single thing Asmodeus had ever told her about.

Her body was on fire, her heart soaring. When Declan pressed his lips to hers her body surged with a need she'd never had a name for.

Her demon lover had never taught her this. Kissing. She knew what it was, had read about it. But to feel this…

Declan's soft, soft lips, pressing onto hers. His tongue slipping out to lick at her lips, then opening them. The wet tip touching hers, then twining. So, so sweet. She didn't understand how his tongue in her mouth could make her feel what she did—as though his tongue were between her thighs. She was wet, hurting with desire.

She arched her hips, pressing hard against his body, and the length of his rigid shaft pushed against her belly.

Soon he would be inside her. Unbearable, to have to wait one more moment. Unbearable, yet exquisite. And the kissing went on and on. Lovely.

He pulled back, his lips moving over her cheek, down her throat, and every single touch was like some tiny climax on her heated skin. She had known desire before, but never like this. She was shaking all over. And as Declan lowered his head, his mouth feathering over the full flesh of her breast, she fell against him, her legs weak, useless.

He laid her down then, murmuring to her. She couldn't understand what he was saying. It didn't matter. All that mattered was his hands stroking her skin: her breasts, her belly, even her collarbone, the insides of her arms, her calves. He explored her in a quiet frenzy. And as badly as she wanted to touch him she was unable to move. Unable to do anything but lose herself in response.

His fingers went to her nipples, caressing, teasing, until they were nothing but two hard points of pure sensation. When he moved down to take one nipple into his mouth, it was better than she could have possibly imagined. The pure heat of his mouth, the sucking, sucking. Pleasure was like a knife, stabbing into her body, deep, deeper.

"Declan, yes…"

His hands were on her breasts, pushing them together, and he released one nipple only to take the other. Once more he sucked, softly at first, then harder, and she was so close to coming she could barely stand it. She wanted to squeeze her thighs together to ease the hammering ache there. But instead she parted them, needing to invite him, to feel the night air on her soaking wet cleft.

"Declan," she whimpered. "I need you."

He grunted, but she didn't need words. No, all she needed was his hands rough on her skin, finding her thighs, spreading them wider. Then his hair brushing the insides of her thighs as he bent over her sex.

He paused and she heard him breathe her in, making her shudder with a quickly spiraling desire. Her hands fisted in the sheets, knowing what he was about to do.

When she felt just the warmth of his breath between her thighs, she pulled in a long draft of the cool night air. And when his tongue flicked out, she gasped. He pressed his tongue to her clitoris and held it there. One exquisite heartbeat, then two. Then another. And she thought she might die if he didn't *move*.

"Declan. Kiss me."

One long, sweet stroke of his tongue and she was hovering on that keen edge. Her hands went into his hair, impossibly soft, adding another layer of sensation. His fingers held the lips of her sex apart, opening her to his tongue. He pressed it against her, then pushed it inside, and she cried out, her hips arching.

His hands, his mouth, hard and soft, all at the same time. And she was dizzy with sensation. Drowning in it.

His tongue pushed into her again, withdrew. His thumbs went to her hard clitoris, circling it, pressing, pressing, his tongue thrusting. A few more strokes and a blaze went off in her head, her body. She shook as she came, her hips bucking. Declan held on to her, pleasure thundering through her like a storm cloud.

When she stopped shaking he moved up over her body and she spread her thighs for him.

"Declan," she gasped, "come into me. Please."

He groaned, rolled off her, and she wanted to cry as he turned away to dig in the nightstand drawer. But he was back in a moment, poised over her on his knees, the muscles in his thighs strong and taut.

"What is it, Declan?"

"This is to protect you."

"From you?"

"Yes. Trust me, Angel."

"I do."

She watched as he opened the small packet with his strong, white teeth, took a strange, pale tube out of it and unrolled it onto his hard shaft.

He looked at her then, his gaze on hers. It was

as though he were seeing her for the first time in some different way. And she realized that he was finally seeing her as a *woman*. For the first time, she truly felt like one.

She grasped his thighs, loving the texture of his skin, the density of the muscle there, the soft hair.

"Come into me, Declan."

"You're sure, Angel? You have to be sure."

"Only with you."

His eyes were dark, glittering. His face soft and loose with desire. He reached out, stroked her hair, her cheek, making her heart beat faster. It was a different kind of need, even more powerful than her purely physical desire.

"Love me, Declan."

His brows drew together and he looked as if he was about to speak. Instead, with a look of awe on his face and with the most tender of hands, he parted her thighs. As he settled his body over hers she drew her legs up, her knees held high on either side of his lean, muscular torso, and waited for him to take the gift she offered him. The one purpose she had spent her life preparing for. It was about to happen. Her heart hammered, her sex clenched in need and anticipation.

"Now, Declan."

He paused. She shivered, held him tighter. Reaching up, he took her hand, their fingers twining, clasping. He held himself over her, his body

pressed to hers. His face was so beautiful. Every
feature, every plane. And as she watched his face,
and he watched hers, he slipped inside.

There was a tiny piercing pain, like a flash of
bright light. Then it was gone. He moved deeper,
and pleasure moved with him like a tide. His blue
gaze was on hers, blazing even in the dark, and she
surged against him, her hips rocking. He moaned.

"Jesus…are you okay, Angel?"

"Yes. Yes. Wonderful. Please don't stop."

He pushed deeper, and pleasure was like a long,
undulating sigh deep inside her.

"Ah, Declan, yes…"

"You're sure you're okay?" he panted.

"Yes, I promise. I need you, Declan. I need to
feel all of you inside my body."

He leaned in and kissed her, whispered against
her mouth. "Angel, Angel…you feel so damn good.
So good…"

He began to really move then, long, slow, lovely
thrusts. And she opened her legs, her body, to him,
taking him in. Desire poured through her system,
that pure, aching need for him filled, then filled
again, until she thought she might overflow with it.

His arms went around her waist, and he held
her close, changing the angle of his thrust. Unbelievable, how good he felt. She was shivering
with pleasure, tensing all over, her legs wrapping
around him, across his wide back.

She had never known it would be so exquisite: to feel his body joined with hers. To feel that low, keening bliss, spiraling higher and higher. To be held so tightly in his arms. His scent was everywhere. On his skin. On hers. He pumped into her, his lips going to her throat, latching on, kissing her, his tongue swirling against her skin.

"Declan, I need more."

He ground harder, driving into her. She hovered at that lovely edge for moments, then fell, tumbling. Her climax was like a fluttering, brilliant light going off behind her eyes, deep in her sex, her belly, her breasts. She cried out. And he held her tighter, drove deeper.

"Angel," he murmured, his breath warm against her throat. "Love you, Angel…"

"Declan, yes."

Her heart was like a small hammer in her chest.

He gasped, tensed, his hips arching hard into her. And it was pain and a new kind of pleasure as he came inside her, his entire body pulsing.

"Angel…Angel…God."

He fell on top of her and they were both panting. She had never felt so wonderful in her life. She loved the weight of his body on hers. Their skin, slick with sweat, pressed together.

He loved her.

She'd known it, but to *hear* it…

She had never thought she could feel so happy.

That sex could be even more pure and beautiful than she'd been taught.

This was what her life was meant to be. Here, with him.

Declan.

This moment, with him, was so beautiful to her. Precious. She wanted it to last forever. She was too impossibly languid to really think, her body still humming with sensation. With him still inside her.

She hung on, her hands clasping behind his head, his hair like dark silk against her palms. Burying her face in his neck, she inhaled, breathed him in.

Forever. This was where she was meant to be.

CHAPTER TEN

DECLAN PULLED IN A LONG BREATH, the night air cool in his lungs. Realizing Angel was still pressed beneath him, he rolled onto his back. She went with him, burrowing into his side, and he took her automatically into his arms, where she laid her head on his chest.

Her cheek was so warm against his skin. Her waist so tiny he could wrap his arm all the way around it. And her hair was everywhere, covering her body and his like a sheaf of silk. He pulled her closer with his other arm, his fingers tracing the scars on her shoulder blades. Whoever had done it had wanted to make space for wings to grow. For her to fly.

He couldn't think about that now. Too horrible, the reason behind those scars. He didn't know why he was thinking about it. He could hardly think straight at all. Could still barely breathe. Could still barely believe what they'd done.

And he was thinking things he'd never thought about any other woman.

But it had felt right. *She* felt right. She felt perfect. Scars and all.

Maybe that was how he was justifying to himself that he'd just taken her virginity. But he hadn't been able to resist. Not anymore.

It was more than the insane attraction he felt the moment he first laid eyes on her, even when she'd been broken and half-alive on the beach. He'd pretty much stopped beating himself up for that. But was it possible he could accept this? That there could be something between them? He couldn't fucking help what he felt for her. There was no way to stop it. It was too powerful.

And God, he wanted to be with her. He never wanted to let her go. He'd never felt this way for anyone. That to simply hold her naked body next to his, to kiss her, *talk* with her, make love to her again, was all he'd ever need.

Was he some kind of bastard for doing this? For loving her?

He loved her. Goddamn it, he did.

He held her tighter and she sighed, pressing into him. Her plush breasts were crushed against his side, her leg sliding over his.

"Declan," she whispered, "I never knew…I thought I did. Let's never get out of this bed."

He laughed, then, all the bullshit in his head slipping away. He pulled her on top of him and kissed her. Her lips parted, her sweet tongue sliding into his mouth. She took control of the kiss, probing, grazing his lips with her teeth.

He lay back while she explored, her mouth moving down his neck, over his chest. He couldn't get hard again—not yet. But every touch of lips and teeth and tongue, every soft sweep of her hand or her hair, was pure pleasure.

She moved lower, took one of his nipples into her mouth and sucked, and he felt a new stirring of desire. Impossible. But she sucked harder, her tongue lapping, and when she bit, hard, his cock jumped, wanting to fill.

"Can we do it again, Declan?" she asked.

"Sweetheart, you have to give me a chance to recover."

"How long?"

"An hour? Maybe less for you."

"Too long."

She slid up his body, her breasts against his chest, her warm stomach pressed to his, her cleft against the soft flesh of his cock. She was wet again. Or still.

"Are you sore, Angel?"

"A little. I don't care."

"I don't want to hurt you."

"You won't. You never could."

He felt a sharp twinge in his chest. He never wanted to let her down. Not here, not now. Not ever.

"Come here."

He pulled her up, helping her to straddle his waist. Her wet sex was slick on his stomach, and he felt his cock stir again. But it was too soon. And if he tried it again now, she would be too sore.

"Rise up, Angel. Hold yourself up on your knees. Yeah, that's it."

She was poised over him; he could see her beautiful body in the dim moonlight. Her breasts were two perfect globes of flesh. Succulent, squeezed together between her arms, her hands on his chest to steady herself. He stroked one nipple and she arched her back, pressing into his hand. He took the nipple between his fingers, pressing and releasing.

"Ah, I love that, Declan. It feels so good. But I need you to touch me. Everywhere. Between my thighs."

God, that she could say that to him, tell him what she wanted without any inhibition.

He reached down with one hand, stroking her. She moaned, arching into his hand. He found the hard nub of her clit and circled.

"Oh, yes…that's lovely."

He rubbed and she moved her hips in rhythm. He watched her as she bit her lip, her teeth coming down on that plush, pink flesh. She was so damn beautiful he could hardly believe it. Really like some angel come to earth.

His angel.

"Declan, this is so good," she panted. "But I need more."

"You'll have to wait a while for me." He laughed, loving the stark need in her voice.

"I need to feel you. To feel a part of you."

"Come here then, my baby."

He pulled her down, until her sweet, damp cleft was laid over his softening flesh. She felt so good he could almost...but not yet. No, this was for her.

He grasped her hips with his hands, showed her how to slide back and forth. And even though it was far too soon to get hard again, it felt amazing— her slippery flesh against his, the pleasure on her face, the look of wonder in her blue eyes.

"Oh, this is good," she murmured, her eyes closing, her head falling back.

Something inside him opened and a strange warmth settled in. Something to do with the sheer wonder of her body, of her beautiful response. To see her like this, watching what she felt reflected in the sinuous writhing of her hips, the expression on her lovely face. Her pink lips parted, her quiet moans.

She moved faster, ground down harder against him. Pleasure filled him: mind and body, as her moans grew louder.

"Declan," she gasped.

"Yes, baby. Come on."

"Oh...ohhh..."

It was a long, keening cry, her body undulating, her sex like liquid fire against his nearly hard flesh as she came.

For her.

Yes, his own desire was nothing right now. It was all about Angel.

She dropped, burying her face in his neck, and he breathed her in: her scent, her *presence.*

She was laid out on top of him, her weight nothing on his body. She was so small, everything except her full, heavy breasts. But he was beginning to realize there was nothing fragile about his Angel.

His Angel.

His.

He rolled her over, until they both lay on their sides. Her arms wound around his neck, her face pressed into his chest.

He couldn't figure out this sense of possession he felt with her. But he was too exhausted to think straight right now. There would be plenty of time to think in the morning. To figure out if he'd just done something really terrible. Reprehensible. Or if this was the best thing he'd done in his entire life.

SHE WAS FALLING, THE WARM wind whispering over her skin. She felt wonderful, light and loose all over. She wished briefly, in some vague way, for

Asmodeus, to share with him what she had experienced. But she was too content to call for him. Too comfortable in the familiar, falling darkness, with the lovely, aching sensations in her body. She would happily fall alone while Declan rested. She knew this empty place, knew it was a place of rest and recovery for her body. When she awoke she would be ready for him once more.

Declan.

Her body lit with need simply thinking his name. Her hands went to her breasts, cupping them through the strands of her long hair that had wrapped around her body in the wind. She thumbed her nipples, luxuriated in the hardening flesh, the urgent pulse-beat of blood in her veins. She pictured his beautiful face, the iris-blue of his eyes, the lushness of his mouth, and she went damp with need.

She spread her thighs, let one hand slip down to stroke her wet cleft. Ah, it was too good. But not nearly as good as when Declan touched her. She could almost come simply thinking about it: the way he touched her, the gentle pant of his breath in her mouth, the heat of his body, the press of his hard flesh inside her.

She pushed two fingers inside, going deep for the first time, since she no longer had to preserve her virginity. That gift had been given, and received. Beautifully.

"Oh…"

Yes, she would come, here. Now. For Declan.

Her hips arched into her hand. She squeezed her nipple, drove her fingers hard into her pulsing sex, pressed her thumb to her clitoris. Her climax rose inside her, hovered. She took in a breath, readied herself.

"Girl!"

"Asmodeus…"

It felt wrong, suddenly, that her demon lover was there with her. Sensation skittered to a stop, faded, her body aching, but unwilling to come in his presence.

She did not belong with him now. She belonged to Declan. *With* him, which was even better.

"You dared," Asmodeus said to her, his tone low, threatening. He didn't have to finish his sentence; she knew exactly what he was talking about.

"Asmodeus, it was right. It *is* right. I am for him. I know that now."

"I trained you, girl." His body, his flawless face, gleamed golden in the dark, heat radiating from him. But it was a different heat than the sensual warmth she was used to. This was a burning heat that singed her skin. But she was not afraid. She was too sure of herself, of what she had done.

"Yes, Asmodeus. And for that I thank you. Truly."

"I did not teach you these things for a mere man."

"Yet you agreed to teach me to be irresistible to him. You helped me."

"I did not teach you for him. Not for *him*."

"The one you taught me for rejected me."

"And what of me?" His voice was tight and low.

Was that fear she heard in his voice? Sadness?

Was it possible that all along he had wanted her for himself?

"You were meant to be my teacher," she told him. "And you have been so much more. Lover and friend and confidant."

"But no longer."

It was a statement, not a question, made in a voice laced with bitterness. Still, she had to think carefully about her answer.

"I must be honest with you, Asmodeus. I no longer know what your role in my life will be. Everything has changed."

"I have not."

"But I have. For the first time. I have changed beyond your teachings, the teachings of The Grandmother. I've grown beyond even the many things I've read in books, most of which did not apply to my existence, but was nothing more than information stored in my head, to ponder over, to wonder at. To amuse myself with. And I am having to reevaluate everything. Every single thing. Who

I am, who and what I'll be. Until now, there has never been any question about any of this. Even having to consider these things is…an epiphany for me. Declan is helping me—"

"Do not say his name to me," Asmodeus growled.

She nodded. "I understand. But I cannot promise you that I will seek you out any longer."

He looked away. She had never seen this sort of emotion from him. Perhaps there had never been any reason for him to feel anything other than pleasure and arrogance and his own power. She had not given him any reason to. She had only ever given him complete power over her. Reason to exist in her dream-life. In her mind.

In my mind…

She remained quiet, waiting for him to respond. Finally, he turned back to her, his voice still low, but softer now. Seductive, almost. "You do not know how to exist without me, little one."

"I never have before. But that, too, is changing."

"And yet, I am here, as I have always been."

"For now."

"You need me still," he insisted.

She shook her head. Her pulse ticked wildly in her throat, but she had to say it. "I don't know. Asmodeus, I have come to question even your very existence."

He threw back his head, exposing the strong

column of his golden throat, and let out a sharp, barking laugh. "Do not be too confident, little one, in the infancy of your self-discovery. Do not let it go to your head, as it apparently has. I am here before you. You feel my heat. My power."

"Your heat, yes…"

"Do not doubt me." Anger in his voice once more. His mood seemed to be shifting from anger to wheedling and back again.

"And yet I do, Asmodeus. I don't know what will happen now. I don't know if I will call you again. I don't know that I need you any longer."

"You will always need me. You will see that for yourself. And unlike you, my loyalty does not waver. I will be here when you call."

He said it like a threat. But she could hear the pain beneath it. Felt her own pain like a twisting knife.

"I appreciate that, Asmodeus," she said quietly.

"Do not condescend to me."

"I never would."

He frowned at her. His face was beautiful even then.

"I have had enough of you for now."

He waved his hand and vanished.

She was left alone, falling. But she let the darkness envelop her, the warm wind carry her, safe for the first time. Safe in her knowledge of love.

SHE CAME AWAKE. THE SUN was shining beyond the curtained window, a pale, golden light casting its rays on the wood floor, across the foot of the bed. Declan was still beside her, his dark lashes resting on his high cheekbones. His mouth looked even more lush to her in sleep. And there was a calm about him that was never there when he was awake.

Twice she had come to him as he slept, but always in the dark. She had never had the opportunity to explore his face, his body, while he rested.

She saw now how the morning sunlight tipped the dark hairs on his arms in amber. How the muscles corded beneath his tanned skin. Saw the small scars on his hands from working outdoors, and from making his wood carvings. Her fingertips went to her own scars: on her thighs, her stomach. To the pentagrams tattooed in red on her palms, where she could feel the raised ink beneath her skin.

Did he see her scars as something she had earned, as she did herself? As she saw his? She wondered again about the scar on his jaw. She'd meant to ask him about it, but the subject always turned just as she was getting ready.

She reached out, traced the mottled line of flesh with her fingertip. His eyes opened. He smiled.

"Hey." His voice was rusty with sleep.

"Hi."

His smile was so beautiful. So open. As though he wasn't awake enough yet to worry, as he so often did. Or maybe last night had left him feeling the same way it had her. Changed. Better.

She remembered her dream talk with Asmodeus. So much was different now. She didn't know if she'd see him again, and somehow, surprisingly, it didn't matter as much as she would have imagined, the idea of giving him up. Although some small part of her was sad, still doubtful as to whether or not she would end up calling him eventually. Perhaps out of habit, if nothing else. But she understood she no longer *needed* him. All she needed was right here, in her waking world.

Declan.

He pulled her to him, kissed her mouth, her cheeks. She closed her eyes and sighed her pleasure, her body heating. Slipping her leg over his hard thigh, she felt his cock go rigid against her leg. Needed him inside of her again.

"Declan, have me."

"You'll be too sore," he murmured against her throat, his lips leaving tiny, hot kisses all over her skin.

But his arms tightened around her, his chest a solid wall of muscle beneath her breasts. And before she had a chance to protest that she was fine, he'd flipped her over onto her back.

His shoulders were broad, rippling with muscle.

She could hardly believe that he was this close, finally, that she could smooth her palms over his skin. His hair was a mess of unruly curls, falling into his eyes. They were that dark, rich blue in the early light. Brilliant. Dazzling. And his hands on her were burning hot, making her body yearn for him, making her sex go wet.

He reached down between them, his fingers teasing at her damp opening. She spread for him, opening her body up.

"Jesus, you feel like silk."

He plunged two fingers inside her, and she arched to meet him. But he slipped them out, leaving her empty.

"Are you sore, sweetheart?"

"A little. But it doesn't matter. I will heal. You heal me, Declan."

He pressed against her clitoris, his fingers rubbing in lazy circles. Desire skittered over her skin, arrowed deep into her body. She moaned. And when he bent his head to take one stiff nipple into his mouth, she went rigid with a pure, steaming pleasure.

"Oh, yes…"

His tongue swept over that hardened tip. Her breasts ached, her sex swelling. She spread her thighs farther apart.

"I need you now, Declan," she murmured. "I need you inside me, please."

"Ah, since you ask so politely."

His voice was low, husky. He seemed enormously pleased as he reached into the night table and pulled out another condom. He began to tear the packet, but she put her hand out to stop him.

"Wait."

"What? Angel?"

"I want to see you in the light. For the first time. May I?"

He smiled, the smile spreading into a grin, and he pushed himself up, settling back on his heels. She sat up, holding on to his muscular thighs. They were covered in fine, dark hair, soft beneath her palms. But it was his cock that fascinated her.

The skin was smooth and velvety; she knew the touch of it from the night before. In her hands. In her mouth. She leaned in, her gaze roving the texture of the skin, watching it swell. She reached out with one fingertip, touched it gently. He moaned, and she looked up to find him still smiling at her. His face was soft and loose with desire. She bent to her task once more.

Experimentally, she ran her fingers up the underside, tracing the barely visible veins beneath the skin. He shivered. She did it again, smiling to herself.

The harder he grew, the more beautiful it was to her, that hardening flesh, swelling with need, with the pleasure of her touch. She felt…powerful, in a way she never had before. This strange sense of absolute vindication of what she was able to do to him. *For* him. Of her femininity. It felt suddenly like more than merely her purpose. She was beginning to understand the value of their exchange of pleasure. Of touch and taste and presence.

She wrapped her fingers around the base of his cock, as she had seen Asmodeus do so many times, and began to stroke. Declan groaned, and she glanced up to see his eyes closing as he wrapped his hands in her hair.

"Ah, God, Angel…"

She stroked harder, faster, her own body filling with a tight, coiled heat, as though she were the one being stroked.

His breath came in short, sharp pants, and his hips were moving, just a small undulating arch and retreat. She loved the sight of the muscles working in his thighs, the earthy scent of man and desire. Loved his quiet moans, the feel of his hand tightening in her hair, the other slipping down to hold her cheek.

When she looked up he was watching her, his eyes a gleam of blue from beneath his lowered lids, the lashes incredibly long and dark and heavy.

She wrapped her fingers tighter and squeezed. He pulled in a short, gasping breath, his face absolutely torn with desire, making her sex throb in response. Rising up on her knees, she bent her head to sweep her tongue over his belly, tasting the salt of his skin.

He growled, his cock jumping in her hand.

"Jesus, Angel, you'll make me come. It's too good," he panted.

She bent lower, flicked her tongue at the juncture of hip and thigh.

"You torture me," he moaned.

She laughed, did it again, and again he flinched, pulled in a tight, gasping breath.

"Angel. Sweetheart. This will all be over in about two seconds."

"No, too soon, Declan."

She sat back and pulled his hands to her breasts. "I need you to touch me. To be inside me. I want you to show me what you enjoy. What you like about my body."

"Everything. I want to do everything with you. And your body is so damn beautiful, so perfect, I can barely stand to look at you every day. I can barely stand that you're right here, and I haven't been able to touch you. Haven't let myself."

His fingertips stroked the curve of her breasts, tracing the fullness before going to the nipples, caressing lightly. "I love your breasts. Love the feel of the flesh here. The pink of your nipples. Watching them go darker when I press them between my fingers."

He did so, a small, aching pinch that was lovely, sending sensation straight to her sex.

"Ah…"

"I love the smooth skin of your stomach. How *female* it is." He brushed his hands over her belly, pressing gently with his palms, then sliding them around behind her. "And I love the flawless curve of your ass. I love the way it feels cradled in my hands. I love the way it looks. The way you're put together. God, the way you felt inside…"

"Do you want to have me now, Declan?" she asked, nearly breathless with his words, with what he was saying, what he was doing to her body.

He exhaled slowly. "I want whatever you want. Whatever you need."

"I want you. Always. In whatever way pleases you. That is what makes me happy. That is what brings me satisfaction."

She lifted his hand, kissed his palm over and over. He watched her, his lips parted, a look of pure pleasure on his face—pleasure, and the same raging desire she felt.

Without another word she turned around, until she was on her hands and knees, her thighs spread to welcome him. When she felt the heat of his body as he leaned over her she felt a new wave of desire. And something else…

Yes, to be taken over by him in this way. To surrender every part of herself.

His hand between her thighs once more, sliding in the seam of her sex, making her shiver.

"You're so damn wet," he murmured. "Are you ready, Angel?"

"Yes, please."

He shifted to reach for the condom packet he'd left on the nightstand. She waited, her breathing ragged with need, while he sheathed himself. He spread her thighs wide with his knees, and already pleasure was like a storm, hammering through her instantly, her sex clenching.

"Please," she told him. "You won't hurt me, Declan. I swear it."

He slipped inside her with a low groan, just the tip, one arm winding around her waist and holding her tight. He slid a little deeper.

Desire shivered over her skin, up her spine. She leaned back against him, loving the tight muscles of his thighs behind hers, his abs and chest pressed against her back. The hardness surging inside her.

"Declan, you don't need to be tentative with me, I promise. My body is ready. I need you deep inside me. I need to feel you."

He kissed her back, between her shoulder blades, left a trail of small, fluttering kisses down her spine. His other arm looped around her waist, his hand slipping between her thighs, pressing onto her tight clitoris.

"Ah…"

"Okay, sweetheart?"

"Yes. Wonderful. Come on, Declan. Please."

He moved deeper, and she loved the stretch of her body, the hard, driving wave of pleasure coming from his fingers on that erect nub of flesh, his cock moving slowly into her. Sensation was like a thundercloud, a heavy wave rolling through her. And as he inched deeper, pleasure drove deeper into her body—she swore she could feel it in her womb.

"Declan, I need to come!"

"Yes, sweetheart. Angel. Come, baby."

His hips pistoned, a steady and gentle in and out, and he rolled her tight clitoris between his fingertips. Her back arched as the first wave hit, coming from everywhere at once: his hand, his cock, his hard body against hers, holding her down, taking her over.

She cried out, her sex clenching. She arched into his fingers, back into his thrusting cock. Her climax went through her like a storm. Powerful. Raging.

"Declan…ah!"

She was still shivering with it when he tensed, his body going rigid all over.

"Angel…baby. My baby…"

He ground into her, a little too roughly, perhaps. But she didn't care. All she knew was his pleasure, and her own. It was all one thing. Almost as if they were one sensation. One person.

"His baby," he had called her. *His*.

Yes.

CHAPTER ELEVEN

SOMEHOW THEY HAD MANAGED to stay in bed nearly all day. It was afternoon; he could tell from the way the sun shone through the window, lighting up the room, making his eyes ache.

They'd napped, made love again, napped some more. He'd only gotten up to feed Liam, to let him outside. He hadn't had such a lazy day in…maybe never. He didn't usually allow himself this kind of indulgence. And the truth was, there hadn't been anyone in his life he'd wanted to spend an entire day in bed with. Ever. Not even Abby. He'd been too young, too much in grief over his mother, he now realized, to really know what it was he'd wanted with her. And then it had been too late to think about it.

He hadn't allowed himself to feel. Hadn't allowed himself to even consider it. Until Angel.

He watched her now as she stretched in her sleep, the sheet pulling away from her breasts. Jesus, they were spectacular. Perfect.

She was perfect. Strange, that it was her that had

gotten to him. Right under his skin. But she was a strange woman. Unusual. Different.

Maybe that was what got him. Maybe that was what he'd needed to open up. She *had* opened him up; he had to admit that. In so many ways.

She made him think about things. Everything. His willingness—or lack of it—to connect with a woman. With anyone. His relationship with his father. The way he'd hung on too long to his past, like a goddamn bulldog with a bone. If she could move beyond the things she'd lived through—and he was damn certain it was a hell of a lot worse than anything he'd been through—then he should be able to do the same. Shouldn't he? He couldn't forget—didn't want to forget—but maybe he could find a way to move on and leave at least some of the bullshit behind. The pain.

Abby...

Still hard to think about her, but Angel made it easier, somehow.

Something went off in his head, a brilliant flash that left him stunned.

Angel.

She *redeemed* him. Made him all right. And more than that, he loved her.

Loved her.

It was like an epiphany to him. Startling and sharp and clear.

He felt his limbs go loose and warm. And looking at her beautiful, serene face, his chest tightened.

He would never let any harm come to this woman. Never.

He ran his fingertips through her long hair. Incredible, how soft it was, how pale and fine, like her skin. He ran his palm over her shoulder, her neck, her cheek. And felt something warm and eager and frightening stir in him.

She woke, smiling, as always.

"Declan."

"I didn't mean to wake you. No. That's a lie." He laughed, his head still reeling from what he'd just realized. "I did mean to. I wanted to see you. To talk to you."

"About what?"

"I don't know. It doesn't matter." He laughed again, feeling lighter than he had in too many years. He didn't trust it yet. But he had to recognize that it was there. "I must sound crazy."

Her smile widened, her teeth a flash of white between her lush, pink lips. "It's not crazy to want something without quite knowing what it is. At least, I don't think so."

"I want you, Angel," he told her. "I don't mean just sex. I want to know you. Everything about you." His heart was racing. "I don't care if it's not all pretty. It doesn't have to be. God knows my life hasn't always been pretty. But I want to tell you about it. Everything. I don't understand why. I don't understand what's happening here."

She raised a hand, touched the scar on his jaw. "Tell me about this, then."

"I was seven, I think. I fell off my bike and I went face-first into a fence post in our front yard. One of my bottom teeth cracked and came out. I remember seeing it on the ground, how white it was. Shining. My dad came and picked me up." His hand closed over hers, feeling the ridged skin on his jaw with his fingertips. "I thought he'd be pissed, but he was just…worried. I guess I scared him."

"He loved you."

He turned to her, saw the light in her eyes, that lovely brilliance that was *her*.

"Yeah."

"He still does, Declan," Angel said.

He was silent for several moments.

He felt himself starting to shut down. He didn't want to do it. "I guess he does," he allowed.

"I can see it. There is love in his eyes when he looks at you." He began to shake his head, but her hand tightened on his jaw. "I may not know much about the world, but this I know," she insisted.

Why did it make him angry to think about his father loving him? To know what she said was probably true? Who was it he was mad at, anyway? His father? Himself?

"I have some…complicated feelings about my father."

"I think maybe it's always complicated, loving someone. But is that enough reason to turn away from love? Tell me it isn't, Declan."

There was something in her eyes, shining. Hope, maybe. He wasn't sure what she was asking, exactly.

"Look, I know I have to make some repairs to my relationship with my dad eventually. But you don't know everything that's happened between us, Angel."

"I would like to see that happen. For the two of you to be close. I feel as though you're missing out on something important. Don't you feel that, Declan? As if enough years have passed. Been lost. Too many."

"I don't even know where to start. With him. With myself."

"You'll find the way. I know you will. He wants it, too. To be close to you. To be your father. All you have to do is allow him to."

"Maybe. Or maybe too much time has passed. Maybe too many bitter things have been said. I don't know."

She sat up, looking squarely at him. There were tears pooling in her eyes. He couldn't stand to see it. But he knew he wasn't going to like what came out of her mouth.

"Declan, I don't understand you! I'm trying so hard. You have a *father*. You have love, just waiting for you to reach out and grasp it."

He ran a hand over his hair, frustration welling up in him like some toxin poisoning the moment.

"I don't expect you to get this."

"Why? Because I've never experienced a complicated relationship?" Her summer-blue eyes were blazing now. "Do you think my relationship with The Grandmother was without conflict, Declan? That even now my feelings for her are not complicated?"

"The woman is crazy!" he burst out. "Dangerous."

Angel's small fist pounded the bed beside her. "I know that! It doesn't make things any easier—not in my heart, where it all happens. But, Declan…" She shook her head, the tears spilling onto her cheeks. "You have so much more…possibility with your father. So much more love. And you are being so stubborn."

A smile threatened at one corner of his mouth. "You're right. I'm stubborn as hell."

She said quietly, "It does not always serve you well."

"You're right about that, too." He sighed. "I have to think about it. Maybe talk to my dad."

Not specifically about all the years he'd kept

him at a distance, his old feelings of rage. But just talk.

"That's all I'm asking. To open the way."

His shoulders relaxed. He hadn't realized how tightly he'd been holding them.

"Come here."

He pulled her into his arms and she went willingly, melting against him. They stayed that way for a while, both of them calming down.

Angel was changing him, making things shift around inside his head. And it was all good, if a little scary. He could admit to being scared.

She was looking up at him, watching him, her face serene now. Certain. And he felt again a startling wave of love for her.

He wished he could feel some of her serenity. Her acceptance. He wasn't sure he even knew how to love, and until he was, he'd better keep it to himself. He couldn't burden her with his feelings. Not now, when she was still just beginning to find her way in the world.

"Angel, remember when we talked about selling your drawings? We should do it. We should go into Mendocino and talk to some people at the galleries, show them your work. Would you like that?"

"I think…it would make me feel more independent, if I were to earn my way. More useful. Stronger."

"That's what I was thinking. We can go tomorrow."

"I would like that. And, Declan, we should take some of your carvings, too."

He shrugged. "I don't know. Those are just my own thing. I don't feel a need to sell them."

"It's private," she said.

"Yeah. It sort of is."

But she made him realize that he had to find his way in the world, too. Maybe every bit as much as she did. He knew television and the internet, and all those things that were brand-new to her. But she knew a hell of a lot more about how people's minds worked, somehow. Their hearts. That's where he was fucking defective. She'd gotten him to open up, to love her, but he still had one hell of a mess in his head.

No, he'd keep it to himself until the right time. And if that time never came, well, maybe he'd get over this. Maybe it wasn't really love at all, but some kind of obsession. What did he know about love, anyway?

All he knew right now was that she made his heart hammer in his chest. And it was a good kind of ache that made no sense to him at all. She made him want to put his arms around her and hold on.

Forever.

He *knew* he loved her, goddamn it. He just didn't know what to do about it.

ANGEL HAD BEEN COMING TO talk to Ruth for three months, a little more, perhaps. And she still hadn't talked to her of Asmodeus. She wasn't sure why. Perhaps because she thought if she did, it would make him less real. Or make her see whether or not he truly was. She hadn't been ready for that. But today was a new day.

She shifted on Ruth's comfortable sofa, rolling the edge of her blue denim sundress between her fingers. Outside the window of Ruth's office the fog rolled by in gray tufts. It was cold today, and she'd had to put a sweater on. But mostly she felt cold inside. She had for the past three days, ever since she'd talked to Declan about his father. About having to let go. She'd understood instantly what that meant for her, as well. And that cold had battled with the lovely, seeping warmth of what was growing between her and Declan.

The past few days with him had been amazing. She'd spent every night in his bed. They'd explored each other in ways even Asmodeus hadn't known of. He couldn't possibly know the touch of human flesh against flesh. The gentle heat that was the human body. The moistness of a tongue, the softness of lips on lips.

Declan went to work each day, and she spent her time reading, walking with Liam, cooking meals. Her body was healing from its wounds. Her heart was healing even more under Declan's care. His affection. His touch. But despite the physical warmth of him, the warmth he brought to her heart, that one part of her was still cold, deep inside. The part that understood it was time to let go of Asmodeus.

"Angel?" Ruth's voice pulled her back into the room. "You seem distracted today."

"I'm sorry. I suppose I am distracted."

"There's something you want to tell me," Ruth said. It was a statement, not a question. She wasn't surprised. Ruth often knew things before Angel spoke. That was her way.

"I have something important to tell you, Ruth." Why was it so difficult to speak? To make her voice come out in anything above a harsh whisper?

Ruth waited, her face calm. She would wait out their entire hour together, until Angel was ready to talk. That was her way, too.

She pulled her gaze from the window to look at Ruth, took a breath, and began. "I've told you about The Grandmother. About how she raised me. The drugs to dream. The rituals. The compound. I've told you about my purpose as The Gift."

"Yes. But there's more?"

Angel nodded, her stomach a tight knot. "I've left something out. Something important."

"Okay."

Ruth waited some more. Angel tried to get her thoughts in order. What did she need to tell? She knew enough now about this world to understand how strange Asmodeus would seem to most people, even though he was as familiar to her as her own skin. Even to Ruth, who accepted everything without judgment.

"I told you I was trained in the art of love. How to please a male. That I was untouched by man. But I didn't tell you *how* I was trained. Or by whom. This has been my one secret from you. And I'm not sure I even understand why I've kept it to myself."

"Everyone is allowed to have their secrets, Angel. You tell me things as they occur to you, or as you're ready to talk about them."

"I'm ready now." She paused, bit her lip as her pulse kicked up a notch. "I think I am."

Ruth nodded, waited.

"His name is…Asmodeus." A hard rush of heat that wasn't entirely pleasant ran up her spine as she said the words aloud. "I don't know why it's hard to say his name here. To say it to another person aside from The Grandmother." She paused, took a long breath before continuing. "When I call to him I am always in the dream place. The place that was shown to me with the dreaming herbs. I came to know it, and can reach it whenever I sleep. I can go there when I want to. To see him. It's *his* place. But he doesn't belong here, on this plane. And so talking about him feels…wrong."

She stopped, unsure of where to go next. Her head was aching.

"The name is familiar to me. I know 'Asmodeus' as the prince of carnality in the Christian hierarchy of demons. Is this who you're telling me about?"

"Yes."

"And he comes to you in your sleep?"

She nodded. "He has been the one to train me since I was twelve years old. He's been my only friend, if you can call him that. He was my teacher. My companion. He showed me so many things. Talked with me. But now…now I'm doubting my need for him any longer. I am doubting his very existence. And I'm afraid of what that makes me. That I am…insane, perhaps, to think he's real."

Ruth leaned forward in her chair and patted Angel's hand. Her touch was warm. Reassuring. "I don't believe you're insane, Angel. I think you've been given certain information, your brain more easily programmed by the drugs and the rituals and what you've been told by The Grandmother, the only person you had in your environment. That can be a very powerful thing for a child. What else could you have possibly known?"

"But I know now. About the world. And I have to question what's real and what were lies The Grandmother told me. I have to begin to sift through it, to separate it all out. I've been doing that since the day I woke up in the hospital and realized my old life was over, that I was out in the world. And I think…" Her heart was beating a million miles a minute. Could she really say the words out loud? "I think Asmodeus was a lie. I am really beginning to think so. Yet he seems so real to me, still. It's as though my mind knows the truth but my heart is afraid…"

"The truth can often be scary."

"But it doesn't make it any less true, does it?"

"No." Ruth smiled. Her dark, beautiful eyes had always seemed to hold the truth of the universe, some ultimate form of comfort and wisdom. She could see it all in her gaze now. "Angel, tell me what you think you might lose if you decide to face what you see now as your truth about Asmodeus."

Her hands twisted together in her lap, her fingers twining until they hurt. But she needed it, needed something to ground her. Something to hang on to. "My only friend. The only thing left that is familiar. The one anchor to my old life. This new one is still so new. It feels…tentative. Except for Declan. Even with him, I am sometimes uncertain if he's any more real than Asmodeus." She stopped, shook her head. "I don't mean that I ever truly believe this is some sort of dream that will vanish when I wake up. But those thoughts are in the back of my mind. I can't help it."

"Most people have thoughts that roam through

their mind that don't entirely make sense," Ruth told her. "It's perfectly normal. Your mind has to weigh things before it makes a decision, that's all."

"It sounds so simple when you put it that way."

"Sometimes it *is* simple. You consider something, make a decision about it and move on. But other things are more complicated. You've been moving forward at a pretty amazing pace for someone who's experienced the things you have, the life you've led."

"Have I?"

"Yes. Absolutely."

"But this…?"

"You know the answer already. You just need some time to accept it. Why do you think this issue seems so pressing now?"

"Because of being with Declan. Knowing what love feels like. Being close to another human being. It's so much *more*."

Ruth nodded. This was the first time Angel had had a chance to tell her about what had happened with her and Declan, and she didn't go into detail now. She never had to, with Ruth. Ruth always understood, and simply accepted.

"Have you told Declan about Asmodeus?" Ruth asked.

"I told him a little while ago. I don't know if he quite believed me. Or perhaps he thought it was some leftover delusion from the drugs. We haven't discussed it again. I haven't told him I continued to talk with Asmodeus. I don't want to talk to him about this. I feel as if it's my own to deal with. Do you think I should?"

"I think you need to decide how you feel about Asmodeus, despite Declan's presence in your life. How you may feel about him, or him for you. Then you can decide what to tell him."

"Do you think this is love, if I keep something from him?" Angel asked.

"You are allowed to have your own thoughts, Angel. You never have to give that to anyone. Only as much as you choose."

She nodded. Ruth's words made sense. Love was without judgment.

"So, you and Declan are together. How have you been feeling since being with him?"

"The same as always. And different, too. He's a good person. Better than he knows. I love him. It grows each day. It's one of the few things I'm utterly certain about."

"And Declan?"

"I believe he loves me. I feel it. And I think it's good for him, to love."

"I think so, too." Ruth smiled.

Angel let her gaze wander to the window again, shivered a little at the grayness outside. "I love Asmodeus, too. Or, I thought I did. I don't know anymore."

Out of the corner of her eye she saw Ruth shrug. "Love is love, Angel. It exists, we can't deny that. And love is always a good thing."

"Even if he is a product of my imagination and the years of drugs? The years of The Grandmother telling me he exists? Programming me, as you said."

"Even then," Ruth said. "For my people, the Hopi, love is central to existence. In humans. In animals. Part of every individual's life path is to find love wherever you can. You're still discovering your path, but love is the guiding light. It always has been for you, I think. That is, in my mind, anyway, part of why you've been so largely untouched by the hard life you've led. You are so *able* to love, Angel. *That* is the gift."

"I hope so. I hope it's enough. But, Ruth, if I love Asmodeus, how can I give him up? Yet, I feel I must if I'm to have Declan. If I am to have a life."

"Love is also letting go. But you already know that, don't you?"

It was true. She and Declan both had to learn it. They were on the same path perhaps.

"I still don't know what to do. If I need to say goodbye to Asmodeus yet. If I'm ready."

"You'll know when it's time, Angel."

She nodded. Ruth always spoke the truth. She didn't doubt the validity of what she was telling her. She only doubted herself. She needed a little more time. To grow. To learn. To love Declan and be loved by him. Love, as Ruth had said, was her guide. Love would tell her what to do. It was the one thing she was ready for.

SHE WAS STILL THINKING of her conversation with Ruth, thinking about love, when Declan came to pick her up from Ruth's office.

He pulled up in his truck where she waited in front of the building, wanting the fresh air, the scent of salt and forest. Now all she wanted was him.

Declan.

He got out of the truck and took her easily into his arms to kiss her. His lips were warm and soft and tasting of *him.* Her body softened all over, and she forgot for the moment her tension and confusion. He did that for her. Made her feel warm and safe. Made her body heat with need, her heart fill with love, until she forgot everything else.

Sometimes it was good to forget.

"Declan, take me home," she whispered into his neck.

"Are you tired after your session with Ruth?"

"No. But I want to be home with you."

It didn't take long to reach the house, or at least, it didn't seem long. They were both quiet on the drive. Dreamy, close. Declan kept his arm around her, and she kept her eyes closed, enjoying his solid body next to hers, the hum in her veins from the anticipation of being with him, his body joined with hers. It was never enough, with him.

They pulled up in front of the house and he turned the engine off.

"Declan…"

"What is it?"

"I need you. I need you inside me. I need to come again and again."

She always wanted him. Always. She felt some edge of desperation, suddenly, and understood what it was about. But she didn't want to think of *him* now. She only wanted to think of Declan.

"Whatever you want, sweetheart. Come on."

He led her into the house, and they gave Liam the briefest of greetings before Declan pulled her down the hall and into the bathroom. He helped her off with her sweater, then pulled her dress over her head, her soaking wet panties down her legs, until she stood naked before him.

"Jesus, you're beautiful, Angel. My beautiful girl."

There was awe in his voice, and a lovely raw desire laced with unspoken emotion, yet she knew it was there. She loved hearing that edge in his voice. That edge that was purely sex to her, the emotion only making it more intense.

"Now you," she said softly, unbuttoning his flannel shirt.

She couldn't wait to see his naked body, to feel the contrast of smooth skin over hard muscle beneath her palms.

His shirt came off, his boots, his pants, and soon he was as naked as she was. Naked and achingly beautiful to her. She reached out and placed both hands over his chest, his dark nipples coming up hard against her palms.

He was watching her, his eyes gleaming that dark iris-blue, nearly purple, the color of a deepening night sky. His features had gone a little slack with his desire, and she glanced down to find he was beginning to harden beautifully.

He leaned in and murmured against her cheek, "I want to have you in the shower, Angel. To feel your skin wet and hot and slippery."

"Yes…"

He let her go, stood back and simply looked at her for a moment, his gaze hungry, before he reached in to turn the shower on.

"Get in," he told her. "I'll be right back."

She stepped into the white tiles, beneath the warm spray and waited, leaving the glass door open for him. She loved the shower. She had only ever taken a bath before she'd come out into the world, and the feel of warm water cascading over her body was always incredibly sensual to her. It was about to become more so with Declan in there with her. She could hardly wait.

He returned in a moment with a condom, stepping in and closing the door behind him.

Steam coiled around them as they came together, white and ghostly. And she felt as though they were completely cut off from the world, in their own warm, cocooned dream place.

Declan's arms came around her, closing her in, the heat of his body and the water on her skin like a single silky sensation. His erection pressed against her stomach, hard and lovely. Standing up on her toes, she reached between them to position the rigid shaft between her thighs, spreading wider for him. He arched his hips, and his cock rubbed over her cleft, pressing against her clit. She was on fire, needing him, drowning in want.

"Declan, touch me."

His hands slid down her back, over the curve of her buttocks, and he held her there, his hands tight on her flesh, pulling her in closer. She tilted her head back and his mouth went to her throat, small, burning kisses that shimmered over her skin, swept down her body along with the water: that liquid, that hot.

"You're so beautiful," he murmured to her between kisses. "I can't ever stop wanting you. It's insane how much I want you."

He pulled back only enough so that his hands could come around to cup her breasts. He brushed her nipples with his thumbs, and desire was an arrow, piercing her: her belly, her breasts, her sex.

She reached down between them, wrapped his cock in her hand, stroked the length of the shaft, loved hearing his moans fade into the white sound of falling water.

"You are ready. I'm ready for you. Now, Declan."

"Yes…"

He did something strange, then—he pulled the shower head until it came off in his hand. She hadn't known it could do such a thing. He took one small step back, and watching her, as he so often did, he aimed the spray of water at her breasts.

"Oh…that's wonderful, Declan."

The water was like a warm spark against her hard nipples, the fleshy globes of her breasts, making them ache, but in some indescribable way. And when he lowered the spray, aiming it between her thighs, she opened them wider with a quiet sigh.

Such pleasure— She'd never felt anything like it before. The heat and the wet. The softest, most teasing touch imaginable.

"Declan…ah…it's almost like your tongue, but different. And so good."

"Come here, Angel."

He took her in his arms and turned her so that her back was pressed against his chest, his stomach. He bent her over, guided her hands until she was braced against the tiled wall of the shower.

"Spread your thighs, baby. Yeah, that's it."

He let go of her for a brief moment, and she heard the tearing of the condom packet, knew he was making himself ready to enter her. She shivered, the anticipation an exquisite throb in her sex.

He moved back in, used his fingers to spread her open, and in one stroke he was inside her.

She shuddered, pleasure moving through her in long, rippling waves. She thought he would reach around her to take her clitoris between his fingers, as he often did. But instead, he pressed on either side of her clitoris, holding her flesh open to the spray of the water.

"Declan!"

"Is it good, baby?"

"So good…oh…"

Pleasure and pleasure; the hot pulse of water on her hard clit, the hard shaft of his cock pressing into her, sliding out. The feel of his body solid against hers.

She began to move, to press back into his impaling cock, to arch forward, into the stream of water. She had never felt anything like it, these dual sensations of hard and soft. She thought again of how like his warm, wet tongue on her clitoris the water was. And with that image in her mind, she came, hard, her body shivering. Pleasure was like a knife, but sweet-edged, sharp and lovely. Behind her, Declan thrust, over and over, driving sensation ever deeper.

"You feel so good, Angel," he panted into her ear. "Like silk. So damn tight. And to feel you coming…it's too much. Too much…ah…"

He drove harder, and she reached behind her, grasping his hips, pulling him deeper as he came.

"Angel!"

She was still trembling with her climax. He slipped out of her, turned her around in his arms, the shower head back on its hook. He held her close. And now that they had both come, now that the urgency was gone from their embrace, she was able to focus on the pure pleasure of being held by him.

Declan.

"Angel…"

"What is it?"

The water fell around them, veiling them from the world. From everything but each other.

"I love you, Angel."

Tears brimmed, spilled over and mixed with the fall of water on her cheeks. She didn't understand why she cried. She wasn't in pain. She wasn't scared. She'd never before cried because something was so *good.* Perfect.

"I love you, Declan."

He cradled her face in his hands and kissed her.

His lips were soft on hers. And she felt in his kiss
the words he had just spoken to her. The words
she hadn't even known she'd been praying to hear.

CHAPTER TWELVE

DECLAN'S ALARM WOKE HIM, the harsh buzzing star-tling him out of a deep sleep. He reached for it blindly, slapped it off. And in the quiet, he heard the gentle whisper of Angel's breath beside him.

It was dark still. But he could just make out the outline of her body: her shoulder, the soft curve of her hip. He realized her long hair was draped over his chest, like strands of silk on his skin. Smelling of flowers and sex and *her*.

"Angel?" he whispered, but she didn't answer. Lost in sleep. Lost in dreams.

He slipped out of bed as quietly as possible. He didn't want to wake her. He didn't want to just leave her, but figured she'd know he'd had to get up for work. She was familiar with his schedule now. She often got up with him and made him breakfast, drank her tea while he sipped his cof-fee, watching the forest turn from black to dark green tipped in gold or the silvery-gray of fog as the sun rose. But today he'd let her sleep.

He stood and watched her for several moments,

listened to her gentle breath. He liked the idea of her asleep and warm in his bed.

The floorboards were cold on his bare feet as he made his way across the hall to the bathroom. The tiled floor was even colder. He turned the hot water in the shower on to blasting and stepped in.

He didn't think he'd ever take another shower in this house without remembering his night in there with Angel. Even as his cock hardened, his chest surged.

Love her.

Jesus. He never thought he'd feel that for a woman again. He'd thought he was too damaged. Maybe too…undeserving. Maybe he still was. But he couldn't help it. He loved her. And everything was changing. His life was changing. *He* was changing.

It scared the hell out of him. It made him feel fucking great.

He wasn't sure what to think of that.

He hurried through his shower, then carried his clothes into the living room, Liam following him, his big paws heavy on the wood floors. He got dressed quickly and was heading to the kitchen to brew some coffee when his cell phone went off. He grabbed it from his shirt pocket.

"Byrne here."

"Dec, it's me."

"Dad? Is everything okay?"

"Yeah, fine. I'm fine. Sorry to call so early, but I have some news."

"About Angel?"

"I just got a fax. It's a possibility."

He wasn't going to ask his dad what he was doing up at five-thirty in the morning. They were both early risers. Always had been. Declan had a quick flash of his father waking him in the still dark of early morning to go fishing. They'd leave his mom sleeping, warm and cozy in bed, as they sat in the kitchen eating oatmeal that sent small wafts of steam up. Sweet on his tongue with the brown sugar Dad sprinkled on it.

"Dec?"

"Yeah, I'm here."

"A friend of mine at the federal level was able to track down some missing kids around the time Angel must have been taken. Three girls who've never been found, and the cases were all closed pretty quickly, for whatever reason. One of them was reportedly blonde."

"You think this could be her?"

Declan's pulse was like a jackhammer in his veins, his head, his mind coming awake fast, despite the fact that he hadn't had his coffee yet.

"Could be. The time frame matches. All three of these girls were taken in California, but one was Hispanic and the other had dark hair. I don't think Angel would have had dark hair as a kid."

"No, I don't think that's even a possibility. What else do you know?"

He heard a shuffling of papers and his father cleared his throat.

"Okay, here goes. Name, Emmi Norling, age five, approximately thirty-four pounds. Reported missing on June 21, 1995. Sixteen years ago, Dec, which would make her twenty-one. That's what the doctors figured for her age and what Angel says, too, right?"

"Yeah." He realized he'd curled his fingers around the back of one of the kitchen chairs so tightly his knuckles were burning. He flexed, let go. "What else?"

"Parents were tourists from Norway. The father spoke some basic English, the mother even less. The kid none at all."

His stomach tightened into a knot and he began to pace it off.

"Dad, you may be on to something."

"What is it, Dec?"

"Angel has this memory of a blonde woman speaking to her. But she doesn't understand what she's saying. Maybe because the woman wasn't speaking English and Angel doesn't remember her first language."

"Okay. Okay. Could be."

"But?"

"But let's not get our hopes up until we look further into this."

"I can tell from your voice that you think this is something, though, Dad."

"Yeah. Could be," Oran repeated.

"So we have to look into this! Come on, Dad! You wouldn't have called me at the fucking crack of dawn if you didn't think this was a real lead. Goddamn it, don't stall here, like you always... Fuck."

He heard a long sigh from the other end of the phone.

"Declan, I know you have some feelings about what happened before, with your mother. Oh, I know—you don't want to talk about it. But look, Dec, I'm trying to help here, okay? We need to do this together, no matter how much you hate it that I'm involved."

"I don't hate it, Dad." He pulled in a long breath, exhaled slowly. "I know you're trying to help. I'm...sorry I'm being such a bastard."

There was a pause from the other end of the line. "Okay, son. Let's just see if we can figure this out. For Angel."

Declan nodded, even though the old man couldn't see it. He took another long breath. "Okay. So, if these people were Norwegian tourists they would have gone back home at some point. Which is maybe why the case wasn't pursued further than it was. There was no one here to press the issue, and they probably wouldn't have known how to deal with the police procedure in the States."

"And in those days they didn't have the same kind of computer systems in place. Nothing as sophisticated as we have now. No AMBER Alerts. Nothing but reports filed, an initial twenty-four-hour search before they'd literally call the dogs off."

"How do we find the parents? Do you have access to the file? Is that what you're reading from?"

"You didn't hear me say it."

"Okay, got it. Jesus." He ran a hand through his hair, blew out another long breath. "Dad, I have to go to work. Are you looking into this more today? I don't know what I can do until I get home."

"Go to work, Dec. I'll follow up and see what I can find. Maybe come by after work and we can sit down and look this stuff over?"

"Yeah, I can do that. But I don't want to say more about it to Angel until we have something solid."

"That's probably a good idea. I'll see you tonight."

They hung up, leaving Declan's heart pounding. If they could find out who Angel was, maybe it would help them find the people who did this to her, took her life away from her. And maybe then she could have some of her lost life back.

Maybe then he wouldn't feel so guilty about trying to make a new life with her.

HIS DAY HAD SEEMED ENDLESS, but finally Declan was pulling up in front of his father's house. His childhood home.

Too many memories in the two-story cedar-shingled house. It had been the same weathered silver for as long as he could remember, the wood colored by time and the salt air. His mother had planted the roses that lined the path to the front door. She'd had a particular fondness for roses in peach and pink. He remembered their names: Juliet, Lucky Lady, Seven Sisters, Bella Roma, Lovestruck. They were just starting to bloom, and he knew he'd smell their perfume the moment he got out of the truck. That they'd remind him of Mom.

Even so, the house hadn't felt like home in a long time. Not since Mom had been gone. He remembered some of the things Angel had said to him. About appreciating the family he had, how lucky he was. He hadn't felt lucky. He didn't feel any luckier now, with the house bringing back memories in an aching flood: helping his mom plant some of the roses in the front yard. The way the kitchen smelled when she was cooking. Helping his dad rake leaves. Playing catch with him as a kid. Learning to build things, his dad showing him how to hold the hammer, then as he got older, how to use the skill saw, teaching him the "measure twice, cut once" rule.

His mother lying weak and in pain in the bedroom upstairs.

He sighed, scrubbed a hand over his head.

Enough philosophizing—now he had to get in there and see what else Oran had tracked down, keep his focus on the present, on what he needed to do for Angel.

He got out and went up to the door, paused with one hand on the doorknob, ran his other hand over his jaw before releasing the knob and deciding to knock instead.

He wasn't ready to believe this was home again.

His father answered, pulling the door open.

"Dec, hi. Come on in. Are you hungry? Ruth left a beef stew in the fridge for me yesterday. She's a hell of a cook."

Ruth.

It didn't mess with him the way it had in the past. Her name. Hearing Dad compliment her. It was almost okay.

Almost.

"Uh, sure. I guess." Why was he still acting like some surly teenager? "That'd be great. Thanks."

He followed his father into the familiar kitchen, with its big, pine-plank table, the copper-bottomed pots hanging from a rack over the stove, the knotty pine cupboards.

It still smelled like home, which seemed almost more alien to him, more *wrong,* than if it hadn't. But the rich scent of Ruth's stew was steaming into the cool air as his dad ladled it into two bowls, brought it back to the table and gestured for Declan to sit. He did, and Oran passed him a basket of bread.

"So…" Why couldn't he seem to get started? He cleared his throat, tried again. But what came out was, "This is…weird."

His father raised an eyebrow. "Weird?"

Declan shrugged. "Being here. Sitting at this table. Eating food at this table that some other woman cooked."

His father's face went red in an instant. "Look, Dec, I've had about enough of you and your attitude."

Declan felt his own face flush. "Don't talk to me like I'm some kid."

"Then stop acting like one. You've met Ruth, so you know the kind of woman she is. You even seem to like her. So what the hell is your problem?"

His hands folded into tight fists under the table, and he felt as though there was an explosion inside him bursting through the long-held dam. "My problem is that you're leaving Mom behind!"

"Jesus, Declan. It's been ten years. That's a hell of a long time to be alone. Is that what you really wish for me? That I spend the rest of my life alone? I'm goddamn lucky to have met Ruth. Just as lucky as I was to have met your mother, and to have spent all those years with her. She didn't want me to be alone. We talked about it. And it was damn hard to hear at the time. But ten years…Jesus, Dec, that's long enough for anyone to mourn. Including you."

He felt momentarily stunned by what his father was saying. But he couldn't let it go. Not yet.

"Maybe for you. She was my *mother*. And you didn't do a damn thing to save her. I fucking *begged* you, Dad."

His father nodded, his face stern. He could see the suppressed rage there, but it was nothing to match his own. "And she was my wife. I did what *she* wanted me to do."

"You should have tried to convince her—"

"It was important to leave her with some dignity, for God's sake," Oran interrupted. "The chances were too slim that more chemo would work. She didn't want to live her last days suffering like she did with the chemo. Would you really have had me take that away from her?"

He was silent for several moments, taking it all in.

"You didn't talk to me like this at the time."

"You were too young—"

"I was not too young. And I was never too young for you to talk to me about Erin, either."

His father ran a hand over his gray hair. He took a deep breath, and Declan could see he was trying to calm himself. "We didn't talk about your sister because your mother couldn't bear it. This is about what your mother wanted, Dec. I loved her enough to give her that. Did you?"

He felt the bile rise in his throat.

He was a selfish bastard. His throat was closing, going tighter by the second.

"I loved her more than anything," Declan managed finally.

"Then it's time to let this go. How long did you plan to stay mad, anyway?"

"I don't know." He shrugged. "I seem to be pretty good at it."

"Yeah," his father agreed, a small grin tweaking one corner of his mouth.

"All right. Okay." He sat for a few more moments, forcing his racing pulse to calm. "I hate to say this—you know I do—but you're right."

His father raised both palms. "Lord knows I won't rub your face in it."

"I wouldn't blame you if you did."

"Dec, it's time to move on. I thought you volunteering to care for Angel meant you were starting to do that. Starting to come out of your shell."

"It does."

"We have to move on, too."

He nodded. "It's going to take some time to get used to the idea. But you're right."

His father nodded. "Okay, then."

"Okay."

"We should eat before the food gets cold."

He knew this wasn't the end of the discussion. But his father was allowing him some time to digest things. He appreciated it.

"So, anything new today on Angel?" Declan asked. He took a bite of the stew. It was pretty damn good.

"Plenty. The missing girl, Emmi Norling, was taken from a campground at Yosemite National Forest. Parents discovered her missing but thought she had just wandered off. Didn't report it until the next day. Possible they didn't know what to do, what authorities to contact."

Declan nodded. "Probably."

"They stayed in the U.S. for another eight weeks, then went back to Norway. Nothing in the records indicates much follow-up on the part of the state police. But after a search through the national forest, it would have been standard procedure to close the case. The parents were never implicated in her disappearance, by the way, so they were free to leave the country anytime."

"Jesus. I can't imagine being them."

"Me, neither. To lose a kid like that…" Oran

shook his head, his gray eyes distant, and Declan knew he was thinking of Erin. "Anyway, I think this could be something, Dec. I just have a feeling."

"Can we get a photograph of her?"

"I should have it tomorrow. But people change a lot from childhood to adulthood. It may not be conclusive."

"Even if it's not, I could show it to Angel. Maybe she'd recognize herself. Or it would trigger some memories, if it is her."

Oran nodded. "It might. How's she doing, anyway?"

"Good. Better. She's pretty amazing. She just accepts everything. She's so calm." Declan shook his head. "She's not what I would have expected. She's so damn smart. And insightful. She knows a lot about people, especially considering she's hardly been exposed to any most of her life."

"Huh."

"What does that mean?" And why did he feel so defensive?

His father shrugged, wiped his mouth with his napkin, taking his time. "Seems to me there's something more going on than appreciating how intelligent she is. I could be wrong." He shrugged again.

Declan looked at him, his body tensing. But maybe this was part of it all. Coming clean with his father about something—anything—might be something he needed to do. And who else could he talk to about this?

"You're not wrong, Dad."

Oran lifted an eyebrow, nodded. "I can't blame you, Dec. She's special, this one."

"Yeah."

"She seems sweet. That same sort of intrinsic sweetness your mother had. They're the same kind of gentle souls. She would have liked Angel."

He felt a hard twist in his chest, thinking about his mother. Wishing she was there. But she'd been gone a long time. Time to accept that, along with a lot of other things in his life, just as his father said.

He rubbed his fingers over the scar on his jaw.

Like the loss of Abby, which he realized was becoming more distant the longer Angel was with him. The fact that his father had a right to move on. To have a life, after all these years.

"Yeah, I think she would have," Declan agreed.

"Ruth likes her. I know it's not the same. I don't ever expect it to be, Dec. I'm not trying to make it the same."

His dad's gaze was sharp on his.

He nodded his head. "Okay, Dad. Okay."

Oran watched him for a moment, then stood up. "All done with your stew? Or do you want some more?"

"I'm done. Thanks."

Oran nodded and took the bowls to the sink.

"So, I'll call when I have a photograph. Meanwhile, I'm trying to locate the parents. Trying to figure out how to work the system in Norway."

"I appreciate it."

"I have more time, being retired. You just worry about work. Taking care of Angel. And, Dec…"

"Yeah?"

"Think maybe you'd like to go fishing sometime?" His father kept his features relaxed, but Declan could tell from the set of his shoulders that he understood how loaded this simple question was, between the two of them. Oran shrugged. "You know, when you have a day off?"

"Yeah. Sure."

Say it like you mean it.

"I'd like that, Dad."

His father gave him a small smile. There was nothing triumphant or smug in it. Just pure pleasure that he was obviously trying to hold back. Trying not to make too big a deal out of it.

"Okay. That'd be good, Dec."

"Okay." Declan pushed his chair back. "I should get going. I don't like to leave Angel alone too long."

"Liam's with her?"

"He hardly leaves her side."

"He's a good dog."

"Yeah."

They smiled at each other. And even though it

was over something as easy as Declan's dog he recognized that they were finally on the same page about something. That it had been happening, bit by bit, ever since Angel had come into his life. That it was necessary. That he *wanted* it.

They said their good-nights and he got back in the truck and headed home. The drive wasn't long. He followed the familiar roads, passing the state beaches, the small clumps of night-dark forest, the occasional house or bed-and-breakfast inn. He rolled down the window just to hear the quiet roar of the ocean, to smell the damp and salty air. To feel the old familiarity.

He loved this coastline, this town, more than he'd wanted to admit. Wasn't that really why he'd come here, after all that had happened to him in the military? And wasn't it natural to crave comfort, the familiar? Why did he think he had to make excuses for himself? That just wanting to be there wasn't a good enough reason? Didn't he at least deserve that comfort?

He'd spent most of his adult life beating himself up over one thing or another. And it was time to stop. He thought he'd been taking responsibility for his actions. But maybe what he'd been doing was taking the coward's way out, after all. Running from his fears by pretending they didn't exist. By pretending he didn't feel anything at all. Love. Desire. Even anger.

He'd been pretending he didn't love his father. That he wasn't angry with him. And it was all bullshit. The anger had been there, simmering beneath the surface. He'd avoided dealing with it by avoiding his father. For ten fucking years. And he'd lost out. On time. On love. Because he'd convinced himself he wasn't worthy of it.

It was Angel who'd convinced him otherwise.

He stepped on the gas. He couldn't wait to get home to her. To see her. Tell her everything.

Light shone through the windows and on the porch when he swung into his driveway. He got out of the truck and moved to the porch, opened the door.

Angel was sitting on the sofa, her drawing pad in her lap. She was wearing nothing but one of his big, bulky sweaters, her lovely, bare legs crossed beneath her. Her hair was streaming over her shoulders, pooling on the cushions beside her like liquid gold. She looked up and smiled at him.

"Declan, you're home."

"Hey."

He leaned down and kissed her, and she pressed her lips to his eagerly, her flesh soft and sweet. He opened her lips with his tongue, slipping into the pure warmth of her mouth. Her hands came around the back of his neck, holding him, and he slid his into her hair. So soft—her hair, her mouth. He was growing hard already, just from the heat of her wet tongue on his, the silk of her hair, for God's sake.

He wanted to feel it draped all over his body. He wanted to feel *her* draped over his body, all long legs and silken skin.

He moved over her, slipped her sketch pad from her hands without looking at it and set it on the coffee table. It was easy enough to undress her. He just slipped the sweater over her head, his hands going immediately to her full breasts.

"Ah, Declan, yes…" she murmured as he brushed his thumbs over her hard nipples.

She was unbuckling his belt, helping him kick his way out of his jeans, then his boxers, helping him get out of his shirt. He was aching, he wanted her so badly. Needed her.

He pushed her down on the sofa, covered her naked body with his, pressing his cock against her smooth belly, his chest against her plush breasts. She sighed, opened her thighs for him, and he felt how wet she was, his cock resting against her cleft.

He kissed her cheek, her jaw. He kissed her neck, where she was warm and fragrant. He kept kissing her, using lips, then tongue, sweeping it over that tender flesh. And she was moaning, squirming, pressing her damp mound against him.

He was rock-hard, desire a hot, keening pulse. Their hips moved in tandem, pressing, rubbing, need growing, spiraling. And all he knew was the incredible wet heat of her pussy against him, the taste and the texture of her skin beneath his tongue, her quiet sighs and moans of pleasure, the hardness of her nipples crushed against his chest.

Hard and soft, texture and flavor. And his heart hammering in his chest, going a thousand miles an hour. Need and pleasure and love.

Her hips moved faster, the slick lips of her sex soft and swollen, sliding against him. He thought he might lose it. Come all over her. Lose his mind.

"Angel, I need to be inside you."

"Yes. I need you, Declan."

"Fuck. Hang on. Let me get a condom."

"Declan, don't go. Don't let me go. Be inside me."

He pushed himself up on his arms so that he could see her face. It was absolutely torn with desire. Her blue eyes were gleaming, her cheeks flushed. She had never looked so beautiful to him. But she was his responsibility. He couldn't forget that.

"Angel, you could get pregnant."

"I know. I need you now, Declan. Please."

Angel watched as his brows drew together, desire and confusion warring on his face. His mouth was dark and lush.

"Angel, I can't—"

"Please, Declan. I understand. I want all of you.

All of you. Do you understand what I'm saying? I'm not a child. I know what this means."

He reached up and held her cheek in his hand, his pupils widening, his features softening.

"Jesus, Angel."

"Come into me, Declan. Come inside of me. Let us be together. Let us be one. I understand, and this is what I want, more than anything."

She reached up and pulled him toward her, kissed him hard, her tongue delving in and searching. She breathed him in, took in his breath as he exhaled. And opened for him.

Just the tip of his cock, at first. He paused, his arms shaking. He pulled away, whispered against her mouth, "You're sure, baby?"

"Yes. I'm sure. I swear it. I love you."

She wrapped her legs around his back, her hands going to his hips and pulling him in closer. He was watching her, his face loose with desire and wonder. He kept his gaze locked to hers as he slid inside, inch by inch.

Pleasure shimmered through her like something transparent, weightless, like light itself. It grew, rumbled down deep, like the sound of thunder— that same kind of elemental power as the man she loved drove deeper into her body.

"Yes, Declan," she murmured. "All of you…"

She smoothed her palms over his stubbled cheeks, exploring his features with her fingertips.

And he began to move, a gentle, thrusting rhythm. Desire was like some small, lovely shiver, making her clitoris go as hard as his cock. She became hyperaware of everything—his thick shaft sliding in and out of her, silken and sleek without the barrier of a condom. His skin, hot against hers. The scent of him: earth and man, sweat and sex, heat and the heady scent of desire itself. And with all of her senses she felt the sheer power of being female. Of being a woman with a man, the two of them together, and the way they each built upon the desire of the other.

"Declan, wait."

"What is it, baby?"

"I need to be on top. I need to…be in control."

He smiled as he shifted, turning their bodies until he was sitting up on the sofa, his back against the pillows, her legs straddling his lap. She poised over him, reached down and stroked his hard cock with her fingertips.

"It's beautiful, you know," she told him.

"Is it?"

"Yes. As you are beautiful to me."

He was quiet. But she could see his chest rise and fall with his panting breath.

She touched one finger to the tip of his cock. Watched as his stomach muscles clenched. She glanced at his face, saw the look of concentration there as he watched her every move.

Keeping her gaze on his, she kept that one fingertip on the swollen head, and slipped her other hand between her own thighs. She pressed two fingers into her own damp heat, gasping a little at the sensation. Watched Declan's sharp intake of breath as he saw her do it. She pulled her fingers from her body and held them to his lips. He leaned forward, took her fingers into his mouth, and sucked.

The heat was stunning, just his mouth around her fingers. She felt it as if he was sucking on her nipples, on her clitoris. And as he sucked, she ground down and impaled herself.

He groaned. Her body clenched with a pure, piercing pleasure.

She rose up on her knees, letting him slide almost out of her, then coming down hard. His hands went into her hair, his fingers threading into the long strands that cascaded over their joined hips, pulling tight. She loved it, that added sensation, that almost-hurting. Loved that he was really losing control as she surged down onto him, over and over. He thrust up into her body, driving deep, but he was letting her control the motion.

He held her fingers to his mouth, sucking, kissing her fingertips. His gaze on her face was like another sensation, dark and full of need. And love.

"Come on, Declan. Harder. Love me harder."

He thrust faster, deeper, their hips clashing,

crashing into each other. As he closed his eyes, his face torn in ecstasy, pleasure came down on her like a wave. She tumbled into it, her body clenching, her sex going tight.

"Ah, Declan!"

She felt his come, hot in her body. Lovely. She swore she could smell it, sharp and earthy and *him*.

"I love you, Declan. I love you…"

She was still coming, still shivering with it.

He released her hair, and held her hand in his, kissed her palm. "Love you, baby. My baby."

He pulled her down, onto his chest. With her head resting there, his heartbeat was a steady cadence against her cheek, his arms around her.

She had never been so happy. Had never known it was possible.

They sat together for a long time. Outside, she could hear the quiet night sounds. Wind in the tree branches, some small animal scuttering, crickets singing. Inside the house was nothing more than the sound of Declan's breath and her own, the soft snores of Liam on the floor, the hum of the refrigerator in the kitchen. All of it warm and familiar. Safe, finally.

For the first time in her life, she realized she was living without fear. Some of it was the way her life had changed, of course. And some of it was her talks with Ruth. Liam's steady devotion. But mostly, it was Declan.

Declan.

She had never been able to *count* on someone—on anything—the way she could count on him.

She breathed him in, as she so often did, that warm scent of the earth and the forest. She lifted her head and placed a kiss on his jaw, on the scar there.

He let out a long breath, his arms going tighter around her, holding her closer.

"Hey," he mumbled sleepily.

"Hey."

"How are you?"

"Wonderful. A little tired. Relaxed. How was your visit with your father?"

"It was good. I have things to tell you."

"Oh?"

"But it can wait. How was your evening?"

"Long and quiet without you," she told him truthfully.

"What did you do to keep yourself busy?"

"I made dinner for Liam—"

"You cooked for him?"

"Yes."

Declan laughed. "He's a dog, Angel. He's fine with his kibble."

"But he likes my cooking. It makes him happy."

"I'm sure it does. What else?"

"I did some drawing."

"Ah. Something new? Let me see."

He shifted, taking her with him, so that he was still sitting on the sofa with her in his lap. He reached for the pad of paper. She tried to stop him, her heart beating hard. But he grabbed it before she could do anything about it.

He sat quietly, her drawing pad in his hand while her pulse raced.

Maybe she wasn't totally without fear, after all.

"Jesus," he muttered. He let go of his hold on her waist, ran his free hand through his hair. "Angel. What the hell is this?"

CHAPTER THIRTEEN

"Declan…"

Her face was pale, her body tense. No more tense than he was, even with his softening cock still inside her. And even with their bodies pressed so close together, he felt cold all over. Some strange chill that reached all the way down his spine, like a coiling snake.

He wanted to recoil, to pull back. But he couldn't do that to her. Despite what he was seeing, what she'd drawn.

It was a humanlike creature drawn in colored pencil, with enormous, bulging muscles, built like some sort of cartoon superhero except that it was drawn in her usual realistic style. The body was covered in a golden shell, the face that same hard gold. The eyes were two dark pits, burning with fire, the expression menacing. Long, pale hair floated around him like serpents. The creature was naked. And from between his thighs sprang a huge cock, done in close detail, one hand closed around the shaft.

It wasn't that the image was sexually graphic. And he had some idea that this creature was the demon she'd talked about weeks ago. But he thought she'd let that shit go, and obviously it was still in her head. It was still happening, her seeing this demon thing. But what disturbed him the most were the words she'd written across the bottom.

My teacher. My lover. My enemy.

"Angel, tell me what this means."

He didn't mean to sound so hostile. He couldn't help it. He didn't know why he'd felt so instantly certain that this was more than some fantastical image to her. Why he felt immediately threatened by it.

She slipped from his lap, pushing off him and retreating into the corner of the sofa. She pulled a pillow over her, covering her stomach, her bare breasts, like armor.

He couldn't blame her. He couldn't stand to see the fear on her face. Part of him wanted to reach out, to comfort her. But he *knew* in some strange way that this picture meant something. Something he wasn't going to like.

"Who is this?" he prompted, making an effort to keep his voice low, his tone calm. He knew what her answer would be. But he had to hear her say it. Had to have her tell him the truth. Maybe he was testing her. Fucking unfair, but he couldn't help it.

"It is Asmodeus," she said softly, biting her lip, her hands fisting in the ends of her long hair.

"Asmodeus," he repeated. "Why are you drawing him now?"

"This picture is meant to be…a sort of…tribute. A way to remember him. A way to bring him here, into my…reality. To help myself figure it all out. His existence. His role in my life, in my past as well as now."

"What do you mean 'now'?"

He wasn't liking this. Was she still caught up in those old delusions? And what did that make him, what he'd done with her, if she was…mentally unstable? He was shivering all over.

She shook her head, her long hair falling like a curtain around her body, her face.

"I have to figure out if he has a place in my life now. He has been with me since I was twelve years old, Declan. He is not so easy to give up." She parted her hair and looked at him then, her blue eyes blazing with hurt and fear and something else he couldn't figure out.

His stomach was pulled into a tight, gnawing knot. All he could do was shake his head.

"He isn't all bad, Declan. He taught me the ways of love. He prepared me for you."

"Come on, Angel. It wasn't for me. Was it?"

"Not at first, no. But I've come to realize that

even though I was trained to a different purpose, my true purpose was to love *you,* Declan."

There were tears in her eyes now. He couldn't fucking stand it.

"I don't understand all of this, Angel. I need to know what this Asmodeus means to you. If you still think he actually exists. If you still see him in your head. If you still want to. Why would you want to, for God's sake?"

"Declan, I was raised to believe in him. And I have. Until recently. Now I am…unsure. Being given this new life has given me a new perspective, but I still don't know what to trust in. I mean *myself.* If my perceptions are correct. About the world. About what my life has been. And mostly about Asmodeus. I feel on some very deep level that he does not exist. That he is a product of my imagination and the drugs and the lies The Grandmother fed me. But how do I know for certain? And even knowing, how do I say goodbye to the one familiar piece left of this bizarre puzzle that is all I've ever known?"

The tears pooled in her eyes, spilled over. He couldn't stand it one moment longer. He reached for her, pulled her into his arms.

"Christ, I'm sorry, Angel. I'm sorry. This is all so damn weird to me. I've never seen anything like it. I don't know how to handle it. And I don't like that. I don't like that you kept something from me. Especially something that's so big for you."

"I was going to tell you, Declan." She paused, shook her head. "No, that's not true. I wasn't certain yet if I should. If I'd need to. But, Declan, you aren't without your secrets, either."

He was quiet a moment. He felt like shit suddenly. Because she was right. Because he was being such an asshole about this Asmodeus thing. "No. I haven't told you everything. There are some things I don't talk about."

Angel lifted her head, wiping her tears with the back of one hand. "There are things which, if kept to ourselves, poison us. I believe you have been poisoned. At least I'm trying to let it out. To figure it out, to put my life in perspective."

"And I need to do the same. I know. That was one of the things I wanted to tell you about seeing my dad today."

"Let us make a deal, then. I will tell you of Asmodeus. And you will tell me about your father."

"I can do that."

Her arms went around his shoulders, slender and warm as she buried her face in his neck. She whispered against his throat, "I am coming to understand that part of loving someone is holding nothing back. History. Emotion. And I love you, Declan. All that I am must be yours. And all that you are must be mine, if we are to love completely.

Ruth does not necessarily agree with me, but this is how I see the truth of it."

"I've sort of come to the same kind of conclusion lately. Maybe just today."

"Tell me what you've discovered, Declan, about your father."

He looked into her eyes, as blue as the summer sky and twice as beautiful to him. He would tell her. And whatever she had to tell him about this demon creature, he would handle it. It was part of her. He would be there to help her figure it out.

He pulled a soft throw blanket from the back of the couch over them both, making a cocoon of heat and flesh. She laid her head on his shoulder, her cheek warm against him. And he began to talk to her about the things he had never discussed with anyone, never faced. But with Angel, it all seemed a little less difficult.

"Some of this you know already. The logistics of what happened when my mom got sick. How I felt about the decisions my dad made. That *she* made." He wrapped his fingers up in her hair, the softness soothing him. "You were right about me needing to hang on to the anger. Because as long as I'm angry I don't have to face the loss and the grief."

He thought about his conversation with his father today—all that he'd come to understand, all that he still needed to wade through.

"I'm realizing that, really seeing it," he told her. "But it's mostly on a cerebral level right now. I know there's more to explore there. It's all been buried under this bullshit that runs through my head every day. Like this blanket of denial. I don't really want to know what's under there, I'll admit that. But I know I have to start dealing with it. I have to start letting go of the anger at my father."

"Yes," Angel said. "But you have to find a way to do it without blaming yourself too harshly."

"I feel like I've been such an asshole to him all these years."

"No, Declan."

"Oh, I have been. But I can't wallow in that shit. I just have to work through it because the blaming isn't constructive. And it'll make me keep my distance from him, which is what I want to stop doing. I did it a little tonight, at his house. Stopped blaming him. Myself. Let the anger go. Maybe I did it a lot. We talked about it tonight and he called me on it. Made me see it. Had a hell of an argument that was a long time coming, but we needed to do it. Hash it out. And, Angel, I have to tell you, you are the catalyst in all this. This would not be happening without you in our lives."

"That makes me happy." He heard her soft sigh, knew she had more to say. She took his hand in hers, twining their fingers together. "Declan. Tell me now about Abby."

He was quiet a moment, his mind spinning a hundred miles an hour. "What do you want to know? You heard the story. You know what happened to her."

"I want to know what happened to *you*. I want to know the emotions, Declan, as you've just shared with me about your father."

He pulled in a long breath. "Okay. Fair enough."

He had to think for a moment. To sort it out. He still wasn't clear about how he felt when it came to Abby. How much was old pain that he was hanging on to because it was familiar and how much he still actually *felt* about it.

The whole thing seemed like a million years ago sometimes. It *had* been a long time. And he hadn't really let it go yet, had he? But talking about it with Angel now seemed easier than it had ever been, with her warm body pressed close to his.

"I think when Abby died, I was still grieving for my mother. It was too much. I mean, seeing something like that would be too much for anyone, but for me…it made me shut down. I haven't…" He had to stop, shake his head, take in a breath. "I haven't let myself love anyone, not even my own family, since then. I guess I've been afraid that I could lose anyone I loved, so it was safer not to."

Shit. Had he just said that out loud? But there was some relief in getting it out, dumping it out of his system. Getting rid of the poison, like Angel had said.

"Your feelings for your father must have been very confusing. The anger and resentment and love you were pretending not to feel."

"Yeah. Exactly."

Angel said gently, "Yet those emotions are always there. I think emotions are *things*. Do you know what I mean, Declan? They exist. They don't just go away. You cannot talk yourself out of them. You can only bury them, sometimes."

"For a long time, in my case."

"And maybe in mine, as well. I've been remembering lately…just a few things. A few moments. Emotions."

Declan squeezed her hand, but she seemed okay. Calm.

"What do you remember, Angel?" he asked.

She could see the memories in her head, like the television playing, even with that same flickering glow. Like the lambent flicker of sunlight through the trees.

She closed her eyes, tried to recapture those images. "I remember a man's face. And a woman's. They look so much alike. Pale hair and skin. His eyes are blue, but not as blue as mine, as blue as hers. I've seen her before. Remembered her before. She's the one whose language I couldn't understand. They're talking to me. Laughing. We're all laughing and playing with a small boy. He's maybe...two or three years old. He has the same blue eyes and blond hair as the rest of us. And we are...together, all of us. I take his hand, the boy's, and we go for a walk in the forest. We are all together. And then we run ahead, the boy and I, through the trees, into an open field. There are wildflowers and sunshine. And then he's gone."

She stopped, rendered quiet by what felt like a dark wall coming down in front of her eyes. Anxiety speared her body and she held tighter on to Declan's hand.

"Angel? What is it?"

"I can't seem to get past that point. I don't know what it means."

"You're sure this is a memory and not a dream?"

"It feels different than a dream." She pulled back to look at him. "Declan, do you think it's only a dream, but I want to make it a memory?"

"I don't know. Maybe you can ask Ruth."

"Yes. Maybe she can tell me."

"But, Angel, it's definitely possible it *is* a memory. I should tell you what else my dad and I were talking about tonight."

She nodded, feeling a strange sort of anticipation building inside, making her shoulders pull tight, her pulse race. Liam stood and nosed at her hand, whining quietly until she stroked his big head. He wagged his stubby tail, helping her to calm a little.

"Okay," Declan said. "I don't want you to get too excited because we don't know anything for sure yet. But we have some leads as to who you might be, Angel. Your name, your family."

"Oh…"

"Are you all right?" Declan leaned in, his hands going to her cheeks. "Jesus, you just went pale as a sheet."

"Yes. I'm fine. I just…it's a shock to think of it. After all these years of being…of having no identity. Of being nothing more than The Gift. The Grandmother's nurse and cook and housekeeper. And then spending these last few months finding *myself.* Figuring out who I want to be. And now…it's so strange to be faced with a past that isn't my own, and yet *is,* somehow. I'm sorry. I'm not making sense."

"No, you are," he soothed, stroking her cheek, her hair. "It has to be a hell of a shock. But you might have a family, Angel. And if you do, we'll find them."

Why was her heart hammering in her chest as though it wanted to burst free, escape?

"Declan, I know this should be happy news. But it scares me."

"What are you afraid of, baby?"

"These people who may be my family—I don't

know them. They don't know me. I *have* family. And that's you and Liam." She smoothed her hand over the dog's sleek black coat. "And your father because he's *your* family. I'm not sure I'm ready for more."

Declan pulled her in, his arms closing around her body, and she relaxed into that lovely, familiar warmth and strength.

"It's okay," he murmured. "We'll take it one step at a time. We still have some tracking to do. It'll take a while. You'll have some time to get used to the idea."

"Okay."

"My dad will have a picture tomorrow, of the little girl who went missing. The one we think might be you. Will you look at it? You don't have to do anything but look. You can have Ruth there with you, if you want. If she's not available tomorrow we'll wait until she is."

"Yes, I'll look at it. And I'd like for Ruth to be there, if you don't mind."

"I don't."

"Truly, Declan?"

"Yeah. I'm working through that."

"That's good. Your father deserves to be happy."

"Ruth makes him happy," he admitted. "I know. I know how important it is. You make me understand that, Angel."

"I meant what I said, Declan. About you being

my family. Do you know how important that is to me?"

"I'm beginning to."

He stroked her hair from her eyes, and in his was everything she needed to know. Strength. Support. Love.

She wasn't certain she wanted to know about some family of strangers, but she also understood she needed to find out who she was. Who she'd been. Because then she would truly be free to move forward, to who she wanted to be.

ANGEL WAS EXCITED TO BE GOING to Oran's house. She was looking forward to seeing him. But she was nervous about what else she might see.

She loved his house the moment they pulled into the gravel drive. It was homey-looking, surrounded by roses in full bloom. Declan led her to the door.

"You okay?" he asked her, keeping an arm around her waist.

"Yes. This is just a little scary. Strange. As if there are all of these possibilities suddenly. And it might be good, or it might be frightening, or it might be nothing at all, which is perhaps the scariest part."

"You don't have to do this," he told her.

"No, I do. Not only for me, Declan, but for you, too."

"What? I didn't mean to pressure you."

"No, it's not that. But I think we can only have a life together after I get past this. And I want that, Declan."

She looked up at him. His brows were drawn together in concern, but there was love shining in his gaze. It made her heart trip in her chest in a way nothing else ever had.

"So do I, baby."

"Then let's do this. Let us see if today will tell me who I am."

He nodded, knocked on the door. Ruth answered a moment later, her face wreathed in smiles. She took Angel from Declan's arm and pulled her in, hugging her close.

"Angel, I'm so glad you're here. And, Declan, thank you for coming." She released Angel and pulled Declan into her arms for a brief hug. "It's been too long since there were young people in this house. Just us old folks tottering around in here."

"Speak for yourself, woman," Oran joked, coming up to hug Angel. He stepped back and patted Declan on the shoulder in the way she'd come to know men did with each other. "Come on in. Have you guys eaten? Can I get you something to drink?"

"We had dinner, thanks, Dad."

"Angel, a cup of tea?" Ruth offered.

"Yes, please."

"Peppermint with honey, yes?"

"Yes." She smiled to Ruth and they all moved into the kitchen.

It was a cozy room, made warmer by the wood cabinets, the big, worn table, the ceramic bowl of fruit on the counter. It felt like a home. She was glad Declan had grown up in this beautiful house.

She sat at the table, Declan right next to her, keeping his hand on the back of her chair. Ruth made tea and Oran opened bottles of beer for himself and Declan before sitting down.

"So..." Oran began. "Angel, Declan's told you what we've found?"

"He told me there's a photograph of a missing girl who disappeared around the same time I did. He told me her family was from Norway, that she was taken from the Yosemite Park. We looked at these places on a map."

"Does any of that ring a bell with you?" Ruth asked her.

"I was telling Declan last night about a memory I've had recently. About being in the woods. About...my family. At least, I think they were my family. No, I'm sure of it." Ruth nodded, waiting for her to go on, as she often did. Angel stopped to sip her tea; it was warm and sweet on her tongue. Comforting. "Maybe I should look at this picture before I say more. Is that all right?" She looked to Ruth, then to Oran.

"Of course." Ruth smiled and covered her hand in hers.

"Whatever you want, Angel," Oran assured her.

Behind her, Declan's arm slid from the chair to her shoulders. And suddenly she wanted to cry. Not because of her nervousness about the picture and what it might mean, but because she was so overwhelmed by this sense of family. Solidity. She understood how much she'd missed in her emotionally sterile life with The Grandmother.

That's over now.

She swallowed back her tears and nodded her head. "I'm ready."

Oran nodded and pulled a color photograph from a folder he'd had sitting before him, slid it across the table toward her. She held her breath for a moment before she was able to look.

She laid her fingertips on the photograph, smoothing the edges beneath her hands, then slowly let her eyes focus on the image there.

It was a child, a small girl of four or five years. She had long, pale blond hair. It was lighter than hers was now—almost platinum—falling in waves around her shoulders. She had a round, cherubic face, a brilliant smile. And she had Angel's own blue eyes.

My eyes.

She was quiet, studying the picture, recognition hitting her like a blow to the chest.

This is me.

Yet she felt distanced somehow. It was as if this child was someone she'd known once, a long time ago. It hurt to see the innocence in her face. To know what she would endure.

"Angel?" Ruth asked, her voice softly prompting.

She let out a long breath, looked up at the expectant faces around her.

"It's…this is me."

"You're sure?" Declan asked.

She nodded. "Oh, yes. I'm absolutely certain."

She felt light-headed, as though the picture, the table, Declan and Ruth and Oran, were suddenly very far away.

"This is me," she said again, maybe simply to get used to the idea. Her own voice sounded odd, tinny in her ears. But she had to tell them what she knew.

"I remember," she said, her throat so tight it hurt to get the words out. "I know what happened to me."

There was a hush around the table. She saw Declan's hand squeeze her shoulder from the corner of her eye. Saw Ruth still holding on to her hand. Saw Oran lean across the table toward her. She couldn't quite feel any of it, but she knew they were there. It helped.

She swallowed past the hard lump in her throat.

"We are in the forest. On a trip away from home. There is a big green tent made of canvas. We each have our own sleeping bags, and mine is pink. The surface is…plasticky. Shiny. And I love it. My parents are there. My father and mother. Pappa and Mor. And my brother, Niklas. He's small, smaller than me. He is three years old. He just had his birthday at home, before…before coming to this forest.

"We are walking in the forest and we come to a big field. Pappa has lunch in a knapsack on his back. The grass is so high I can barely see over it. Niklas is running through it. Laughing. I chase him."

She stopped, her chest pulling tight. She wasn't even certain what was going to come out of her mouth next.

"Then, Niklas is…gone. We can't find him. Mor-mor asks me where he is but I don't know. We all look. Pappa calls for him. His voice is loud. I try to find him. I run and I run. And Pappa is calling for me, too, but I have to find Niklas.

"At the edge of the field there is a woman. She is holding Niklas's hand. He smiles when he sees me. I go to him. But when I try to take his hand the woman lets him go and grabs my hand. Hard. She's pulling me away and I don't want to go. But when I try to tell her she puts her hand over my mouth. I can't breathe. I don't know where Niklas is. Then, it is dark."

She stopped, pulled in a deep breath. Her chest ached so badly she didn't know how she was still breathing. Yet a part of her was still distant from everything, as though this memory belonged to another person.

"It's okay, Angel," Ruth soothed her.

And she knew it was. Because she was safe now. With Ruth. With Declan.

"Angel, do you know who the woman is?" Oran asked, keeping his voice low.

She nodded. "It is The Grandmother. She was old, even then."

"Do you need to stop now?" Declan asked, his palm smoothing across her back, over and over, helping her to come back into her body, into the moment.

"I'm okay. I want to tell you."

"What else do you remember?" Ruth asked gently.

"Everything is sort of…blurry after that. I think they probably kept me drugged for a long time. They taught me English."

"Ah, I thought so," Oran muttered.

"Thought what?" Angel asked.

"If the girl in this picture is you, Angel, then your native language would have been Norwegian. Your English is a little strange. Maybe because it wasn't your first language. Maybe partly because of the way you were taught by the old woman."

"Yes, that makes sense. Yes."

"Were you always alone with this woman, The Grandmother?"

She turned to Declan. His face was calm but she could see his eyes were dark with emotion, glittering in the warm light of the kitchen.

"I saw the others only during the rituals, but they were hooded then. People would sometimes come to The Grandmother's house and I would be sent to the garden or to my room. I would hear them talk. And I could hear activity every day on the other side of the garden walls, but they were too tall for me to see over."

Declan watched her talking, felt the tension in her shoulders beneath his hand. It was always hard for him to hear her talk about her life with the old woman. But now, with this photograph to remind him how young she'd been when she'd been taken, it was even rougher. That, and the blank expression on her face. It spooked him, to see her like this. And a terrible thought occurred to him.

"Angel, this is important." He leaned closer, his heart hammering in his chest. "Were there other girls there? Girls like you?"

"There were others. I was never allowed to see them, speak to them. But I sometimes heard their voices over the wall. And there was at least one other before me who was meant to be The Gift. The Grandmother would sometimes rant about how badly she'd failed. She told me I must do better."

"Jesus." His gut went tight.

"Are you thinking what I'm thinking, Dec?" Oran asked him.

"Yeah. That without Angel, they'll need another girl. If they haven't taken one already."

"We have to try to find these people."

"Angel," Ruth asked, "do you have any idea where you were? Where they kept you all these years?"

"I don't know. I have no idea how far they traveled to bring me to those cliffs. I was too full of drugs. It could have been minutes or days. I'm sorry."

"It's okay," Ruth soothed.

"I'll never get over what they did to you," Declan said, the words slipping out. He touched her hair, as if he needed to reassure himself that she was safe now. "Christ, I'm sorry. That must sound selfish as hell. You were the one who went through it."

"It's okay to feel something when those we love have been through pain," Ruth said.

"Yeah, son, don't be so hard on yourself. Look, I'm going to make some calls, send a few emails. Now that we have a little more information I want to see where it'll lead. And we have enough to make it clear that these people are a very real and current threat. That this needs to be looked into right away."

"Thanks, Dad."

The two men exchanged a look, and he could feel the love between them, even if they were both still a bit guarded. It was there, buried beneath the rubble of their history together. The rubble of his own bitterness. But he was trying to change that.

Meanwhile, there was work to do. Work they could do together. Finding out who had done this to Angel, who had taken her fucking life from her. Hopefully before those people did it to anyone else.

He looked at Angel. The blank expression had eased, but there was a line of worry between her brows, her mouth tight. Ruth had her hand, was murmuring to her. He knew she was in good hands with Ruth. But all he wanted was to get her out of there. To get her home. Into his bed, tucked safely away next to him.

"Angel, you look a little worn-out," Ruth said. "Why don't you two get going?"

Declan nodded his thanks, stood up and helped Angel from her chair. She still had a small limp, but it wasn't that. He just couldn't bear for her to be anyplace where he couldn't touch her right now.

"Dad, call me if you find anything."

"Of course. Angel, get some rest, honey." Oran

leaned in and kissed her cheek. "I know you'll take good care of her, Dec." His dad smiled at him.

"Always."

He realized he did want to take care of her always. Forever. And he felt scared and relieved and a little foolish. He turned to help Angel on with her coat so his father wouldn't see his face.

Just get her home. Get her alone.

Angel was quiet on the way home, forgoing her seat belt to snuggle up next to him, but he didn't have the heart to say anything about it. He liked having her there. Liked that she came to him for that basic physical comfort.

A sleepy Liam greeted them when they got to the house. He got up from his favorite spot on the floor next to the desk, his stump of a tail wagging, then went right back as soon as he'd been petted.

"How are you doing?" he asked Angel as he helped her slip her coat from her shoulders.

"I'm all right. Tired. A little dazed." She rubbed a hand across her forehead, then dropped it to her side. "I can't even think right now about what this all might mean. It's too much to take in."

"Don't then." He rubbed her arms with his hands. Her skin was cool to the touch even through the sleeves of her dress. "Let me put you to bed. Just curl up and get warm."

"Only if you'll come with me, Declan. I don't want to be alone now. Is that okay?"

"Of course."

He took her to the bedroom, helped her undress, handling her carefully. He saw the scars that laced her skin, some so pale he knew they must have been there since childhood. He'd always accepted that they were simply a part of her, had to force himself not to think too much about how they'd gotten there. Reminding himself how strong she was helped. But tonight he saw her fragility, how the evening had overwhelmed her, made her raw. And it made him more fiercely protective of her than ever.

He helped her into her cotton nightgown and put her to bed, changed into his pajama bottoms and slid in next to her. She moved into his arms, her soft, fragrant body against his. They lay quietly together for some time, and he thought she might have dozed off. But when he shifted to look at her he found her eyes open, staring back at him in the dim moon glow coming through the window.

"Declan?"

"What is it, baby?"

"I don't want to think anymore tonight."

"Don't then. Just sleep."

"I don't want to sleep. I want to forget. Will you help me forget?"

She wrapped her arm around his body, pulling his hips toward hers, and slung one leg over him. The warm, damp press of her mound on his leg made him hard instantly. That and the smell of her hair. Flowers. Pure female. Purely a creature of the earth.

His.

He slipped her nightgown over her head, tore his pajama bottoms down over his legs. Holding himself up on his elbow for a few moments, he stared at her. She was bathed in moonlight, washed in gleaming silver. Her hair was spread out around her, long silken strands. So long they draped off the edge of the bed. And her face was so damn sweet, her mouth so lush, he could hardly stand not to kiss her.

He rolled over and did just that, opening her lips with his, his tongue slipping inside. She tasted faintly of the mint tea and honey she'd had earlier, which made his chest go tight for some reason he didn't understand.

Love her. Have to have her.

He shifted until he was on top of her, her plush breasts soft against the wall of his chest. He could feel her nipples hardening as he kissed her. And when he slid one thigh between hers, he felt her wet heat. Incredible, how wet she got.

His cock pulsed with need. He kissed her harder, heard her quiet moans, felt her breath tangling in his own. He inhaled, inhaled *her*. And she opened for him and let him slip between her thighs.

Soft and hot and wet. Her pussy was a tight sheath around him as he pushed inside. She was warm in his arms, her mouth eager on his, her hands all over his skin. Her legs wrapped around him, her hips meeting his thrusts.

"Declan...more. I need you. I *need* you."

"Baby..."

Together they moved, one breath, one body. Need and a sharp, simmering pleasure that rose, higher and higher. Until finally, they came, both of them crying out. And he felt a strange warmth that went beyond the pure physical pleasure of being inside her beautiful body.

Forever.

He would have to do something about that. But first, he had to catch his breath. Had to breathe her in once more. Had to sleep with her in his arms. And wake up to her beside him.

CHAPTER FOURTEEN

THE WEEKS PASSED IN A lovely blur. Angel was remembering more each day about her past: her time
with The Grandmother, as well as her early years
with her family. Yet she still felt disconnected from
them, as if that life had happened to another person, someone she'd just met or had seen in a movie.

Meanwhile, she had Declan. And Ruth and
Oran. They had spent some time with them, once
going to Oran's house for dinner, twice going to
eat at a restaurant, all of them together. And she
had spent a little time with Georgia, one of the
waitresses at Bitsy's. They'd had pie and coffee
at Bitsy's while Declan had gone to the hardware
store. They'd talked about gardening and baking,
and Georgia had promised to take her to a movie,
something Angel hadn't tried yet, but was eager
to experience. Georgia was so nice to her. It was
strange having a friend. She wasn't quite sure how
to go about it, but Georgia was patient with her.

Declan had taken her into town, and two of the
local art galleries wanted her drawings to sell. She

still couldn't quite believe it. But she liked the idea of having some *place* in the world. A job. Declan told her she was an artist, a professional, which made her a little giddy.

She was still getting used to going places. She enjoyed it, but found she was easily overwhelmed. Ruth assured her that would ease with time. Meanwhile, she was happy in Declan's house in the woods. Happy with Declan.

She knelt on the front porch now, Liam at her side, planting basil in a terra-cotta pot. She had a whole herb garden on the porch in planter boxes: thyme and rosemary and lemon balm. Oregano, sage and an enormous pot of lavender. It reminded her of her old garden. Except that this time, it was truly *hers.* Hers and Declan's.

They'd grown closer. As her strength grew and she was able to do more she realized Declan's view of her had shifted. He was still protective of her, but she felt they were on increasingly more equal footing. He had more confidence in her, and she had more confidence in herself. It felt good. Their relationship felt balanced, as though each of them had a place in it, their individual responsibilities to each other. That in itself was some sort of epiphany to her, something she had never imagined. But now that it was happening, it felt exactly right.

The sun was just beginning to lower in the sky, casting dusty light and shadow over the trees. She loved this time of year, midsummer. Loved that it was still light out at the end of the day, when she knew Declan would be coming home from work soon. Loved the warmth of the summer days. Sometimes she walked with Liam while Declan was at work, just the two of them. She appreciated Liam's quiet companionship. He was her protector every bit as much as Declan.

She was happy.

She'd never known she could be happy. So much of her life had been about surviving the strange and terrible events she was put through over and over again. In between those times she had worked to find whatever tiny moments of joy she could: her garden growing, discovering a nest of baby birds, those rare nights when The Grandmother would really talk to her, mostly about the books she read. But now she had true happiness.

She couldn't wait for Declan to come home from work each day. Loved even more those days he had off from work, when they would walk on the beach together, or in the woods with Liam, or drive into town to eat at Bitsy's or the small Italian restaurant down the highway, where Angel had tasted pizza for the first time. Some days they stayed at home, sitting on the porch together. She would draw while Declan worked with his wood, shaping it into animals and trees. Some days they spent hours in bed, getting up only long enough to eat. Those days were her favorite.

"Almost time for him to come home," she told Liam, wiping her hair from her eyes with her arm, her heart beating a little faster.

And as she worked her hands into the soil, patting it down around the newly transplanted basil plants, Declan's truck pulled into the drive.

Liam got up and ran to greet him as she dusted the potting soil from her palms. Declan got out, rubbed Liam's head, then moved to the porch, smiling. He wrapped her up in his arms, kissed her, his lips soft on hers.

He pulled back, brushed his lips across her cheek, picked up her hand to kiss it, as he often did, and paused. "You're dirty."

"I am."

"I like it when you're dirty."

She grinned at him, and he kissed her again.

"How was your day, baby?"

"Good. Trina from the Zimmer Gallery in town called. She wants more of my botanical prints."

"That's great."

"I still can't believe people buy them."

"Why wouldn't they? They're beautiful."

She shrugged. "I don't know. It's just something I've always done. The idea that anyone would pay money for something I love to do anyway. Actually, the whole concept of money is still a little strange to me."

"Don't worry. You'll get it. You've come so far already."

"I feel that I have. That I've made good progress in adjusting to the world. But, Declan…do you ever imagine moving away from here? Living in a big city somewhere?"

"What? No. Never. I'd hate it. Why do you ask? Are you thinking of moving away, Angel?"

"I never want to live anywhere else, either. I want to stay here, where it's quiet and safe. I know it's that I'm still a bit afraid of the world. I think to some extent I always will be."

"I'd be surprised if you were ever able to get used to the noise and the pace of a big city. Hell, I'd be surprised if *I* did. I'm not going anywhere. You don't have to worry about that."

He was looking down at her, his features soft and loose. That small spark of desire in his eyes that never dimmed entirely, but there was emotion, too.

"Are you hungry?" she asked him. "I made poached salmon for dinner."

"I'm always hungry."

His hands slid down to cup her bottom as he pulled her hips close to his. His hard flesh pressed against her. She arched her hips into his, felt that answering pulse of desire in her sex.

"Come on, Declan. Take me inside."

"Mmm…can't wait that long."

He swept her down onto the porch stairs, some-how slipping her panties off from beneath her sun-dress as he went. She was ready, panting, when he unzipped his fly and she reached in to take his cock out. He was all warm, solid flesh in her hand. She wanted to taste him. But she needed him in-side her just as badly.

"Come on, Declan."

"Ah, you're impatient, baby."

"I am."

She pushed her dress up and spread her thighs, leaning back on the stairs. He knelt before her, using his hands to part her thighs farther.

"So damn beautiful," he murmured before bending over her and sweeping his tongue over her aching cleft.

"Oh…do it again."

He did, his tongue sliding up, then down the seam of her sex. He parted her then, his thumbs spreading her flesh wide as he delved in with his tongue. He pressed it against her hole, and she whimpered with need, pure driving desire.

"Declan, don't tease me."

She grabbed his head, her fingers going into his dark hair, and held him to her while he licked her in long, flickering strokes.

"Oh…"

Her climax came down on her like a summer storm. Flashing through her body like heat lightning, sharp and electric. And before she was done he was leaning over her, his mouth latching on to her throat as he slipped his cock inside.

"Jesus, that's so good. You feel so good, baby," he murmured into her neck. "I love to feel how tight you are. How wet. I love it when you're around me. Yeah, just like that."

He drove into her, and the stairs were a little too hard, digging into her back. But she didn't care. All she wanted was right here. In her body. Flesh to flesh.

She hung on to his shoulders, her nails digging in as he thrust harder and harder. Pleasure rose once more, and she came again, in short, sharp jolts.

"Ah, Declan!"

Then he was coming, his hips arching, hard and wild.

When it was over he kissed her neck, her face.

"Jesus, Angel."

He was still panting, his body still covering hers so that she could feel the heaving of his chest against her breasts. She ran her hands over his sides, his buttocks, his strong thighs. He was so much a man. So solid.

"Declan?"

"Hmm? What is it, baby?"

"I love you."

"I love you, too."

"No, I don't know if you understand what I'm saying."

Why did she feel like crying? She couldn't explain it to herself.

"You're saying you love me, and I'm saying I love you, and it's all good." He stroked her damp hair from her face, kissed her chin.

"Yes, but it's more than that. I didn't know how much more it could be. How precious you would be to me. How much your love and being able to trust you means to me."

"Sweetheart…"

He kissed her again, a sweet brushing of his lips against hers. She knew he wasn't as verbal as she was. Knew that men generally weren't, or so Ruth had explained to her. But she felt it all in his touch.

After a while, they got up and went into the house, Liam pushing his way first through the screen door. Declan changed out of his work clothes while Angel went into the kitchen to finish making dinner. Declan's cell phone, which he'd left on the kitchen table, went off.

"Declan, someone is calling you," she called down the hallway.

"Who is it?"

"Your dad."

"I'll call him back in a minute."

Her heart started to pound. Just a small murmuring beat that was a little too hard. She was still standing by the table, frozen, a wooden spoon in her hand, when Declan came into the kitchen.

"Angel? What is it? Did you talk to him? Is everything okay?"

"I... No, I didn't talk to him. I don't know if everything is okay."

Declan's brows drew together as he stepped toward her. He laid his hand across her back, his palm resting between her shoulder blades, over the two long scars there as he dialed Oran's number.

"Dad? It's me. You just called?"

He was quiet for several endless moments. She could hear Oran's rumbling voice on the other end, just the low notes. She couldn't hear what he was saying. Declan was nodding his head, but he wasn't saying anything. But he was looking at her, *watching* her face.

"Jesus." A long pause, and then he asked, "You're sure, Dad?" Another pause. "This is great news. Incredible. Yes, I'll tell her right now. Wait for Ruth? No, I don't think so. This is good news. The best. Yeah. I'll call you later. Thanks, Dad. Bye."

He flipped the phone shut. His eyes were gleaming, his face flushed. He smiled, a wide, beatific smile.

"Angel, I have the most incredible news."

She reached blindly for a chair, sat down. Why couldn't she calm down? She felt as though her heart would beat right out of her chest.

Declan knelt in front of her, took her hands. "They found her. The Grandmother. They've got her. She tried to take another child, another little girl, those bastards. But because of an AMBER Alert they found her. And discovered the whole damn compound. The old woman, the whole lot of them. Nine people arrested in all. They've got her. They took her to jail. She's going to be in there for the rest of her life." He stopped, squeezed her hands. "Angel? You're pale. Are you okay?"

She shook her head. She didn't know how to answer him. She was…in shock. Grateful that a child had been saved from the years of punishment she'd endured. And horrified by the idea that The Grandmother was going to be locked up somewhere. Perhaps treated harshly.

"Angel? What is it?"

She wrenched her hands free and twisted them together in her lap. Tears crept over her cheeks. She could do nothing to stop them.

"Baby. You're safe now. Really safe, finally. It's okay."

She shook her head, harder and harder until her hair flew in her face. "It's not okay. Don't you see?"

"What? I don't understand."

"That old woman—she was all I had most of my life. Do you have any idea what that means to me? And you're here celebrating."

"But, Angel, after all the horrible shit she did to you…"

"Don't you think I know that?" She hadn't meant to yell, but the words simply came out that way. She tried to take a breath, but all she did was draw in a deep sob. "I can't forgive her. But neither can I condemn her. It's not in me to do that."

Declan was quiet for several moments. She could hear his harsh breath. "I'm trying to understand. But this is crazy. She took you from your family. She drugged you. She *cut* you, for God's sake. There are scars all over your body." He pulled her hands into his, turned them faceup. "Look. She tattooed you, a child. You'll wear these marks the rest of your life!"

She yanked her hands back, twisted them in her lap. She couldn't look at him.

"She shoved a bunch of insane rhetoric down your throat along with the drugs," he went on. "She told you your entire life's purpose was to be some sex slave to Satan. How can you find anything even remotely forgivable there?"

"To forgive is divine," she murmured, hiding her face in her hands.

He didn't understand. He didn't want to try. Her heart was breaking.

"Jesus, Angel. Okay. Okay. I get that. But isn't there some small part of you that's glad these people have been stopped? Made to pay for what they've done?"

"Stopped, yes. But punished? What purpose has punishment ever served, Declan? That part I do not understand."

He got up, began to pace. Her stomach rolled, knotted. She felt sick.

"Angel. Shit. Finding these people has been my only purpose since I found you on that beach. Retribution. These people are monsters."

"The Grandmother is not a monster. How can you say that? She raised me."

"She abducted you from the people who should have raised you! From the family who loved you."

"You don't know that. We don't even know them, the Norlings."

"They're your parents, Angel. Your brother. The only reason we haven't contacted them is because you asked for more time. But they must have spent all these years grieving."

"They are nearly strangers," she insisted.

"Jesus."

He ran a hand through his hair. She could see the rage in his eyes. The confusion. There was no less confusion and rage within her. She couldn't stand that he was so unable to see what she was feeling about this. That he was unwilling to. She felt frozen inside. Frozen and full of pain.

"I need...I need to be with Ruth."

"Okay. I'll call her, make an appointment."

"No. I mean I need to *be* with her. For a while."

"What?" His eyes were blazing, full of blue fire. It reminded her suddenly a little too much of Asmodeus, of the endless burning black of his gaze. A small shudder ran through her.

She said quietly, firmly, "I'll call her myself. Have her come pick me up."

"What are you saying?"

There was shock on his face. But she was too much in shock herself to take it all in. Tears were a hard, bitter lump in her throat.

"I need to go. I can't stay here while you crow about the only family I've ever known being taken away. Punished. Suffering. I cannot do it. I won't do it."

He reached for her, but she rose from the chair and moved away.

"I need to go, Declan."

He looked absolutely overcome, bewildered. He didn't say anything as she went into the living room to call Ruth. He remained in the kitchen while she went to her room and gathered some clothes, took her toothbrush from the bathroom, stuffing everything into a pillowcase. He still hadn't moved from the kitchen when Ruth's old blue Mercedes pulled into the driveway and Angel walked outside.

Declan stood, stunned, in the kitchen. He couldn't even look out the window, listening to the swing of the front door as Angel walked out, the slam of the car door. The tires crushing the gravel in the driveway as they pulled away.

She was gone.

He couldn't comprehend it. He'd done everything he could for her. Protected her, cared for her, kept her safe. Done everything in his power to help reopen her case and hunt down these fucking lunatics who had taken a five-year-old child from her family and kept her locked up. Abused her. For sixteen years. Her whole goddamn life. And now it was as though none of that counted for anything. That crazy old woman's pull on Angel was bigger, stronger, than the fact that they loved each other. And just like with Abby, with his mother, she was gone, and there wasn't anything he could do about it.

Not again.

His whole body froze up, the chill creeping over him a little at a time. That same sense of being fucking paralyzed taking him over. He could not move.

He stood by the chair, his fingers gripping the back of it as the sun set, the sky turning dark outside. Liam settled on the floor at his feet. Declan stayed there until his knees ached, his fingers stiff from gripping the chair. And the whole time there were a thousand thoughts and images flying through his brain, like some sort of chaotic movie, playing itself out over and over.

His mother in the hospital bed, wasting away, while his father stood silently next to her. Abby's face, the shock in her eyes, as she bled out in mere moments, into the Bahrain street. Angel telling him she wanted to leave. And through all of it, he was frozen. Paralyzed.

Powerless.

Fuck.

Mom. Abby. Angel.

Angel.

Finally he moved, and went to pull a bottle of bourbon from the cabinet. Poured two fingers into a glass, took a swig.

He wasn't much of a drinker, and it burned going down his throat. But the sting of it helped to clear his head.

He didn't have to be powerless, goddamn it. Not this time. He could choose differently. He could *choose.* He had to hope Angel would choose, too. That she would choose to let the bonds of her past go.

That she would choose him.

Angel lay on Ruth's sofa in the dark, listening to the night sounds. They were different here than they were at home.

At Declan's home.

She wasn't sure it would be hers any longer. She wasn't sure she could go back.

Ruth had talked to her a little in the car, but mostly she had let her be. Once at her small cottage, Ruth had made up a bed for her on the sofa and a cup of tea, and they'd listened to an opera together in quiet companionship before Ruth had gone to bed.

Ruth had told Angel she sensed she had to work this issue out for herself. She was grateful for Ruth recognizing her need for independence while offering the comforting solidity of her presence, as well as a safe haven. And she understood she had to figure this out on her own. Understood this was a crucial part of her growth, of creating her new self. With or without Declan. And either way, she knew it would mean saying goodbye to Asmodeus. Forever.

She was anxious now to reach the dream place where she would see him, tell him what she must do. But she also dreaded it, making it official. It felt so finite to her. So far sleep had eluded her, but she'd been lying in the dark for several hours and her eyelids were growing heavy. Still, she fought it, afraid to make that final commitment.

She plumped the pillow, turned over and closed her eyes. She knew what she had to do. *Had* to do. Come what may. She would be strong enough to handle it. She *was* strong enough.

She forced her eyes to close and it felt good. In her mind she imagined her garden, all her growing things, the happy sounds of the birds. She pulled in one long, slow breath after another, willed her body to relax, her nerves to calm.

This was necessary. This was what she wanted. What she *chose*.

The garden was lush and green. Flowers grew among the herbs and vegetables. The scent of the earth was all around her, the warm scent of a summer sky. She reached out to stroke the long, narrow leaf of a corn stalk, that lovely deep velvet-green, inhaled the soft air.

It grew dark, bit by bit. There was nothing threatening there, only that summer softness fading around her. When the garden disappeared, she knew she had him.

Asmodeus.

She felt his striking heat before she saw him. Felt his unhappiness like some viable aura.

"Asmodeus."

"You call, and I come. I am ever your faithful servant." His voice was as deep and rumbling as ever, like a heavy thundercloud.

"I don't want you to be. Not anymore."

"Yes. I always sense what is in your heart."

"What do you see there now?" she asked him, some part of her wanting him to *know,* so she wouldn't have to say the words. But she must be braver than that.

"This man. Your connection to him. To the earthly plane. A parting of ways for us."

"Yes." Her heart was heavy. But she knew this was right. "This has been coming, Asmodeus. We've both known it, you and I."

"It makes it no less painful. I will cease to exist in your reality. Perhaps altogether."

He sighed, and steam blew out in a hot breath from his perfect nostrils.

"Asmodeus, I have to tell you, I have come to understand how you are a manifestation of my own fears and dreams. I must accept that in order to be free to be my own person. To put my past behind me and move on, move forward to whatever my future might hold. I am coming to see for the first time that I truly have one."

"You have always had a future. Time moves, with or without our noticing."

"That's too vague for me. I want a *specific* future. I want a life of my choosing. I want a *life*. I thought I'd chosen before, but I didn't know enough. I knew nothing of the possibilities."

"And now you do." Another sigh. His sadness

radiated from him like energy, like an electric crackling in the still, dark air.

"I will never fall with you again, Asmodeus. And my heart is broken. But I know I will recover. I know what I must do. I must say goodbye. Here. Now."

One tear fell from his coal-black eyes, gleaming blue as it traced its way over his golden cheek. So hard. So utterly perfect. He nodded. She reached out to him, but he began to drift from her, farther and farther away, until he disappeared altogether.

The pain was a small searing in her chest. It spread and the pain melted, turning to a pure light that was nothing more than a brilliant, piercing ache. But bearable, something she knew would fade in time.

She would have a life now. She was her own person, finally.

Her mind drifted, into the simple dreams of one who did nothing more than sleep, who had no larger task than to rest. Her anger and confusion drained away and left in its place a certainty she had never felt before.

She would be okay.

HE'D LET A DAY GO BY. He wanted Angel to have the opportunity to talk with Ruth, to let Ruth get her calmed down.

Declan had spent a sleepless night without her

in his bed. Had finally gotten up and sat in the amber glow of the porch light, Liam at his side, working a piece of wood. Working some of the frustration and regret out of his system, his mind turning everything over, searching for clarity. Facing some hard truths about himself.

He was beginning to have a clearer understanding of what Angel must be feeling. And his own insensitivity to her. Why hadn't he brought the news to her with less of the victory in his tone? He could have kept that to himself or shared it with no one but his father. But the whole being-her-protector thing had gone to his head.

He had to get over that shit. Had to get over the lousy job he'd done taking care of his mom, of Abby. Angel was not either one of them. He wasn't the same person he'd been back then, either. Hell, he'd practically been a kid.

He had to start looking at the fact that part of the protector thing was natural, but for him it was also about control. That role made him feel like he had some control over his life, and it was fucked up to lay that on Angel.

Time to deal with his issues, he'd realized while his knife bit into the wood in his hands, while the crickets sang in the darkness and Liam snored softly. Why was it the still and lonely night was when people usually had this sort of epiphany? Didn't matter. It was long overdue.

In the morning he went to work exhausted. But he'd gotten through the day somehow. The minute he was done he'd jumped into his truck and called his father.

"Oran Byrne."

"Dad, it's me."

"Hi, Dec."

"I guess you know what's going on. That Angel is with Ruth."

"Yeah. Ruth called me last night to tell me."

"You don't sound surprised."

"I thought Angel might have a bad reaction to the news—that's why I suggested you wait and have Ruth there when you told her. I don't mean to rub your face in it. Just to tell you I think this is normal, under the circumstances."

"I should have listened to you."

His father was quiet a moment. "I never thought I'd hear you say that, Dec."

He almost smiled. "Yeah, me, neither. Look, Dad, I need to go and see her. I need Ruth's address."

"Are you sure that's a good idea, son? Maybe you should call."

"No. I need to see her. Face-to-face. I know Angel, Dad."

"All right. Ruth lives out by Noyo Bay, up Highway One."

Oran gave him the address and they hung up.

He sat in his truck for several moments. As anxious as he was to see Angel he really did not want to blow it. He owed her an apology, at the very least. Owed it to her to let her know what had been going through his head all night, the conclusions he'd come to. He sure as hell wasn't the type to open up, confide in anyone. But everything was different with Angel. He wanted to be different for her.

He turned the key in the ignition and the truck started with a low rumbling purr. He pulled onto the highway and headed north.

He'd driven this route dozens of times when Angel was in the hospital. Hundreds, maybe, over the course of his life. It was familiar. Comfortable for him. He'd always liked the comfort of being in a familiar place. Physically. Mentally.

Emotionally.

He was way the hell out of his comfort zone now. But he had to break out of it or he'd end up alone.

Without Angel.

Not acceptable.

He found Ruth's place easily and parked on the road in front of the small yellow cottage. He hardly noticed it as he got out of the truck and swung the door closed. Until he was on the porch. Then it hit him—the scent of roses. He looked around, and in the dying light of day he saw that the place was surrounded by roses. White and lavender and pink. Coral, peach and dark red.

In the past he would have been annoyed by this similarity to his mother. Now it pleased him somehow. But he had more important things to think about. Like Angel.

He lifted his hand, his pulse racing.

He'd better make this damn good.

He knocked and Ruth answered the door. She smiled when she saw him, which surprised him.

"Declan, hi. I was just on my way out to see a client. An emergency of sorts. Angel is in the living room. Go on in. I'll be back in about two hours, so you'll have the place to yourselves." She smiled again, put a hand on his arm. "It's good you're here," she told him, her voice low. Her dark eyes were sparkling.

"Is it?"

"You two need to talk."

He nodded, unable to say more. She seemed to understand, just gave his arm another pat as she moved past him, car keys in her hand. He went inside.

It was warm in the cottage. When Angel came into the living room, his breath stuttered in his chest.

She was so beautiful. He could never get over it, the purity of her face. Her blue, blue eyes. The cascade of hair like golden silk swinging almost to her knees.

And right now everything felt so damn important. Fucking crucial.

Calm down.

Angel stopped with her hand on the back of Ruth's floral sofa for support. She had heard him arrive, had taken a moment in the kitchen to calm herself, to breathe.

"Angel, before you say anything, please hear me out."

She nodded, emotion making her throat too tight to speak. She had so much to tell him. But she would listen first.

He took a step toward her, seemed to think better of it, stopped.

"Okay. Okay. I've been thinking. A lot. All night, if you want to know the truth. And I've come to some hard conclusions."

Her heart twisted, stalled. Was he going to tell her he'd decided he didn't want her anymore? Seeing him standing there with his emotions so naked on his face, she knew she wanted to be with him. *Needed* to be with him.

He took another step closer. He was so beautiful to her. His dark hair was mussed, as if he'd been running his hands through it. He probably had. His eyes were brilliant, that iris-dark-blue, the lashes black and full. He hadn't shaved, which seemed impossibly tender to her for some reason she couldn't explain.

"Declan—"

"No, let me say this, Angel."

She nodded.

"I've been an idiot," he told her. "And…closed off for most of my adult life. Which has only added to my stupidity. I've let my past rule me. My thought process. My emotions. Or my lack of emotion." He stopped, shoved his hands into the pockets of his khaki work uniform. "The truth is, I've been living in fear. It's been a component in everything I've done. But mostly in my relationships with other people. My dad. You. And there's enough of the macho jerk in me that I didn't see it. I didn't *want* to see it. But I do now. I understand I have to get over this shit, that I have to let it go. Losing my mother. Losing Abby. Or I'll be as trapped as you ever were, in that compound in the mountains."

She felt the tears behind her eyes. They pooled, began to blur his face, as though she were looking through a rain-streaked window. She could still see, though, how hard this was for him.

"Declan, I've been unfair to you, too."

He shook his head. "You were dealing with a trauma I can't even begin to imagine. I knew something about how that kind of thing can work. Ruth told me. About how a victim can sometimes become emotionally attached to their captor. But my damn ego was in the way of me really listening. I wanted to believe you could put it all behind you just because I'd ridden in like some white knight to save you. Because saving you— saving *someone*—was so damn important to me. I needed that."

"I don't see that as being something terrible," she said.

"No. What was terrible was that it became more important to me than anything else."

"Is that really true, Declan?" she asked, almost afraid to hear his answer. "More important than me?"

He moved toward her then, a few long strides and he was right in front of her. He laid his hands on her shoulders and she felt the heat of him like a soft, lovely glow.

"Angel, *nothing* is more important than you. I just had to risk losing you to see that. I'm sorry. I'm so damn sorry."

"Declan…" She swallowed her tears, her throat closing up. She had never before imagined how crucial it would be to hear him say this now— that she truly mattered to him. She started once more. "Declan, I've been hard on you, too. I need to understand how unusual my situation is, that you were behaving as most people would. And I needed to let go of my past every bit as much as you. More, maybe. And I've done it—I need to tell you that. I've said goodbye to Asmodeus. That's over. I found that I don't need him any longer, and whether or not he ever truly existed almost doesn't matter to me. What matters is that I am my own person, finally. That I am of *consequence*. I am recognizing my own strength."

"I see it, sweetheart. The stronger you become, the more I love you."

He brushed her hair from her face, so much love in that simple motion.

"I have been emancipated, Declan. Some of it was with Ruth's help, and much of it has been with yours. And much simply from myself, which is important. I have a long way to go. I understand the strangeness of my life may mean that I will always be dealing with the fallout, to some extent, that I may be able to go out into the world only so much."

"That's true for me, too, to some degree. It has been for a long time."

"We have both been damaged," she said.

"I don't like to admit it, but yeah. We have. And it's time for me to face the truth about a lot of things. But the most important truth, Angel, is that I love you. I need you. And I have to let go of my fears and my need to control my whole damn world so that we can be together."

"I want that, Declan. I'm sorry I was angry with you."

He shook his head, his brows drawn together. "Don't be sorry. We're here and…we're together. Are we together, Angel?"

"Yes. I love you, Declan. Just as long as you can be patient with me. I still have so much to learn."

"So do I. But it has to be with you. *Has* to be."

She slipped her arms around his neck and he smiled, in a way she'd never seen him smile before. There was no restraint in it, for once. Purely unselfconscious. Beautiful.

He pulled her in close and she felt the inevitable heat of his body against hers. Love and desire were united in a way she knew it only could be with him. The man she loved, and who loved her in return. The man she *chose*.

She knew, in that moment, that choosing love was what had truly set her free.

* * * * *

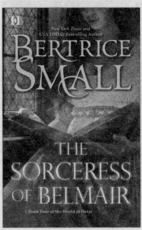

REQUEST YOUR
FREE BOOKS!

2 FREE NOVELS
FROM THE ROMANCE COLLECTION
PLUS 2 FREE GIFTS!

YES! Please send me 2 FREE novels from the Romance Collection and my 2 FREE gifts (gifts are worth about $10). After receiving them, if I don't wish to receive any more books, I can return the shipping statement marked "cancel." If I don't cancel, I will receive 4 brand-new novels every month and be billed just $5.99 per book in the U.S. or $6.49 per book in Canada. That's a saving of at least 25% off the cover price. It's quite a bargain! Shipping and handling is just 50¢ per book in the U.S. and 75¢ per book in Canada.* I understand that accepting the 2 free books and gifts places me under no obligation to buy anything. I can always return a shipment and cancel at any time. Even if I never buy another book, the two free books and gifts are mine to keep forever.

194/394 MDN FELQ

Name	(PLEASE PRINT)	
Address		Apt. #
City	State/Prov.	Zip/Postal Code

Signature (if under 18, a parent or guardian must sign)

Mail to the **Reader Service**:
IN U.S.A.: P.O. Box 1867, Buffalo, NY 14240-1867
IN CANADA: P.O. Box 609, Fort Erie, Ontario L2A 5X3

Not valid for current subscribers to the Romance Collection
or the Romance/Suspense Collection.

Want to try two free books from another line?
Call 1-800-873-8635 or visit www.ReaderService.com.

* Terms and prices subject to change without notice. Prices do not include applicable taxes. Sales tax applicable in N.Y. Canadian residents will be charged applicable taxes. Offer not valid in Quebec. This offer is limited to one order per household. All orders subject to credit approval. Credit or debit balances in a customer's account(s) may be offset by any other outstanding balance owed by or to the customer. Please allow 4 to 6 weeks for delivery. Offer available while quantities last.

Your Privacy—The Reader Service is committed to protecting your privacy. Our Privacy Policy is available online at www.ReaderService.com or upon request from the Reader Service.

We make a portion of our mailing list available to reputable third parties that offer products we believe may interest you. If you prefer that we not exchange your name with third parties, or if you wish to clarify or modify your communication preferences, please visit us at www.ReaderService.com/consumerschoice or write to us at Reader Service Preference Service, P.O. Box 9062, Buffalo, NY 14269. Include your complete name and address.

Summer love can last a lifetime....

A dazzling new story from
New York Times **bestselling author**

SUSAN MALLERY

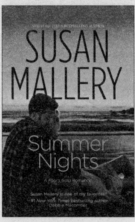

Small-town librarian Annabelle Weiss has always seen herself as more of a sweetheart than a siren, so she can't understand why Shane keeps pushing her away. Shane has formed the totally wrong impression of her but only he can help her with a special event for the next Fool's Gold festival. And maybe while he's at it, she can convince him to teach her a few things about kissing on hot summer nights, too—some lessons, a girl shouldn't learn from reading a book!

Summer Nights

Available now!

PHSSM687